The TOUR

A Novel

Also by this author:

The Pendulum's Path

The Race: A Novel of Grit, Tactics, and the Tour de France

Link to additional articles and stories at DaveShields.com

The TOUR

A Novel

by

Dave Shields

Three Story Press
Salt Lake City
2004

Library of Congress Number: 2005908944
ISBN-13:   978-0-9748492-1-8
ISBN-10:   0-9748492-1-9

Published by Three Story Press
P. O. Box 17141
Salt Lake City, UT 84117

Manufactured in the United States of America

For Elle,
thank you for your undying support.

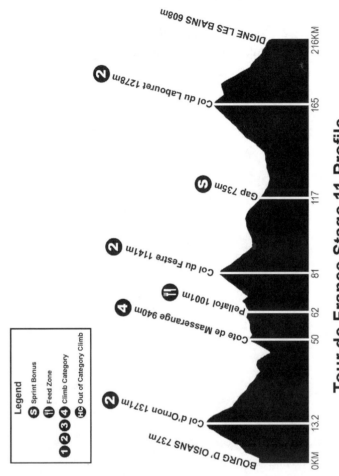

Tour de France Stage 11 Profile

Legend
- **S** Sprint Bonus
- **⏸** Feed Zone
- **①②③④** Climb Category
- **HC** Out of Category Climb

BOURG D' OISANS 737m

Col d'Ornon 1371m ②

Cote de Masserange 940m ④

Pellafol 1001m ⏸

Col du Festre 1141m ②

Gap 735m **S**

Col du Labouret 1278m ②

DIGNE LES BAINS 608m

0KM 13.2 50 62 81 117 165 216KM

Chapter One

Children clanged cowbells, women cheered, and men waved colorful banners in the thin alpine air. Passion supercharged this corridor through the outskirts of centuries-old Bourg d'Oisans. Blistering mid-day heat rose from the tarmac. One hundred and sixty-two men had survived a week and a half of bicycle racing to reach this point on the road, more than eleven hundred miles from the start of the Tour de France, yet still almost a thousand short of the finish line in Paris.

Riding near the crest of the peloton, shoulder-to-shoulder with the world's greatest cyclists, Ben Barnes savored the electric moment. What a journey he'd taken in his twenty-four years. Today he stood within reach of his ultimate goal: winning the Tour de France. He vowed to make his supporters proud.

On either side of the narrow Romanche River Valley, limestone peaks scratched at the clear sky. Where the cliffs were too sheer for vegetation, exposed swirling strata signed testament to the powerful forces that had shaped this land. Trees, vines, and grasses clothed the lower slopes. Ben wondered if eyes like his, having spent their formative years in the Southern Utah desert, could ever take in enough greenery. In the river basin, every arable patch of land had been sown, but no one worked the fields today. The families who called these hills home stood side-by-side with bicycle lovers from every corner of the globe.

A Swiss band, complete with an accordion and three twelve-foot alpenhorns, yodeled an impossible tune. Fans danced in the street, screaming joyfully. In the athletes' struggle against elements, terrain, and competitors, these enthusiasts seemed to have discovered the perfect microcosm for their own lives. Raw grit set them on fire. They worshiped warriors incapable of giving less than everything.

Yesterday Ben had turned in the sort of legendary performance that the fans loved. He'd bested everyone in a six-hour quest that ended atop cycling's most legendary climb, l'Alpe d'Huez. His exhausted muscles had tightened and seized overnight. Now underway, renewed effort deadened the pain. He cruised along behind his teammates, hiding from the wind and conserving energy for later in the day. He needed to gather his strength for another explosive finish.

The route veered onto a new highway, and soon bent upward. The clickety-clack of shifting gears reverberated like the grumbling of a huge, metallic stomach. The sound brought to mind the peloton's insatiable appetite. One day ago Ben had been the prey. Today he was, as usual, a part of the beast itself.

Soon the route confronted a cliff so abrupt that the road scaled it on a sloping viaduct built adjacent to the rock. The fight against gravity ignited a pleasant burn in Ben's legs. Today's race would cross four alpine passes on the way to Digne-les-Bains. While the profile wasn't nearly as difficult as yesterday's, exhaustion ensured that the ten remaining stages were going to be even tougher than the ten the riders had completed.

"*Aaaahhhh! Il mio amore!*"

Ben recognized Luigi Figanero's voice. Widely recognized as the world's best climber, he bragged of even more prowess as a lover. Thousands of women seemed anxious to find out for themselves. Ben scanned the roadside for the Italian's most recent conquest.

Luigi sprinted ahead of the peloton, and then stopped among the crowd with arms spread wide. He embraced a shapely blonde while he kissed the gorgeous brunette next to her. Then he switched his lips to the blonde while the peloton cheered. "*Avete amiche?* There is enough Luigi to go around."

The peloton rolled by as an appreciative roar rose from the fans. Ben glanced at his Italian friend, still at roadside and now giving passionate attention to a very large German woman.

Ben turned forward, chuckling. How did the guy get away with it? Not in a million years could he play a crowd like that. On top of everything else, it took guts to drop behind the pack, even early in the day before the racing turned fast and furious.

As Ben approached the village of Ornon, the hill relented and the pace increased. The village was packed with spectators. Ben watched a flag blow from a fan's grasp. It floated across the route, colors swirling. For a moment, he thought he might reach up and grab it, but then the emblem made a swan-like dip directly into his path. With cyclists on three sides, where could he go? Suddenly the spokes of his front wheel grabbed the banner and devoured it.

"*Zute!*" The village back-flipped as he cartwheeled, his feet still locked into the pedals and his bicycle inverted above him. He slammed onto his head and shoulder. Pain shot down his spine. Skittering down the road, rubber side up, his left eye was so close to the pavement that approaching pebbles resembled boulders.

The front tire from a trailing bicycle closed the gap to his face. Ben shut his eyes and braced for impact. No collision. He opened his eyes as someone's rear wheel soared over his cheek. The cyclist had bunny-hopped his head.

A second bicycle skidded toward him. Rubber tires screeched across the pavement. The front wheel bumped into his chest and stopped. He breathed again, even as the familiar sting of road rash warmed the left side of his body. Cringing, he grabbed his tailbone. He evaluated his injury quickly: a deep bone bruise. Painful, but not debilitating.

His shoulder, arm, and hip were also bruised but not broken. Ben rotated his neck from side to side, trying to relax and clear his head. With a twist of his toes, he disengaged his shoes from the pedals and separated himself from the bike. Cyclists streamed by on both sides for what seemed an eternity. Ben climbed to his feet, points of light swirling through his vision. The vehicle caravan approached. Someone handed him his sunglasses and he put them on.

An urgent voice asked, "Are you okay to continue?"

Ben nodded, still gathering his senses.

Fritz, Banque Fédérale's lead mechanic, sprang from the team car like a greyhound lunging from its trap. The ends of his long black moustache trailed behind like twin tails on an exotic kite. He looked worried. In his left hand he carried a spare front wheel.

Fans crowded in from all sides to watch. Support vehicles threw dust into the air as they veered wide to get past. Honking. Braking. Revving.

The caravan numbered well over fifty cars, most with a half dozen bicycles mounted on their roofs. In addition to two logo-covered support vehicles per team, there were other cars for race officials, neutral support, and press from around the world. Swarms of motorcycles zipped among them carrying television cameramen, course marshals, still photographers, and others.

Ben's teammates gathered near. First lieutenant Albert chewed gum nervously. His sleek physique and bony face reminded Ben of a gazelle, built for endurance over hilly terrain. Beside him, Rikard, the team's charismatic sprint specialist, looked huge and angry. A thoroughbred racehorse, hard charging even at a standstill, his specialty was speed on the flats. Men like Rikard were dead meat in mountainous terrain, but give them a long, level straightaway and they'd eat the climbers alive.

These support cyclists were called domestiques, literally "servants." They played integral supportive roles, often sacrificing personal results to put their team leader atop the podium in Paris.

Yesterday, Rikard had made it clear that he didn't approve of using a French team to support an American cyclist's efforts. Yet he was here when needed most. Ben owed these men, big time.

Fritz fought to remove the damaged wheel from the bicycle. With a wrenching tug he jerked it free. "It takes a licking…" He snapped the new wheel into place, cinched the quick release, and spun it hard. "…and keeps on ticking." He gave the other components a once over then patted Ben on the back.

Still feeling groggy, Ben swung a leg over his bike. All seven remaining Banque Fédérale teammates watched. The only member of their squat who'd dropped out of the race so far was three-time champion Thierry DePerdiux, the victim of a crash the day before. Ben looked up to the man like a big brother. Thierry had broken his ankle in the accident but, relentless as ever, he'd returned today to become their new directeur sportif, their coach. He drove the vehicle carrying Fritz. One good foot was sufficient for that job, provided it was attached to a mind like Thierry's.

Ben nodded to his teammates, signaling them to shove off. Fritz gave Ben a running push, sending him up the road. Ben rose from the saddle and sprinted up to speed. The men settled into their draft line while, beside them, the convertible roof of a neutral support car disappeared into its trunk, revealing the Tour's doctor kneeling on the back seat. He waved Ben over. "Ah, Monsieur Barnes. I must see you."

Ben looked at him helplessly, and then gave in. The other Banque Fédérale cyclists kept pace as he grabbed the windowsill of the moving vehicle.

"Safety first," the doctor said.

Ben followed the man's swaying index finger with his eyes. He'd been through this drill before.

The doctor put a firm hand on Ben's shoulder and squeezed. "Any pain?"

He felt tenderness but no sharp sensations. "I'll be fine."

The doctor nodded, lips pressed together.

Ben looked down. Asphalt-blackened fabric edged the hole around his bloody shoulder wound. His brand new maillot jaune, the yellow jersey that spotlighted him as overall race leader, had been baptized by fire. "What a start to the day."

"*Oui*. But you ought to be thanking God for your helmet." The doctor used a water bottle to wash gravel from the road rash on Ben's left shoulder, elbow, and leg. "Better to destroy a bit of high tech foam than your skull. *Non?*"

Ben nodded. The doctor unhooked the chinstrap and removed the head protector, showing it to Ben. The outer shell still held it in one piece, but the impact had shattered the core.

"Call your support vehicle and get a new one." The doctor rose to sit on the rear dash and inspected Ben's head through his stubbly haircut, looking for blood or signs of trauma.

Ben activated his radio. "Busted my brain bucket."

"Fritz will dig a spare from the cargo bin," Thierry answered.

"What's our gap?"

"About a minute." Thierry sounded unimpressed by the crash. Mishaps were part of the sport. Professionals were expected to handle them and move on. Thierry's concern at this moment was brokering deals with other teams and building key alliances to keep Ben in a strong position. No one could win the Tour de France without lots of help. Complex maneuverings formed the backdrop to everything.

Ben gritted his teeth at the stinging sensation as the doctor sprayed antiseptic onto the wounds. The physician finished and waved Ben forward. "*Allez c'est bon.*"

"*Merci.*" Ben let go of the window and hurried toward his teammates' protective draft. The purple-and-green Banque Fédérale bicycle train quickly got up to speed again. Ben sat in the caboose position as his companions escorted him toward the main pack. Had this spill occurred twenty-four hours earlier, he would have been left to his own devices. Today, since he wore yellow, his squad sliced a path through the wind for him. One of the strategic keys to bicycle racing was preserving as much of the team leader's energy as possible so he'd have strength late in the day. Ben could get used to a change like this.

Soon they reached the vehicle caravan and wove their way through. To gain additional protection from the wind the athletes stayed close to the cars. It was a dangerous proposition. The drivers were alert, but a fall here could be the last one a cyclist ever took.

The Banque Fédérale car pulled alongside and the mechanic handed out a new helmet. "You're in good hands with Fritz-state." Fritz loved American culture, so much so that he'd invented a unique way of expressing himself that he called "Ameri-jibberish." He always had the appropriate jingle at his fingertips.

Ben smiled, clipping the helmet into place without slowing.

The car kept pace, and Ben crouched down to glance inside. In the back seat Coach Bill and Fritz worked intently on some component. In the front passenger seat Thelma looked his way and smiled. She was the closest thing to a mother he'd known since his own mom died on his eighth birthday. Ben still couldn't believe that Thelma and Coach had traveled halfway around the world on a moment's notice just to show their support.

Ben keyed his radio. "I need a 'fix' at dinner tonight."

Thelma grinned at his reference to her spaghetti, famous throughout Southern Utah. In his youth, Ben used to cycle over the top of Boulder Mountain regularly to get his fix.

He returned his concentration to the wheel in front of him, anxious to close the gap to his rivals. Five minutes later, relieved and exhausted, he and his team rejoined the peloton. The air current created by this mass of surging cyclists enveloped them like a mother's arms.

The sensation of catching the group from behind was entirely different from being captured by it at the front. Every pro understood the love/hate relationship. Within the pack the punishing headwind disappeared, and a neutralizing tailwind took its place. A rider could reduce his wind resistance by up to forty percent by remaining in the draft of others. The effect was less evident on an incline like this, but slipstreaming wasn't the only benefit of the peloton. Pace making also played a key role. Following wheels simplified decision-making and reduced stress. This big pack served as a great equalizer, complicating tactics and enabling some men to complete the distance while expending far less energy than others. Until the mountains blew things apart, the peloton could be the perfect place to hide.

The Banque Fédérale men sagged over their handlebars. They'd spent a lot of energy closing the gap created by Ben's accident. Finally hidden from the wind, they needed a moment to recuperate. Ben didn't have that luxury. He had to work his way toward the front. Leaders couldn't risk being trapped deep in the peloton should a key rival launch an attack.

He eased forward, noticing that his competitors were in a somber mood. His crash in a rare lighthearted moment had apparently caused many of the other athletes to consider how quickly things could go wrong. Hundreds of rubber tires whispered along the asphalt while men from various teams asked after him.

"Bit of bad luck there."

"*Bien?*"

"Ouch."

"*Nya krafter, nya tag!*"

"Thanks. I think." Even though Ben didn't understand everything they said, he nodded acknowledgments. In addition to English he spoke fluent French and pretty good Spanish, but not much more. With nineteen native tongues in this year's peloton, only a smattering of words could be understood by all.

Cycling had become increasingly international. Each team had a home country, but the athletes who made up the team often came from around the world. Even those squads that emphasized local connections tended to have foreign talent. That was lucky for Ben, who had found a new home on the primarily French Banque Fédérale squad after losing his job with the mostly American Megatronics team.

While Ben rode he surveyed his competitors for potential weakness: a wrap on a previously naked knee, redness in someone's eye, an unexpected change in equipment. He loved the hidden intensity in these moments when the racing wasn't going full throttle. A rider could rest his muscles and forge alliances. Men might learn, or be tricked into believing, that cooperating with various rivals could advance their goals. Competitors spent breath on bits of conversation, laying groundwork for chaos later in the stage. The coalitions were necessary because working solo was nearly always suicidal.

The cyclist ahead of Ben wore number thirty-one. Curly black locks reached to the shoulders of his red shirt. He had no water bottle in his cage, preferring that his teammates carry liquid for him whenever possible. It was Kyle Smith of the American based Megatronics team.

Three years ago they were both neo-pros, rookie cyclists, for Megatronics. On the bike they pushed each other hard. Off the bike they couldn't see eye to eye. Kyle continually chased Ben's girlfriend. Eventually that escalated into sabotaging Ben at the U.S. Cycling Championships. Kyle had ended up winning the race, and then he used his resultant influence to force Ben from the team. The guy was a master of PR, and he used those skills to promote himself at others' expense. The fallout nearly cost Ben his career. To him, the backside of Kyle's jersey served as a matador's cape.

"Looks like you passed your first test," Kyle said as the two drew even.

"Bouncing down the road on my head is a test?"

"Yeah, but you're the only one dumb enough to take it."

Typical. Ben pedaled harder. He'd rather not think about his aches, and he definitely wasn't interested in discussing them with Kyle. The real test, as always, had been getting back on the bike.

Kyle accelerated to stay alongside. "You sure act cocky for a guy with only two seconds to spare."

It was a reference to Ben's General Classification lead, the standings that listed cumulative times for each competitor. Was he fishing for congratulations on second position or something? It didn't matter. Ben had better things to worry about than Kyle's opinion of him.

Kyle ripped open an energy gel with his teeth, and spat the package top onto the road. "Still the same motherless cowboy you always were. Let me tell you something, Barnes. You ain't fit for yellow."

"We'll see about that," Ben said, touching his shoulder through the torn fabric. The maillot jaune wasn't holding up too well, but somehow it felt better than ever. He powered forward, separating himself from his nemesis and moving beside the next guy in line, Gunter von Reinholdt.

Ben wished Kyle were his only concern. Gunter stood third overall, a mere second behind Kyle in the General Classification. The German led a super-strong team called Deutscher Aufbau. It was rare for the top of the leader board to be so crowded this late in the race.

Gunter looked over, a friendly expression masking his famous killer instinct. Blonde eyebrows arched over intense blue eyes. Criss-crossing scars on his chin spoke of multiple meetings with the pavement. He patted Ben on the back. "*Sind sie verletzt?*"

Ben crinkled his brow.

"Hurt?" Gunter translated.

"Naw. Just needed to sand off some irregularities."

Gunter laughed, "We hoped you were okay."

Ben smiled. Why did the German always refer to himself in the plural? He liked this guy, despite his quirks.

Ben's lead was tenuous. He could be overtaken by both Kyle and Gunter in the time it took to swallow. He could hardly believe he led such cyclists at all, let alone the entire rosters of eighteen more teams. Settling on his saddle, he removed his sunglasses and fit the arms into helmet vents so they were available but out of the way. He spotted a boy, about twelve years old, beside the course. The kid straddled a too-large bike, just like Ben had in his early teens. As the boy noticed Ben's stare, a grin exploded across his face and he shot a thumbs-up sign. Ben winked.

He loved helping kids. He knew firsthand what it felt like to grow up without parents. Ever since he'd turned pro, visits to disadvantaged children had become a regular part of his routine, a sort of repayment for the investment others once made in him. Four months earlier, the evening after he'd settled into his European training base of Gerona, Spain, Ben dropped by the local orphanage to say hello. The children were in the midst of celebrating Toma Subic's thirteenth birthday. He was a frail little waif with a smile that filled half his face. Ben smiled back, noticing that the kid had pasted cycling photographs over every inch of his meager personal space, including the backside of his headboard.

"Do you know Thierry DePerdiux?" Toma asked when he learned how Ben made his living.

"*Sí.* I've just joined his team."

Toma's eyes grew round. "He's my hero."

"Mine too."

"King Thierry never gives up. I love him for that."

Afterward, each time Ben visited, Toma followed him around. Ben answered the boy's endless questions while noticing the children's tattered clothes and lack of books. One day he pulled a caseworker aside. "What can you tell me about Toma?"

"Not much. As outgoing as he seems, he keeps his thoughts private."

"I've noticed. How did he get here?"

"He was evacuated from Croatia about six years ago. A labor camp left him behind when they moved to a new location. He nearly lost his left foot to gangrene. It was months before he uttered a word. Once he did, he told us he'd seen his mother murdered. No details."

Ben sucked air through his teeth.

The caseworker continued. "Toma's a smart kid—speaks three languages."

"What happened to his father?"

The caseworker shrugged. "He gets jittery if you bring him up. My guess is that he doesn't remember having a dad. At the time of Toma's rescue he was seven years old and had been in forced labor for at least a year. Despite all that, he's still got an insatiable thirst for life."

"That I do know. Every time I'm around him I feel better for it."

Ben saved money and gathered donations for two weeks. He'd never felt happier than the day he delivered books, some clothes, and a shiny new bike to the orphanage. He spent his free time training Toma. The boy wasn't particularly talented, but his raw determination resulted in an age-division victory by his third race.

Toma embraced Ben on the day he left for the Tour and kissed him on the cheek. "I love you, Ben. Good luck!"

At that moment, neither of them could have imagined the luck Ben would have on l' Alpe d'Huez. Yesterday's victory on the Tour's toughest mountain stage had been unthinkable. Today it wasn't Thierry's name painted all over the road, but Ben's. He felt obligated to live up to his mentor's reputation, and to make Toma proud.

Overnight, American flags had sprouted like dandelions. He even noticed a Utah flag waving in the wind. Ben had never realized he held feelings for that dark blue bed sheet of a banner, but today it energized him.

A group of women cheered, "Barnes-tormer, Barnstormer, Barnstormer!"

"You're making me jealous," said Luigi.

Ben laughed. "I'm not interested in those women. Bridgette is the only girl for me." Yesterday, in the midst of all the excitement, he'd asked her to marry him. She'd said yes.

Luigi breathed easily, hardly tested by riding in the draft at the current pace. "Ahhh, to love just one woman. How can you do it? Monotony will never be for me."

Ben chuckled.

The Italian furrowed his brow. "I tell you a better idea. Luigi will take care of your spare women. Think of it as my engagement gift. Bene?"

There were spare women. There was an abundance of people of every kind, all wanting a piece of him. Whether in person or through the lens of a television camera, everyone sought a glimpse of the yellow jersey. Millions of eyes weighed upon him. The expectations of generations were his obligation to fulfill. He would give everything he could.

Today, even the French believed in Ben Barnes. Yesterday, the day their legendary hero went down, Ben had transformed a disastrous stage for Banque Fédérale into an unforgettable triumph. As a result, in the span of twenty-four hours he'd gone from outcast to adopted son.

He looked at the fans gratefully, then noticed a red-faced boy holding up today's edition of the newspaper *Français au Fond*. Ben's smile faded. The paper bore a photo of him crossing yesterday's finish line. His raised arms appeared to hoist the gigantic superimposed title: "Doper?"

Ben stopped pedaling as a sickening chill shook his spine.

Chapter Two

The cheers of the roadside crowd rang hollow. Someone had painted the outline of a syringe with long needle on the asphalt. "B-E-N" was printed in the chamber. He'd never imagined his success would be turned against him like this. If the only evidence required to assassinate his reputation was the strength of his performance, then the harder he worked, the guiltier he looked. Could anybody ever win a battle like that?

Some people obviously assumed there was something behind these accusations. Most of Europe, plus large chunks of the rest of the world, paid close attention to the Tour. This sort of innuendo could spread like fire in a hayloft. Who had started it? Why? How would Toma react? What about other young cycling hopefuls, kids Ben tried to set a positive example for?

He keyed his radio. "What's this *au Fond* headline about?"

"Ignore it," Thierry said.

"It's slander."

"The press will say what they like as long as you are relevant. When the gossip stops … that's when you should worry."

That may be true, but Ben sure wouldn't mind coming face to face with the journalist responsible for this lie.

Kyle pulled alongside Ben. "Did you really ask for a 'fix' over your radio? What kind of an idiot are you?"

Ben stared in disbelief. He moved away from his rival and activated his radio. "Why did Kyle just ask me about a 'fix.'"

Thierry's calm voice came over his earpiece. The directeur sportif's words flowed into all remaining Banque Fédérale teammate's headsets as well. "They mentioned it on television. Apparently a journalist was listening in on your conversation with Thelma. He believes he's connected the dots."

"He thinks Thelma's a drug dealer? Are you kidding?"

"Isn't that what it sounded like?"

Ben couldn't believe his ears. First there was the scandalous headline and now this misunderstanding added to it? What else could go wrong? The idea of Thelma as a criminal was comical. "This is ridic..." Albert looked back and sliced at his throat with his level palm. Then he crossed his lips with an index finger. Ben shut his mouth.

Albert drifted beside Ben and whispered. "Thierry's always been driven by the opinions of skeptics and assumes you will be too."

Ben gritted his teeth.

"Can you use anger to your advantage?" Albert asked.

"Huh? This is character assassination."

"Who cares? You can't worry about how they twist your words."

Ben's pulse had soared with his rage, but Albert was right. He fought for calm. Time for deep breaths. He could only expend energy on the things within his control. Drug accusations weren't one of them. He knew he rode clean. Nothing else mattered.

Two cyclists sprinted past the Banque Fédérale-led peloton. Three more flew forward to join them. The slight disorganization at the front of the group had enticed these men to take a shot.

The radio hissed then Thierry's voice came through. "*Huées.* Those weren't the guys we planned on letting go." Ben heard television commentary in the background. The team directeur continued to analyze events as they played out on his dashboard TV screen. "One of Gunter's men sneaked into that break. Reel them back."

With a man up the road, Gunter controlled a chess piece in the attack zone. It gave him a wide array of tactical options. Banque Fédérale needed to remove the threat. Ben up-shifted as his teammates increased the pace. He glanced over his shoulder and found Kyle Smith grinning broadly. No wonder. With Banque Fédérale forced to assume the workload, Kyle and his domestiques could tuck into their draft.

Things weren't going according to plan. As team leader, the energy of Ben's support riders was almost as valuable to him as his own. It killed him to burn them out so early in the day.

Kyle sneered. "Bore me a great big hole in the wind, boys."

Ben sat in Albert's draft, cursing himself as his teammates hammered away up front.

The effort increased as the peloton neared the summit of the 1376-meter Col d'Ornon. Ben stood on his pedals, fighting for position. The scent of lavender laced the wind as the cyclists charged through dappled sunshine. More than two hundred kilometers, over 126 miles, still to go today.

Despite the rapid pace, the five breakaway cyclists remained out of sight as the ribbon of asphalt switched back upon itself and gave the riders a view of the road they'd just climbed. Villages gathered around church spires dotted the canyon below. Similar outposts clung to the steep faces of mountains far in the distance. The scene looked like a masterfully designed model: too quaint to be real.

As the gradient increased the pace did, too—a painful relationship. Ben fought for position. He resisted the urge to look back at Kyle, fearing both what he might see and what he might show. Best to keep his gaze locked straight ahead. If any of his rivals recognized his distress the attacks would be relentless. It was too early in the day to be in such misery. He concentrated on the spinning spokes just in front of him and ignored the signals wailing within his body.

Ben had half expected this jersey to give him strength, but it didn't. Legend claimed that wearing it lifted ordinary men to great performances. Despite the lore, today Ben's legs felt more like wet noodles than iron pistons. If something didn't change soon he'd face trouble. Nothing felt right as he fought to maintain the narrow gap to Albert's wheel.

Even though the breakaway group remained clear as the peloton crested the pass, Ben felt enormous relief. Ahead lay thirty kilometers of downhill road, considered by some the most enjoyable decent in all the Alps. It began with three quick whoopty-doos, rolling bumps that nearly tossed the men airborne. They soon entered a hanging glacial valley. The peloton poured onto the slope like liquid mercury, its mass stretching thinner as speeds increased, but the whole remaining intact.

The road took a half dozen long, sweeping turns, like the path of an expert skier schussing a beginners' run. It was as safe a descent as the Tour ever confronted—moderate grade, no drop-offs, clear visibility, few blind corners, a headwind to check the speed, and fresh black pavement without defect.

The breeze invigorated Ben. Today he felt more comfortable descending than ever before. Downhill tentativeness used to be his biggest weakness as a cyclist. The fear of crashing often tempted him to brake for corners harder and longer than necessary, costing valuable time and energy. Today he and his machine were one.

He whipped through a bend, leaning low to fight the centrifugal force. The sensation of rubber biting asphalt thrilled him. Then he righted his machine and rocketed through a straightaway.

The route entered Chantelouve. The air surrounding each object he passed—trees, cliffs, buildings, spectators, automobiles, garden walls—made it's own sound and had a distinctive aura. Ben's eyes were on the road where he must be wary of rocks, dust, potholes, oil spots, and worst of all, dogs.

Thelma's voice emerged from the earpiece. "Goodness! Is this safe? We're going awfully fast!"

Ben grinned, imagining her gripping the dashboard in the passenger seat of the support car. Several teammates looked back and smiled. They were flying down the hill, but to a pro cyclist this was almost a lazy descent. A recreational bicycle rider wouldn't dream of taking his eyes off the road, even momentarily, under such conditions, yet these men did it almost casually. One cyclist separated himself from the field and rode without hands while he slipped into a windbreaker.

"You asked me to win," Ben answered.

"Oh my. I wouldn't have asked for anything if I'd known it would put you in such danger. It looked risky from my living room, but this … Wow!"

"Enough chit chat," said Thierry. He probably regretted inviting a chatterbox like Thelma on board.

In Les Daurens checkered linen danced on the line, appearing to toss wind up the hill. A flop-eared donkey with a baffled expression watched the entourage navigate the perimeter of his pasture. The cyclists crossed the river Le Bonne on a covered bridge, and continued carving turns through small vineyards.

As the descent slowed, Ben massaged his right thigh, trying to work lactic acid out of the muscle in preparation for the next climb. He would have liked to unclip his foot and shake the entire leg out, but he might as well sign his own death warrant as admit to weakness or even discomfort. Finally the road left the wide valley through high, narrow walls.

The course leveled out. They pedaled through Valbonnais, a hodgepodge village of stucco and asphalt whose streets were defined by the open angular spaces between scattered buildings. On the opposite side of the wide valley ahead the gargantuan l' Obiou rose like an inverted fang.

Cyclists crowded the right hand edge of the pavement, trying to gain the largest radius possible for the left turn onto a new road. Men leaned on their machines and dove through the corner, only centimeters between wheels, pedals, and handlebars. A single touch of the brakes could cause a pile-up. Rivals or not, trust in every competitor's ability was fundamental to getting through safely. Once pointed in the new direction they righted their machines and sprinted to regain the slight loss in momentum.

The highway they had just joined was known as the Route Napoléon. On his way to reclaiming power after exile on the Isle of Elba, Napoléon traversed this same route over a six-day span in late winter, 1814—the beginning of his Waterloo Campaign. The cyclists rode in the opposite direction than the emperor and his band of loyalists had taken through the Alps. Like Napoléon before him, Ben needed to sneak through this passage, only within plain sight of his foes. Just then, a crazy idea occurred to him.

He dropped back between Gunter and Kyle, removing his left foot from his pedal and shaking his leg violently. "Maybe I'll attack again, like yesterday."

Gunter laughed. "Good one. We'll admit you fooled us once. It won't happen again."

A pair of domestiques looked over, clearly annoyed that anybody would have the energy to talk. They would bear the brunt of the workload for most of the stage.

Ben clicked his shoe back into the pedal. Then he removed the opposite foot while looking at Kyle. He made a show of shaking that leg out. An invigorated feeling flowed through his muscles. "How about you, pal? Ready to face the wind?"

Kyle glared.

"Guess not. No need to be in such a foul mood." Competition, ethics, and desire for the same woman had driven successive wedges between Ben and Kyle, but passion for cycling kept their lives intertwined. Ben respected Kyle, even if the feeling wasn't mutual.

Around them, thousands of butterflies, resembling spastic flower petals, bobbed on the wind. Orange, black, or white, each seemed magnetized to a matching mate. They'd collide in mid-air again and again as if determined to exchange wings. What a day for a bike ride!

Ben clipped back into the pedal and took two strong strokes forward to rejoin his team. There were still three tough mountains to climb. Even two seconds lost to unmet challenges would cost him the maillot juane.

They left the Route Napoléon for a minor highway to the right. It plummeted to the shore of Lac du Sautet where bright catamarans skated through frothing turquoise waves. The cyclists raced along the water's edge and crossed a lattice-like bridge where it spanned a narrow gorge. To their right a gray cement dam plummeted so deep that its base wasn't visible.

The road rebounded up the opposite wall. Atop the Côte de Masserange, the cyclists reached another fertile shelf. A farmer had positioned his rain bird sprinkler to shoot a soaring arc down the left-hand side of the road. Ben drenched himself, thankful for the cool shower. The water evaporated quickly in the oppressive heat. The gradient kicked up and they began climbing the category-two Col du Festre. In the old days, categories corresponded to the automobile gear necessary to cross the summit. Category-four hills were moderate bumps that a driver could cross without downshifting. Category-one climbs took everything the jalopy had in its lowest gear, but those weren't the most challenging tests. The toughest ascents ruptured the scale. These killer pitches were classified as hors catagorie: out-of-category. In the early 1900's even the sturdiest automobiles couldn't conquer this sort of climb until the passengers got out and leant their elbow grease.

Nowadays the categorizations also took into account average gradient, length, road surface, placement in the stage, and other factors. The rating determined how many climbing competition points would be awarded to the first men over the summits. It also gave the cyclists a heads up on what they faced next.

Fortunately, there were no hors catagorie summits on today's route. There had been a trio of these killer climbs on yesterday's stage to 'l Alpe d'Huez alone, and three more were scattered among the Pyrenean climbs slated for next week.

Near the midway point on the ascent of the Festre where the road switched back upon itself in the village of Angiéres, the peloton finally caught sight of the five-man breakaway. They were all sitting up, hands atop their handlebars. It was the most comfortable position to ride in, but under these conditions it signaled surrender. Ben heaved a sigh of relief just as three new escapists took off.

His gut wrenched as this new threat disappeared beyond a bleating flock of freshly shorn sheep. Before he countered, Thierry's calm analysis came over the radio. "Let those guys go. None endanger Ben's position. Their lead might discourage our rivals from attacking."

Banque Fédérale let up on the gas, and since no rival team was motivated enough to move up front and push the pace, the peloton slowed. Ben knew the escapists would be happy about this. The initial success of most breakaways had as much to do with the peloton's desire to chase the men down as with the strength of the riders involved. If a man had enough friends he was likely to escape off the front often; if he had enough enemies he would never build a substantial gap.

Ben's legs still felt hollow, so the slackened pace came as welcome reprieve; but recovery didn't come. His thighs burned. His lungs felt scorched. Fear, an emotion he couldn't afford, nagged at him. He stole a glance behind. Kyle seemed to be coasting along. Would an attack come soon? Could he counter it? Was the weight of the yellow jersey pulling him down instead of invigorating him?

Deep breaths were the answer. Think clearly. Kyle would wait to make his move. That made sense. He couldn't risk attacking too early and blowing up before the line. The yellow jersey was too important a prize. He'd go late and attempt to overpower his rivals to the finish. Ben needed to conserve energy to shadow his adversary once that attack came. He needed to ride tactically, neutralizing Kyle in the rush to the line.

The men gained the pass. Beyond the crowds Ben eyed a gleaming brass statue depicting the Virgin Mary with a smiling Christ Child in her arms. The six-foot tall base was mostly obscured by floral offerings. Ben unzipped his jersey. He grabbed his water bottle, took a long swig, and then squirted the remaining water onto his face and body. The cool evaporation refreshed him in the increasingly muggy air. He tossed the empty container to the side of the road. A domestique handed him a fresh water bottle and Ben slipped it into his cage.

Spokes sang in the wind as bicycle wheels spun faster on the descent. This road was steep and fast. Ben pulled his sunglasses low on his nose so that he could see over the top of them just as he entered a winding tunnel. His eyes weren't fully adjusted, even as he shot into full sunshine again. He pushed his glasses back into place and concentrated on the road. Within less than five kilometers and without passing through a single village they reached level ground.

A pink hang glider swooped over them from behind, and the unlikely looking pilot, a 50-something farmer with a large paunch held in by blue coveralls, yelled down at them. "*Vive le Tour! Vive le Tour! Vive le Tour!*"

The peloton rushed down a curving descent into Gap. A pair of policemen watched the readout on their radar gun. Ben looked at his cyclometer: Sixty-eight in a fifty-kilometer per hour zone. If regular rules applied he'd be paying a hefty fine.

The cyclists charged through town and then left on a road beneath shimmering silver maples. It eventually hugged the eastern foothills of a flat-bottomed valley. The orchards and vineyards extending to the opposite canyon wall resembled a patchwork quilt.

Then the day's final climb, the assault of the 1240-meter category-two Col du Labouret began. Judging effort and spending it only at crucial moments would be the key to finishing strong.

At the foot of the hill the three breakaway riders came into view. Despite the peloton's pace, these men hadn't established much of a gap. A roar rose from the crowd. Domestiques charged forward. Their respective leaders tucked behind them and sprinted for the front of the group. The road clogged with sudden activity. The space at the head of the race that might have comfortably contained five athletes now housed twenty-five. Cyclists jostled through traffic, shoulder to shoulder and brake hood to brake hood, in the suddenly tense environment.

Ben churned his legs to maintain contact with the crashing wave, burning energy he hadn't known he had. If he fell to the back, an unbridgeable gap would surely form. He clambered toward Albert's rear wheel near the front of the frenzied group.

One by one, athletes fell off the pace, but a dozen were still vying for membership in the lead pack. Then, as if blasted from a cannon, Kyle Smith shot up the hill: a mind-boggling display of strength. Here was the moment Ben had been anticipating. He dug deep, driving strength into the pedals. It wasn't enough.

He looked to the crowd, hoping to feed off their energy, but they stared back in near silence, witnesses to the moment the yellow jersey wearer cracked. Instead of feeling their enthusiasm, he read doubt.

"*Dopage!*" yelled an angry looking man.

The one word question on today's newspaper flashed into Ben's mind. How many of these people believed the lie? He tried again to stand on the pedals, to get away from this place as quickly as possible, but his muscles wouldn't lift him.

His bike slowed further. Ben drifted miserably toward the back of the small group as Gunter, muscles knotted and teeth gritted, launched himself in pursuit of Kyle.

"Come on, Ben. Now is the moment," Thierry pleaded over the headset.

Ben steeled himself and tried again, but his legs were fried.

Albert glanced back. Ben shrugged an apology.

"Dammit, Barnes! No excuses!" Albert gasped.

Ben rose again, but the front wheel dropped into a pothole he hadn't noticed and he jolted forward. As he recovered, a loud hiss and a jellylike sensation in his handlebars told him he'd flatted.

Chapter Three

"Take my bike!" Albert yelled.

Ben squeezed the brakes and jumped off his machine. He handed it to a surprised fan, and then grabbed Albert's bicycle. He clipped his right foot into the pedal as he stepped over the crossbar. Albert gave a running push and Ben snapped his toe clip into the other pedal.

"*Allez! Allez! Allez!* No regrets," Albert yelled.

Albert's words reminded Ben how he'd feel if he didn't give everything to the chase. He stood on his pedals and sprinted for the group. Because of their similar size, the teammates had discussed trading bikes rather than switching wheels in an emergency situation, but the assumption had always been that it would be Ben giving Albert his machine. Ben hadn't even sat on this bike before.

It surprised him that he immediately liked it. The small differences in configuration felt good, allowing him to access muscle fibers that weren't yet spent. For the first time he felt the energy boost he'd assumed the yellow jersey would bring.

He caught the group of cyclists with surprising ease, and then dropped into his saddle, increasing the revs as he worked his way through their ranks. These men were hurting, silently suffering beneath the roar of the crowd. Even Luigi's form had disintegrated. His shoulders swayed from side to side as he struggled to overcome the slope. Ben patted his friend on the back as he moved past. Luigi lifted his eyes and grinned; then he dropped his head and resumed his labor.

Overtaking the lead cyclist in the group, Ben focused his thoughts on the only two men still farther up the road: the two he needed to beat. Winning the Tour de France didn't require winning every day. No cyclist could do that, but victories in key moments could crush a rival's spirit, preparing the way for the overall title. If Ben could win today, he would take a big step toward victory in Paris. If he lost, the maillot jaune would be stolen from him, and the overall title would be up for grabs.

"Do that jersey proud," Coach breathed through the headset. The man was in his element, having organized and directed hundreds of amateur races during his life. "Do me proud, Ben!"

Ben churned the pedals, past ancient church spires and gorgeous pine forests. He eventually entered a fertile valley of such jaw-dropping beauty that even on a route like today's it stood out like a diamond among emeralds.

On the straightaway ahead he spotted Gunter, still visible amid crowding fans. Ben couldn't waste energy looking back to see if he was clear of the other riders. It didn't matter, anyway; his battle was with Kyle, the man who wasn't even in sight.

He fought his machine forward, hungry for every meter. He rounded a corner and saw Gunter again. He'd pegged the German, neither losing nor gaining any distance, but what about Kyle? He'd taken off looking like a motorcycle rider. Had he maintained such a pace? Impossible.

"Gap?" Ben asked into the radio.

"Eleven seconds to Gunter, twenty-eight to Kyle," Thierry said. "Just concentrate on the German for now."

The road crested another false summit before tilting up again. In a way, these changes in effort were more challenging than a constant gradient. Hopefully his rivals didn't enjoy them any more than he did.

"That's better, son!" Coach encouraged. "Maintain rhythm. Find your pace. Reel those suckers in."

Suckers riding bicycles? Something about an unexpected image of lollipops on wheels struck a chord. The cartoonish vision amused Ben. A smile tugged at his cheeks. He noticed a motorcycle cameraman zoom in on his face. Viewers must wonder what he could find funny. Grinning forced some of the pain away, but Ben couldn't maintain the humor.

A group of spectators sipping wine cheered his renewed vigor. Some deep recess of his brain acknowledged the encouragement and lifted him from the saddle. He bore down and accelerated.

Another long straightaway opened ahead. Gunter moved up the hill amidst a wave of enthusiastic fans. Still no sign of Kyle. Were Ben's eyes playing tricks on him? Was the man in the red jersey invisible because of the surging humanity? Ben clawed forward, feeling his earlier exhaustion creeping back. He held it at bay, returning his focus to Gunter.

"Scotty, we need more power," Fritz yelled in his best Captain Kirk impression.

A man carrying an enormous French flag ran alongside. "Courage! Courage! Courage!"

This climb, even though designated a lesser category-two, seemed to have no end. The gradient hurt. Running fans easily kept pace for short distances. Ben sensed a citadel to his right, but didn't dare look for the summit for fear the unnecessary motion would derail his rhythm. Or maybe he couldn't bear finding that the remaining task required more strength than he had left.

Ben didn't worry about finding space through the teeming crowd. He trusted that the route would clear as his progress forced the fans aside. A fly landed on his cheek, its footsteps tickling him. Ben didn't shake the bug off. He just kept the path clear for messages being relayed from brain to legs, lungs, and heart. He vaguely processed the encouragement streaming through the headset from his friends in the car behind. First Thierry, then Thelma, Coach, and finally Fritz. Then it was Thierry again and another cycle was underway.

Suddenly ice water jolted him. He tensed as it coursed down his skin. The flood evicted the fly. A fan must have dumped a bottle over his head. Ben turned angrily to see where it had come from. Water was appreciated, but ice?

Instead his gaze found the intense expressions of Thierry, Thelma, Coach, and Fritz, pasted like caricatures to the front window of the support vehicle. They looked like they meant to will him over the mountain. He had to reward their faith.

"No! No! No!" Thelma shrieked. "Look the other way!"

Ben laughed again. What other cyclist had such a sage advisor? He straightened his thoughts and redoubled his efforts. The gap to Gunter had collapsed by half, and the top of the climb was in sight. Surprisingly, this now came as bad news. The finish line was nearing and Kyle remained out front.

"Gap?"

"Twenty-five seconds to Kyle," Thierry said.

Ben crossed the summit close on Gunter's heels. He threw himself into the descent. If they joined forces they could further increase their speed. A long hard road remained, with plenty of false flats and small climbs thrown in. Alliances of convenience played a crucial role in cycling strategy, often working against stronger riders. Kyle deserved nothing less.

Gravity flushed them through the shaded stucco canyons of a village so inviting that even a downhill racer had to resist the urge to stop.

With his bike in its highest gear, Ben drove his legs, reaching for the German. He yelled.

Gunter turned his head. A pleased expression broke across his face. He swept an arm wide, inviting Ben to race past. A pair of high tech gliders flying in formation whooshed past them. The sleek aircraft banked against the sun.

Ben felt Gunter tuck in behind as the two bicycles cruised out of the town. Gunter stored up momentum and shot by. Ben dove into the vacuum behind the German. He held the gap at inches, taking maximum advantage of the draft.

The road zinged left, right, and then left again. When Ben felt strong enough he pulled back into the lead. As he did, an invisible swarm of gnats sandpapered his face. It was a good thing he wore sunglasses.

Working as a team, the two cyclists increased their speed, even though the gradient relented. With wind wailing through his ears Ben couldn't make out anything being said over the headset. Surely he'd spot Kyle soon.

A dead tree beside the road had been filled with purple and green balloons in honor of Banque Fédérale. The men powered over another steep intermediate summit, and then hung on tight as technical turns came fast and furious on a ten-percent descent. Senses on high alert, Ben experienced a sort of euphoria as he screamed down the hill.

The two men worked well together, jamming out of the forest and into the outskirts of Digne-les-Baines, today's finishing town. Neither man wanted to play the cat and mouse game that often ensues when two cyclists near a finish line together, positioning for a prestigious win or finishing bonus. The stage winner would be awarded a twenty-second premium. That precious time would be subtracted from his cumulative score. The second-place man would earn a twelve-second bonus while a final award of eight seconds would be deducted from the overall time of the man who took third. Ben would rather drive hard for the line than squabble with Gunter over four seconds of bonus differential. His legs seared by the days effort, he pushed on.

As Ben and Gunter charged past the two-kilometer to go marker, Ben realized his yellow jersey was lost. No way could he catch Kyle in time. His rival would wear the maillot jaune tomorrow. His shoulders sagged. Gunter powered into the lead.

Ben clenched his teeth as the German's pace increased. It was too much. He couldn't hang on. The gap to Gunter widened. Beneath the flamme rouge, the triangular red banner that designated one kilometer to go, Ben seemed to be moving backwards.

"Keep it together," Thierry ordered. "Only 900 meters left. You'll answer to me if you hold anything back!"

Ben fought to regroup. The finishing straight opened ahead between ancient stone buildings. Two digital clocks stared back at him, mounted atop a temporary archway constructed over the road. The elapsed time clock had stopped. That meant Kyle was in. Beside it, the time gap clock counted higher. It already read twenty-three seconds. As Gunter crossed the line it read twenty-nine seconds. Ben twisted and pulled his machine to conquer the last few meters, practically bending the bike frame. His lungs felt on the verge of exploding when he finally collapsed across the line, forty-six seconds behind Kyle Smith.

Ben sagged over his bike, his yellow jersey tattered and limp, ready to be stolen. He'd let so many people down. If only he could have pushed a little bit more. The team had performed so well, protecting and keeping him supplied with food and liquid throughout the day, but he'd failed to reward their efforts. Third place wasn't good enough. How would he face those men? They'd made enormous sacrifices on his behalf, and he'd let them down in return.

Despite exhaustion he forced himself to face the failure. He needed to fully experience the disappointment. He'd use the loss to drive himself back into the lead.

He'd broken his promise to Thelma, the first person ever to believe in him unconditionally. He'd let down Toma and the little boy with the big bike he'd seen this morning, plus so many other fans who had urged him to victory. He'd failed to capitalize on Albert's sacrifice. And what about Thierry? His anger over the radio wasn't merely an act. If the former champion hadn't crashed the day before, he would have kept the yellow jersey for his team. The list went on and on: Coach Bill, Bridgette ... too many to process. So many people had heaped hope on Ben's shoulders. He'd accepted it, reveled in it, believed in it. Then he'd gone out and squandered everything.

He looked up. Bridgette ran toward him. How would he explain?

Chapter Four

Ben could hardly find the strength to keep his head up as he watched his fiancée approach. He gasped for breath, wiping stinging sweat from his eyes. His body was entirely used up.

"You were wonderful!" Bridgette's voice lilted musically. She moved with an easygoing, athletic grace. She sure could make shorts and a t-shirt look good.

They'd been through some tough times together, and emerged stronger for it. Pursuing a pro cycling career demanded huge sacrifices. He would have been forced to give up long ago, if not for her tireless support. No athlete ever made it to this level without hitting the wall many, many times. In his darkest hours, she'd always been there for him. Ben couldn't imagine anybody he'd rather spend his life with. It still hadn't completely sunk in that she'd chosen to spend hers with him. He looked at her, fascinated by the way her blue eyes sparkled and the sun shone off her auburn hair.

When she kissed him, he caught a scent of wildflowers. He didn't mean to accept congratulations for failure, but it felt so good to be near her that he couldn't help kissing back. She'd told him yesterday about her thing for men in yellow. He wore the leader's jersey at the moment, but didn't she realize he'd just lost it?

"I'm so proud of you." She hugged him.

Ben winced.

"Oh, *désolé*. Let me take a look at that shoulder." Bridgette examined Ben's wounds. Her degree was in sports medicine and her comprehensive understanding of diet, training methods, and the human mind explained her loyal clientele. Not just cyclists, but many other top athletes sought her advice. Ben got better attention than any of them. She'd taught him proper hydration, diet, and supplementation. She'd shown him how to peak at the perfect moment. He meticulously followed the schedules she set. But her insight was far greater than that. Bridgette understood the inner workings of Ben's mind. She'd figured out ways to get more out of him than he knew how to ask of himself. Along the way, she'd also become his best friend.

"Your wounds are superficial, but I'm sure they sting."

"They're not a problem. It's thirst that's killing me. I'd love a slice of Green River watermelon right now."

"Yeah. Right. Here's an electrolyte drink instead."

He lifted it to his lips, visualizing the bleak Southern Utah outpost where Interstate-70 crossed the Green River. The town sat on the sorriest patch of acidic dirt in the state, but there wasn't another gas station for seventy miles to the east, or a motel for seventy miles to the west so the economy always plugged along.

Then, one day, somebody spit a watermelon seed onto the riverbank and a miracle happened. The combination of limy soil, tons of water, and day after day of blazing sunshine somehow created the perfect anecdote to heat exhaustion. As far as Ben was concerned, Green River watermelon put ordinary melons to shame.

"The press will be anxious to see you." Bridgette nodded to the right. Kyle was surrounded by reporters, looking refreshed.

"I need to catch my breath," Ben said.

"Breath-catching is for domestiques. You're a star. Life has changed."

Simone Sardou, a mainstream television reporter known for her love of cycling, caught Ben's eye. "Can I ask some questions?"

Bridgette held up a hand as she fished in her purse and then handed Ben a pen and some documents. "Another moment, *s'il vous plait*," she said. "Ben must complete some paperwork."

He suppressed a chuckle, allowing his breathing to slow as he pretended to look the documents over. After a while, he scribbled, "You are so damn hot," at the bottom of the first page and handed it back to her.

She looked at it, satisfied.

He wrote, "You complete me," on the second one and passed it over as well.

She smiled impatiently as she gathered the rest of the papers from beneath his pen and pointed toward the reporters. By now a half dozen journalists waited. Ben wiped his brow and stepped forward.

Simone Sardou raised a hand while the other journalists around her yelled questions. Ben had admired her work for a long time. Now he appreciated her demeanor, so he asked for her question first. "What was the hardest thing about today's race?"

Ben cleared his throat. "That Kyle and Gunter were so good. It's not the roads that make the Tour de France the toughest endurance event in the world. It's how your competition forces you to deal with them. Those guys made things difficult today."

The reporters nodded, jotting notes. Cyclists continued to flow across the line. Every man must finish each stage within a percentage of the winner's time. The cut off was determined using a table that took into account terrain and average speed. Today the deadline would be around 110 percent. Men who didn't beat the clock would be disqualified.

Another journalist yelled over the crowd. "So, are you equal to the competition?"

Ben shook his head. "We'll know that in Paris. A couple more days like yesterday and I'll be fine."

"You honestly believe you could take them by surprise again?"

"No. But surprise isn't the only way to gain time. I'll give the race everything I've got."

A third reporter grabbed the spotlight. "How do you answer allegations that yesterday's performance was drug assisted?" The man's credential said *au Fond*.

Blood heated Ben's face. "Apparently you know something I don't. Does your paper require evidence, or do you write whatever you want?"

"Is asking for a 'fix' over the radio evidence?"

"Only if you know a law against ordering spaghetti."

A reporter looked up from his notes.

"My friend, Thelma, calls her secret recipe, 'The Fix,'" Ben explained.

The *au Fond* writer scowled. "Our readers find it suspicious that a back of the pack athlete could suddenly turn in a dominating performance like yours, yesterday."

"I've worked hard. I'm in the best shape of my life. Does anybody else have a question?"

The *au Fond* man shouted over the others. "If you're in such incredible shape, why did you start producing results only yesterday?"

Ben shook his head. The journalist's aggressive demeanor was really derailing him. Ben had been involved in an accident two years earlier that had killed Thierry's younger brother. Thierry had forgiven him long ago. Yesterday's performance and the crowd's acceptance made Ben think the memory was finally fading for the rest of the country. This guy apparently didn't want to let it die.

"After a week and a half of working as a domestique, on the stage to 'l Alpe d'Huez I got the chance to show what I could do at the front of the race. Fortunately, things turned out well."

The *au Fond* man twirled his mechanical pencil like a miniature baton. "So, why didn't you repeat it today? After all, you've now forced your former director out of the way and taken control of the strongest team in the race."

Ben wanted to drop this subject, but he couldn't stand to let these inaccuracies go unchallenged. The premise was all wrong. He hadn't played a role in the decision to axe the former directeur, though it had been made because of him. When the team owner discovered that his directeur intended to prevent Ben from winning, he'd canned him. "I didn't have anyone fired. I don't control this team."

The reporter spread his hands, palms to the sky, as if his conclusions were inescapable. "It appears you've maneuvered your way into a position where you can do whatever you want."

"Not true, and even if it were, why would you assume that I'd break the rules just because I could get away with it? Is that what you'd do?"

"You defend yourself by attacking me?"

"I'm simply saying I don't cheat."

"Isn't it true that cyclists are put in positions where their choice is either drugs or retirement?" the *au Fond* reporter asked. Some people were obsessed with drug accusations. They believed the sport was saturated with corruption. This guy seemed to be the poster boy for the movement.

"I've never faced a decision like that. Does anybody else have a question?"

Another reporter spoke up. "Have you ever taken injections to race?"

The journalists leaned in. The most influential group he'd ever spoken to waited to hear the sort of information he was least prepared to deliver. He'd never expected to be confronted with the specifics of drug use. Ben knew some competitors used banned substances, but nothing good could come of speaking out under these conditions.

"It's a simple question. Have you ever taken injections to race," the *au Fond* reporter said.

Ben stared at him. The query hung like a blackening cloud. The impatient expressions on the faces of other media members told Ben he had to answer.

He cleared his throat. "It's a pro cyclist's job to make unreasonable demands on his body. Legal medication is often necessary, injections included. I don't take illegal drugs of any kind, and I never have."

Ben looked at Bridgette. She would be so much better at answering these sorts of questions. He was at his best when focused on clear objectives. Life as a pro cyclist increased that inclination. On course, he followed markers and was never asked to decide which way to turn. Off course, the team handled every detail. He'd become used to being allowed a laser-like approach to his job. When forced to handle distractions he dealt with them in black and white, more concerned with getting back on track than with understanding intricacies.

Bridgette's positions were more nuanced. Her sports medicine background often formed his last line of defense. She advised him on medical issues whenever questions arose about the team doctor's methods. He felt fortunate that he could turn to her in time of need, but he was flustered about turning to her now.

She shrugged.

"Do you believe your key competitors are using illegal drugs?" a reporter yelled above the crowd.

Ben looked back at the group of journalists. "No. Kyle and Gunter were simply better than I was today. I'll do my best to beat them tomorrow."

"*Merci*, everybody," Bridgette said. "Now I must tape this man back together so we can enjoy his efforts tomorrow. Will you excuse us, *s'il vous plait?*"

Ben reached gratefully for her hand. He concentrated on minimizing his limp as he walked away. His muscles were knotted, but he was determined not to signal weakness to the competition.

Bridgette didn't speak until they were alone. "That was interesting."

"I'm not so good with the press. Let's get to the Banque Fédérale bus and sit down."

The two walked hand in hand. She led him to an ancient stone stairway. It rose to a narrow corridor where their footfalls echoed softly between timeless buildings. Through various windowless openings they heard sounds of life: silverware clinking against a plate, a child's giggle, sloshing dishwater. A Tom Jones recording of "It's Not Unusual" played softly over a transistor radio. Somehow, even sounds as foreign as trumpets and American vocals fit the setting perfectly. Citizens of this old city lived compact lives, always cognizant of the impact their activities had on neighbors. Ben found the atmosphere soothing.

Bridgette led him up more stone stairs, around a beautiful ridge top cathedral, down a curving stairway on the other side, and into another pleasant alley. Around a slight corner this one opened onto a gravel parking lot surrounding a supermarket housed inside a huge tin shed; from the best of ancient architecture to the worst of its modern equivalent in a few easy steps.

They entered the parking lot and navigated corridors of Tour support vehicles. A Megatronics soigneur crossed their path. On a pro cycling squad the traveling support staff usually outnumbered the athletes. Soigneurs were the often-underappreciated people charged with doing whatever it took to keep the cyclists comfortable. Whether the job at hand was giving a massage, fixing a registration error, or moving luggage between hotels, soigneurs were the ones most likely to be doing it.

This man had once cared for many of Ben's off-bike needs, but now he worked exclusively for Kyle.

"*Salut*," Ben said.

"*Salut*," the soigneur answered. "You looked good on the television today."

"Not as good as Kyle. Your man was strong."

The soigneur nodded, looking left and right. He moved a step closer and whispered, "Strong? *Oui*. But it wasn't water."

Before Ben could ask more, the man hurried away, disappearing behind a nearby van. Ben and Bridgette stared at one another.

"Let's get inside," she said.

Ben let her pull him toward the team's purple and green custom bus.

"We need to think this through carefully," Bridgette said as she dragged him through the door.

Ben's legs ached as he climbed the stairs. "I doubt there's anything we can do about it."

She looked back at him with clear blue eyes. "You're joking, right?"

Chapter Five

Ben and Bridgette stepped into the Banque Fédérale bus. There were no purple or green team colors here. Instead, there were oak cabinets, slate floors, grey leather upholstery, and enough room for all nine athletes, along with key support staff, to travel in style; it was the most luxurious transportation in the fleet.

Coach bounced to his feet, arms spread wide. "Hi ho! There's our hero!" His silver hair and etched face gave away his fifty-nine years, but he had the energy level and agility of a man half his age. Coach was the wisest man Ben had ever known. Ben never referred to him without the title "Coach." As insignificant as it might seem to some, the name conveyed the respect Ben felt his friend deserved.

He set down his helmet and stepped forward to embrace Coach, but then he noticed Thelma struggling to escape the gravitational pull of the too soft couch. She was bigger than ever, close to a hundred pounds overweight, but it was the joyful sort of excess that comes from sharing good times with good friends. She was the undisputed best cook in an eight-county region, and no one blamed her for eating a bit extra.

Ben clasped one of her hands and put his other hand beneath her opposite arm, heaving her to a standing position. Her trademark infectious laugh bubbled forth. Thelma's hair was even whiter than Coach's, and her smile broader as well.

Ben threw an arm around each of them and the three hugged tightly. "That had to be the biggest thrill of my life, seeing you two cheering at roadside."

"The thrill was mine," Thelma said.

"And you, Coach," Ben said. "I saw a tear on your cheek."

"Let's keep that between us," Coach said. "It's unfair to tarnish my reputation over a single moment of sogginess."

"Single moment, my eye," Thelma said. "He was teared up all the way across the Atlantic. We both were. Just watching your performance and knowing we'd soon be at your side … it was emotional. The flight attendant didn't know what to make of us until we told her we were headed to see you; then she cried too."

"How did she know about me?" Ben asked.

"Boy," Coach said, "You're living in a bubble. Your victory yesterday led off every newscast in the states."

Ben let go of his old friends and turned to Bridgette. "Imagine that!"

Bridgette looked stunned. "Where have you two come from?"

"Boulder, Utah, of course. Now, get over here and give me the sort of welcome I deserve." Thelma threw her arms wide.

"I'm in shock. It's wonderful to see you two." Bridgette stumbled forward and traded kisses, first with Thelma and then with Bill. She'd gotten to know them when she followed Ben to Utah two years earlier, determined to convince him to return to the pro peloton. "How did you get here?"

"In a big hurry. We left Utah yesterday, right after Ben's victory!"

Ben stepped into the bedroom area and pulled the curtain, anxious to get out of his Lycra racing clothes. He maneuvered them carefully over his wounds and then pulled on a pair of sweat pants.

Thelma talked to him through the barrier. "By the way, I brought you a present. Your Walkman and tapes have been at my house for years. I know these tunes used to inspire you. I figured maybe they could work their magic again."

"Thanks." Ben doubted he'd use the bulky old thing. These days he stored his music on a tiny MP3 player. He pushed the drape away and walked toward Bridgette. "I spotted this pair standing along the course this morning. Thierry took pity and loaded them into the team car for the day."

"That's right," Thelma said. "I still can't believe I'm actually going to see the south of France before I die."

"You're going to love it," Ben said.

Bridgette pointed to the couch. "Can we continue the reunion with Ben lying down? I've got to dress those wounds and get some fluids into him."

Ben removed the radio receiver from his jersey pocket and fit it into its slot on a wall-mounted battery charger. Then he grabbed a bag of clear liquid from an overhead bin. He handed it to Bridgette, pulled his jersey over his head, and dropped onto the couch. It felt good to get off his feet.

"Lactated Ringers," said Bridgette, reading the bag. "This will be perfect fluid replacement." She hung the solution on a hook, and began preparing an intravenous drip.

Ben took Thelma's hand. "I'm sorry I let you down. I did my best to win today."

"Let me down? Why, this was the most exciting day of my life. I still can't catch my breath. I sure felt bad about the trouble you got into for talking about my spaghetti, though."

Ben waved a dismissive hand. "Oh, that will blow over."

Thelma nodded in agreement. "I couldn't believe it on the last mountain when you rose like a desert thunderstorm and chased those guys down."

Ben laughed. "Is that what happened?"

Coach chuckled. "It's as good an explanation as I can come up with. The television commentators were reading your obituary when you sprang to life. Wonderful ride, son. But what were you two so excited about when you stepped in here?"

Bridgette slipped a needle into the spot she'd prepared on Ben's arm. She glanced at him. "Just business. We'll take care of it later."

"I don't keep secrets from these two." Ben looked toward Coach. "A friend from my old team claims that Kyle Smith is doping."

"Doping?" Thelma shouted. "Why, that little shit. Did you turn him in?"

"Can't do that," Ben said.

Thelma's brow scrunched. "Why not?"

"The only thing my friend actually said is, 'It wasn't water.'"

Thelma scratched her head. "What wasn't water?"

"Exactly. It doesn't mean anything outside the cycling world, and even within it he could explain that comment away, not that I'd ever force him to."

Bridgette stood to open the drip flow on the bag. "'Not water' is cycling lingo for illegal doping products. But saying that something isn't water obviously doesn't mean much."

"So, why did he say anything?" Coach asked.

"I guess he wanted me to know, as a friend. Getting a real accusation out of him would be like nailing gelatin to a tree."

Coach shook his head. "Who needs an accusation? Kyle will take a mandatory drug test as the winner of the stage, right?"

Bridgette laid out sterile bandages and gauze on the kitchen table. "He'll pass his test. If he thought he might not, he wouldn't have risked winning."

Thelma spoke up. "But —"

"But nothing." Bridgette held her with her gaze. "The dopers are ahead of the testers, and they probably always will be."

"There must be a way to catch him," Coach said. "What did he use? Amphetamines?"

Coach was the best in the business when it came to motivation and technique, but the bulk of his experience had been developing amateur athletes in America, the little leagues where cycling was concerned. The professional European peloton played the game many levels higher, across the board.

"Amphetamines are old fashioned. They're easily detected these days." Bridgette seemed thoughtful as she sprayed another dose of antiseptic onto Ben's various patches of road rash.

"Maybe he panicked when I passed him in the standings," Ben said.

Bridgette nodded. "That's likely. He's probably using something designed to increase the oxygen carrying capacity of his blood. That's the primary way to get quick results."

"So, what do you think he took?" Thelma asked.

Bridgette pulled a gauze sleeve over Ben's left arm and then, modifying it with scissors, positioned it to cover the wounds on his shoulder as well. She taped everything into place as she spoke. "The number one suspect would be blood doping, probably using cells donated by somebody else. Hemoglobin is injected just before competition. That enables the blood stream to carry more oxygen than normal."

Thelma's lips turned down and she looked queasy. "He'd really do something like that to win a bicycle race? Before I had surgery the doctor made me donate my own blood for safety."

Bridgette was now at work on Ben's leg. "Transfusions are definitely dangerous," she said. "Not only are adverse reactions possible, but blood is an ideal carrier for disease. I wouldn't put it past Kyle, though."

"Are there safer choices?" Coach asked, motioning for Thelma to sit at the table. When she did, he slid to the wall on the opposite side.

"Sure." Bridgette continued to bind the wounds. "He could use an artificial oxygen carrier."

It surprised Ben that she talked as if these products were readily available. He'd heard artificial hemoglobin was in development, but not that it existed.

"Are those his only choices?" Thelma asked.

"Hardly. If he came here with the intention of doping he might be injecting EPO, a hormone that fools the body into manufacturing excess red blood cells. EPO is a miracle drug for anemia victims, but athletic cheats have discovered it works pretty well for them, too. I've heard rumors of undetectable designer variations. Another possibility is transfusing his own red blood cells, similar to what your physician asked you to do, Thelma."

Thelma's expression darkened. "That takes months of planning."

"You're right. He'd probably have to donate his blood back in January or so, before the cycling season began. It would indicate a serious commitment to cheating," Bridgette said. "Beyond that, there are all sorts of other potential drugs: human growth hormone, steroids, oxygen therapeutics, blood lubricants, animal products … I'm sure there are options even most doctors aren't yet aware of."

Ben stared silently at his friends' faces as they processed the information.

Finally, Thelma spoke up. "There's got to be a way to prove what he's done."

Bridgette finished her work and sat down beside Coach. "If his hematocrit is abnormally high you'd have a clue. That's a measure of the percentage of oxygen carrying red cells in the bloodstream, but they'll be giving him a urine test, not a blood test."

"If we could get his hematocrit reading, what would we look for?" Coach asked.

"Several years back, pro cyclists agreed upon a fifty percent max for safety. If he's higher than that he'd receive an automatic two-week suspension."

"Safety?" Thelma asked.

"In its relaxed nighttime state the heart can have trouble pumping thickened blood. When the red cell concentration gets too high the blood becomes sludgy and presents serious risks such as clotting and heart attacks."

Ben started this race just below fifty percent. He could push himself above that limit naturally by living at altitude and training at lower elevations, so the rule created a paradox. The suspension applied whether an athlete exceeded the limit through legal or illegal methods. The team held each man responsible for getting his numbers in-line before competing.

"A tough race like this pushes the numbers down," Bridgette

continued. "So a cheat could be safely below fifty percent, but still well above his rivals. At the moment, Ben might not even have the ability to deliver oxygen to his brain or muscles as effectively as you, Thelma."

"Good heavens! That can't be healthy."

Ben smiled. Thelma always made him laugh. "Neither is falling off a bike at fifty miles per hour. I've picked a dangerous way to make a living."

"So, is doping the healthy choice?" Coach asked.

Bridgette's eyebrows arched. "Interesting question. These treatments are in use because they're the healthiest alternative for some patients, but I don't believe pro cyclists are in that group. These men will push themselves beyond their limits, no matter what those limits are. If we artificially increase them, they'll just ratchet their effort higher until they're in the same situation again."

Coach chewed his lip. "You're right."

Bridgette put her hand on his. "Some people make the opposite argument. They believe we should legalize everything."

"Well," Coach winked, "there's no denying that the cheating would stop if they scrapped the rules."

From outside they heard others nearing the bus. The team would be boarding soon.

Thelma spoke in a softer voice. "How does anybody ever make sense of it all?"

Bridgette sighed. "Most don't. Some play by the rules as written. Some believe unspoken rules put the limits at another point. Still others live by the maxim, 'It isn't cheating unless you get caught.'"

Ben rolled onto his back as his teammates began to board the bus. "Cheating is cheating, whether they get busted or not," he whispered to himself.

Chapter Six

Bridgette LeBlanc worried about Ben's doping frustrations as she made her way toward the town center, retracing the winding route through man-made canyons. The Banque Fédérale bus had left for the Hotel Campanile. She'd made her reservation at the same hotel, but she wasn't about to ask for a ride in the crowded vehicle, or any of the team cars for that matter. Turning toward the shopping district, she savored the atmosphere.

The streets of Digne-les-Bains were enlivened by the visit of the world's greatest sporting event, and she wanted to experience them. The weather had cooperated, enticing merchants to display their wares on the street. Nearly every shop window contained a Tour de France welcome message of some sort, some made of jewelry, some of pastry, others of paper.

Bicycles swerved this way and that, the majority of them ridden by partisans wearing their favorite team's jerseys. Good-natured jibes shot back and forth between rival fans.

A black limousine pulled even with her and rolled alongside. The rear window went down and a pungent cloud rolled out. A gravelly voice emerged from the haze. "*Bonjour*, my little flower."

"Monsieur Robidoux?" Bridgette leaned down and looked inside. She'd never seen the owner of Banque Fédérale in person; though she would have recognized his smoky voice immediately even if he hadn't addressed her in the same unusual way he had yesterday when she'd spoken with him by phone. He'd convinced her to take a spur of the moment trip via his private helicopter from her Paris office to the top of l' Alpe d'Huez. He wanted her there to motivate Ben. The man was known for going to incredible lengths to get the most from his athletes.

Robidoux wielded his massive influence mostly from the deck of a Mediterranean-based yacht. Rumor had it that he was as large as any three of his cyclists combined. She could now see that such dimensions were an exaggeration, but not by a huge margin. He probably weighed at least as much as any two riders on his team. Long ago, he'd been a pro cyclist himself. Puffy eyes and cheeks now overwhelmed the chiseled features so prominent in his old cycling photos. Robidoux wasn't the first athlete whose appetite hadn't decreased when his metabolism slowed, but he did seem unusually comfortable in his large body.

"Would you do the honor of joining us for a drive?"

"Um. Okay."

A valet sprang from an entrance near the middle of the vehicle. He opened the rear door for her.

"Where are we going?" she asked.

"Nowhere in particular. I'd just like to talk."

She stepped into the cabin. The door shut behind her. It felt like being sealed into an alternate reality. Raucous street noises were replaced by elegant tones of Bach. The interior was rich, black leather, offset with beautiful red wood—probably cherry. The thick odor of cigar smoke permeated everything.

"Mass in B Minor?" she asked.

"Correct. You're to be commended." He closed his eyes and tilted his head slightly skyward, seeming to draw strength from the music. When the piece ended he opened his eyes and spoke in English. "My tastes are simple. If it's not baroque, fix it."

She smiled. "What did you want to discuss?"

Robidoux tapped the ash from his cigar. "Before we get to that, can I offer you a drink?"

"Ice water, please."

He looked surprised, as if it hadn't occurred to him that such a simple beverage was fit for consumption. "Very well." He looked at the valet who now sat attentively in the forward corner of the passenger cabin.

Bridgette accepted her drink.

Robidoux's nod had the grace of a bow. "Where were you headed?"

"To the Hotel Campanile."

"Only a short drive. We'll take the scenic route."

The valet whispered into an intercom. The vehicle jolted as it moved into traffic.

Robidoux cleared his throat. "Let's get to the point. You did a remarkable job of motivating Benjamin yesterday. I want to hire you. You will tend to Benjamin's needs for the remainder of this race."

"I run a clinic. I have to return to my clients after the weekend."

"I'm sure you have associates who can cover for you. I know your hourly rate. I'll double it and pay you fourteen-hour days. Of course, your travel expenses will be handled as well."

Bridgette's full concentration was barely enough to keep her jaw from dropping. Sure, she could shuffle her appointments. She would have done it for a fraction of the price. And caring for Ben? She'd have done that for free. She extended her hand to shake on the deal.

Robidoux took it gently in his meaty palm and kissed the backside. "No ring?"

The limousine had climbed a rise where they were able to look back at the town. The red-tiled roofs were nestled into a picturesque notch between twin hills, each crowned with gray streaked cliffs. "The engagement took us by surprise."

"*Oui.* What wonderful television that was." His black eyes shone with satisfaction.

She'd forgotten that Ben's proposal was seen by the world. Somehow, the moment had seemed so intimate.

"You make a beautiful couple. You'll have a wonderful life together."

"*Merci.*"

Robidoux clicked open a brief case and drew out some documents. He filled in a few blanks then set the papers on the console beside her. "Here are two copies of an agreement. Initial the first page of each document and sign at the bottom of the last one, if you please." He handed her his pen.

She scanned the front page. Terms and conditions of employment with Banque Fédérale. She executed both contracts. Handing one back, she folded the other and slid it into her handbag.

"Benjamin looked exhausted today," Robidoux said.

"He limited his losses. There's only so much you can expect after yesterday's performance."

Robidoux shook his head. "I must tell you, such talk concerns me. A champion always maximizes his gains."

"He did well and he'll do better tomorrow. I promise you that."

"How do you know?"

"Because I know Ben."

Robidoux nodded. "Then I'll hold you to your word."

She considered the implication as, outside her window, two cane-toting Frenchmen seemed to regard passing clouds through raised glasses of red wine.

"If I have a reservation about Ben," Robidoux said, "it's his competitive drive."

She looked at him curiously.

"He's not as consumed by the need to win as I'd like."

"Are you kidding? Ben's entire life is designed around cycling. "

"Around being a domestique, you mean. It's not just that, though. Sometimes I get the impression that fan acceptance is more important to him than victory."

She shook her head even as she recognized how on target the words were. Ben had endured fan hatred ever since the accident that killed Thierry's younger brother. For him, earning forgiveness had become an obsession.

"He ought to recognize that victory will bring acceptance. If only Ben were as obsessed with winning as ... you, for instance."

Was Robidoux aware she'd undergone counseling to quell her competitive instincts? As an amateur swimmer, and again in her early medical career, there were times when she'd gone too far in order to win. It cost friendships and put her on the wrong side of ethical boundaries. Thank goodness that was behind her.

"Bridgette. Are you prepared to do whatever it takes to help him?"

It wasn't difficult to guess the answer he wanted to hear. He'd probably tear up the contract if she said otherwise. She nodded. The town rolled by just beyond the tinted windows.

"Including the use of PED's?"

Performance enhancing drugs? She couldn't believe he'd ask so openly. Maybe he was testing her. "Of course not."

"Very well." Robidoux held out both palms as if defending himself from her reply. "I was merely curious because of your history."

Bridgette's throat dried. She couldn't swallow. Glancing at him, she wondered how much he knew. For four years her mistake had followed her around like a renegade shadow, threatening to blacken her name forever. When she landed her first job in cycling, straight out of the University of Montpellier, she'd felt equal parts elation and pressure. This was her dream opportunity, but if she didn't make something of it she'd embarrass herself. The team had to win

Bridgette promised her boss that if he took a chance on her, results would follow. Her confidence sprang partly from her brand new degree in sports medicine, and partly from her in-depth knowledge of pharmaceuticals. An opportune internship with a leading drug manufacturer had resulted in unique understanding of a cutting-edge medication. Eventually it would be banned, but at the time its existence was unknown to the authorities.

"Christoff DuPonte responded particularly well to your ... treatment," Robidoux said in a coarse whisper.

Bridgette's heart raced. She turned to the window. He knew her secret! Back then it felt like she'd been handed the keys to a secret kingdom. With childlike enthusiasm she turned DuPonte, a very good cyclist already, into a great one. Just as the season started, the drug she'd been using was added to the banned list.

Bridgette had gone to her boss and told him the bad news.

He held up a hand once the topic became obvious. "I haven't heard a word you said, and I refuse to discuss this subject again. Do you understand?"

She'd nodded.

"Good girl. Now, understand this as well. You've spent a lot of money. The sponsor paid willingly, but the company must be rewarded with results. The athletes risk career-ending injury every day. Everybody on this team is under tremendous pressure to win. None of us are willing to be let down by support personnel who don't understand what's at stake."

Ultimately, Bridgette had decided she had to administer the remainder of their current stock. Shortly afterwards, DuPonte won one of cycling's Monuments, an excruciating one-day classic called Liege-Baston-Liege.

Bridgette's boss was thrilled, DuPonte was thrilled, the sponsors were thrilled. Everything should have been perfect. But as Bridgette watched the second place finisher cross the line she shivered at the agony etched in his face. Here was a man who'd given everything for his passion, a warrior who had reached deep inside himself and delivered a great performance, yet it hadn't been enough. She wanted to tell him that he should have won the race, but she didn't even dare face him to acknowledge his second place.

When she told her boss about her decision never to participate in doping another athlete, he'd acted surprised, but not at her remorse. He pretended that the drug use was news to him. Then he'd fired her. Bridgette had walked away, embarrassed yet thankful that everything had ended in relatively quiet fashion.

The contacts she'd made kept her working in the sport as a

freelancer, and over the years she'd produced more than her fair share of winners, in this sport and others, all through legal means. Her worry about having to answer for the DuPonte affair had gradually faded—until now.

Not until Robidoux spoke again did she realize how long she'd been silent. "I always do my homework."

She took a sip of water. "I made a mistake, but that was years ago. Everyone involved has moved on. I've gotten my competitive juices under control."

Robidoux smiled. "Of course you have."

She looked straight at him. If he'd investigated her recent reputation, and surely he had, he knew she wouldn't administer illegal products. Her earlier thought must be right. He was testing her to make certain she was now committed to doing things the right way.

Robidoux didn't flinch. His gaze burned through her. Finally, she had to look away.

"Can we please discuss strategies that fit within the rule book?" Bridgette asked.

"We will speak honestly, as professionals should." He puffed on his cigar. "Rules are for fools. Everybody knows they're only in place to appease fans. Are you really so wracked by guilt over the favor you did Monsieur DuPonte?"

"What are you saying? It wasn't a favor. We stole another man's victory."

"Stole his victory? Isn't that the very definition of competition? Wouldn't the last man finish first if only those ahead hadn't outplayed him?" Robidoux picked up his drink. "Should we place limits on how dedicated an athlete is allowed to be? After all, is it fair to a cyclist who craves balance that his rivals force him to train at near unhealthy excess?"

A recently retired athlete had complained of exactly that. His career had become miserable because certain competitors were forcing everybody to work too hard.

"That's not the same at all. DuPonte beat a man who turned in a heroic performance." Bridgette shifted uncomfortably.

"What makes you so sure your second place hero wasn't doing the same, only not as well? If he wasn't, he should have been. A true professional will go to whatever length is necessary to accomplish his goal. If he didn't use all means at his disposal to win, he deserved to lose. I'll bet he learned a valuable lesson that day."

She didn't answer.

"If you gave Benjamin PEDs, would he be stealing Kyle's victory?"

Bridgette lifted the ice water to her lips again. Was he aware that Kyle was using? He seemed to know almost everything.

"You ought to consider it."

What point was there in telling Robidoux that she didn't even have a source for most of the cutting edge medications, much less the current knowledge to use them?

"An interesting proposition, eh? Benjamin will do as you ask, you know. You've controlled him masterfully so far. Take the next step."

"I don't control Ben." The suggestion angered her. Their love was a partnership.

"Listen to what you're saying. Ben wouldn't even be in this sport anymore if not for your insistence." He regarded her coolly, and then seemed to reevaluate things. "Of course you won't admit to it. After all, you're a woman, and an incredibly persuasive one at that. Look at the lengths Benjamin went to for you on the Alpe d'Huez climb. Sure, he wanted to win that for himself, but he never would have accomplished it without your influence. You must know that. He'll gladly give you everything, and who can blame him?"

The car hit a pothole and ice water splashed onto her leg. A chill raced up her spine. "Don't talk that way."

"Oh, come now. You master every man you meet, whether you want to or not. Even I am under your spell. Benjamin must be putty in your hands."

She wasn't a manipulator. Anybody who knew her would agree. "This conversation is making me uncomfortable. What do you want from me?"

"I'm sorry, my dear." Robidoux patted her knee. "Since we're working together I thought it best that we understand one another. If you forget everything else about this conversation, here is something you ought to keep in mind." He paused, loading the moment with importance.

She knew she'd better pay careful attention to what came next.

"I always do whatever is necessary to reach my goals."

"Without limitation?"

He stretched his eyebrows high and nodded almost imperceptibly. "Ordinary people admire such single-mindedness, whether they're willing to admit it or not. Men and women with the guts to make tough decisions always rise to the top, whether in business, politics, or sports. Ethics don't matter; results are everything. It's the way of the world."

She looked at him, amazed.

"Don't be so surprised. Why do you think I'm so well paid? My job is to present my company in the best light possible, and I am good at it. Ben, handled correctly, can be a valuable cog in that plan."

"You talk about him as if he's a thing."

"As far as the corporation is concerned, he is." He paused to inhale from his cigar; then he blew two smoke rings. "You are a thing, too. So am I. If the corporation thrives, we are all rewarded. As long as each of us plays our role, we'll remain valuable bank assets. If we lose sight of the big picture ... Well, let's make sure nobody loses sight."

She shivered. "Nothing but winning matters?"

"You're not paying close enough attention. Perception is what matters. People love compelling stories with strong protagonists. The bank's reputation hinges on the public's impression of the athletes it sponsors. Therefore, it's incumbent upon us to create the best story possible. Multi-million dollar decisions hang in the balance. Benjamin's rise has created some unique opportunities. Because of the American market, he could take things to a new level for us by winning this race. I believe he can do that—provided he takes proper precautions."

She swallowed hard. Drugs and precautions had become synonyms. "And if he doesn't?"

"I'll be forced into using harsher measures to get my point across?"

Was he threatening to expose her, revealing her mistake to Ben and the world? As humiliating as it would be, it was time she faced this demon. "I won't be blackmailed. I'll admit publicly to my error."

The car stopped. They were in front of the Hotel Campanile. The valet opened his door and climbed out.

Robidoux exhaled a thick cloud. "Who said anything about blackmail? You're not forgetting what an opportunity it is for Benjamin to be in this position, are you? If you want me to continue aligning resources behind him, I need assurances that he won't handicap the effort by remaining less committed to the task than his rivals. That's only fair, right?"

Bridgette fingered the door handle. How had she overlooked this? That's where potential disaster lay. Robidoux controlled the team, and without a team's support, even the best rider didn't have a prayer. Ben had worked too hard to have his opportunity stolen. To protect him she needed to insure that the boss was happy with the program.

She stared blankly. In truth, some of his arguments hit home. But if she administered PEDs for a second time her nightmare would begin anew. She felt cornered.

"Do you know what these are?" Robidoux tossed a vial of pills her way.

She caught them on reflex, already shaking her head in fear. Then she read the label: not a banned product. She looked up curiously. "What benefit would a cyclist get from these?"

"None."

She opened the lid and dumped a couple of capsules into her hand. They appeared to be exactly what the label claimed. "Then why use them?"

"Masking properties. Please have Benjamin take two a day, that's all I ask. Just in case the moment comes where more significant measures become necessary. Can you do that?"

Bridgette tried to clear her thoughts. Mostly, she wanted to be out of this limo. "Can I have some time to think about it?"

"I'll make you a deal."

"What?"

"You promised me earlier that Benjamin would do better tomorrow. If he retakes the yellow jersey, I'll stay out of the way and allow you to use whatever methods you see fit as long as he retains the lead."

It felt like the sun had moved from behind a cloud. Here was her out. Ben could win tomorrow. He had to.

"One final thing you should know." Robidoux finished his drink and swirled the ice cubes around in his glass. "If we are forced into taking the next step, I won't ask you to administer medication. I have a physician who can take care of that. Your role will simply be to make sure Benjamin is agreeable to the program. Now, what do you say?"

She breathed slightly easier, grateful for the concession. She'd do all she could to make sure it didn't come to that, but if it did at least she would be there to protect Ben. The alternative was forcing him to face Robidoux's demands alone. She spoke without looking up. "I'll do as you ask."

Robidoux lifted her chin with an index finger and turned her face toward his. His gaze chilled her to the bone. "Wonderful. I knew I could count on you, my little flower."

The door opened from the outside. How had the valet known the exact moment when Robidoux got what he wanted?

She rose to her feet. The door shut with a click and she started to walk away.

"*Madame.*"

She turned. "*Oui?*"

"Proceed with caution."

She saw compassion in the valet's eyes. "*Merci.*" He was a very small man. Maybe that's why Robidoux had selected him. He was so unobtrusive that he seemed almost like an accessory.

She turned away and walked toward the entrance of the chalet style building, Robidoux's words muddling her thoughts. Just this one time, manipulating Ben was in his best interest. What good would it do him to cloud his thinking with such complications at a time like this? It wasn't as if there were legitimate decisions to be made. Unless she didn't handle things perfectly, his dream would be lost. The critical thing was preparing him to perform at his highest potential tomorrow. He had to win. Everything hinged on that.

Chapter Seven

Ben sat next to Thierry as the team bus forced its way through the post-race crowds. It felt good to be a part of this group. As far as clubhouse relations went, he'd come a long way in the last couple of days.

The athletes were anxious to get to their hotel. Ben winked at Thelma. She looked so out of place among these men. Thierry had somehow found a room for her and Coach to share in each of the team's hotels for the rest of the tour. It was a fortunate favor, because every lodge within range of the race was normally booked months in advance.

Coach Bill had bummed a ride back to Bourg d'Oisans to pick up the rental car he'd abandoned when they got the surprise ride in Thierry's support vehicle. He wouldn't reach the hotel until late that evening.

Clogging the road ahead, fans held up pen and paper, hoping for autographs. A man in a pointy jester hat banged on the driver's window, begging for his race program to be passed around for signatures. The driver wouldn't give him so much as eye contact.

Rikard, sitting at the kitchen table, lifted the window blind beside him and peeked out. The crowd roared in anticipation, as if they believed they'd soon be welcomed inside. He lifted the blind further and blew a kiss. The passionate screams of young women rose above the din.

"It's a crazy crowd today," Rikard said. He dropped the blind, and the fans groaned.

The driver made his way through the last of the pedestrians, and the bus gained speed.

Ben looked at his teammate's weary faces, blackened with grime and sweat. Their exhaustion reflected his own. "You guys were great today. Sorry I couldn't close the deal."

"You're very tough on yourself," Albert said. "I respect that. We're in for a real fight, but I believe you have what it takes. I'm with you all the way."

Most of the other men either grunted or gestured

acknowledgement, but Rikard merely lifted his blind and stared out the window again. Ben already knew Rikard had reservations about helping him win, but the big sprinter had been there after Ben hit the pavement. He'd done his fair share of pulling to get Ben back into the race. What more could be asked?

"*Merci*, I won't let you down," Ben said.

Thierry rose from the passenger seat and turned to face the team. Wearing a determined expression, he held onto the bulkhead to balance himself in the swaying vehicle. "Rikard, close that blind. I need everybody's full attention."

Rikard narrowed his gaze but dropped the blind.

"This is war, men," Thierry said. "Anybody who thinks of it as sport is underestimating his role. This is not about having fun. There will be plenty of time to enjoy your memories from your rocking chairs. Right now you are my hired mercenaries, and I expect no less of you."

"You'll get no less," Albert said.

It reassured Ben to see Thierry putting his thumbprint on the team. He brought the same intensity to this job as he had to his role of team leader.

Thierry nodded. "Ben is strong, but so is his competition. They are confident, too. We must break their spirit to win. It's going to take every man here to accomplish that. I'm warning you right now, I'm going to push you harder over the remainder of this race than you've ever been pushed in your lives. Are you ready?"

"*Oui*," answered a chorus of male voices. The tone had resilience. These men were eager for more. Ben's heart quivered, anxious for the coming challenge.

Thierry spent the rest of the ride talking tactics while discussing the strengths and weaknesses of the competition, and of Banque Fédérale's riders. His intensity breathed life into the team. By the time they reached the hotel, their swagger had fully returned. Backslaps and laughter filled the air.

A crowd had gathered outside the Hotel Campanile. It was more of a motel, really. The quality of the accommodations hardly mattered; Ben couldn't wait to lie down. Every room was essentially the same when his eyes were closed.

He let his teammates exit ahead of him, each taking their room key from Thierry as they stepped out. The group snaked their way past the fans, signing an autograph per step, and then into the building.

Once Ben finished with autographs he headed straight to the second floor, opened his door, and sat on the bed. His suitcase sat alone atop the dresser. No roommate, a first for him as a pro cyclist. What a luxury: no one to share the bathroom counter with, no one else's routines to work around, and best of all, no snores coming from the other side of the room.

Stripping, he went into the bathroom and turned on the shower. He stepped beneath the stream of water before it warmed. The shock closed his pores. As the water heated, liquid fingers beat life into his weary muscles. He moved directly beneath the showerhead. Salt from the day's effort flowed over his lips. The grittiness of hours in the saddle streamed from his body. No shower had ever felt so good. He might have stayed there for hours, but his legs were too exhausted to hold him up.

Ben wrapped a towel around his waist and walked back into the room. He sat down on the bed. He needed a massage, food, and sleep. Little else mattered.

He lay back, intending to play the race's final sequences through his mind, but then he noticed an unusual box on the nightstand. It was white, about six inches long, an inch deep, and two inches wide. He reached back and grabbed it. Across the lid, a message was written in an even hand:

Dear Benjamin,
Please select your favorite and return the others to Thierry.
Compliments,
Monsieur Robidoux

Ben glanced around the room, feeling as if he were being watched, but there was no sign of anyone. He removed the long lid. Inside were three velvet jewelry boxes, one red, one pink, and one white. He palmed the red box and worked the hinge.

A dazzling diamond shone back at him. He couldn't believe his eyes—or the gem's size. He removed the golden ring and put it on his left pinky.

Next he selected the pink box. Inside was a ring of white gold. Channel set diamonds glistened around half the circumference, and a perfect stone sat on a podium at the center. He slid it onto his other pinky and reached for the last box.

This ring had an ornate look. It was traditional gold with lots of tiny diamonds and a big rock crowning the arrangement.

Ben looked over the three engagement rings. Eventually he became certain that the white gold ring with channel-set diamonds was perfect for Bridgette. Its modern elegance matched her style. The others were more ostentatious—and probably far more expensive.

Ben wasn't sure he should allow Robidoux to buy the ring for him. What obligations might this gift bring? But he appreciated the team owner simplifying the shopping. Bridgette deserved to wear a beautiful ring, and Ben definitely wouldn't have found time to select one for at least a couple of weeks.

A knock came at the door. He replaced the rings in their boxes and slid everything beneath a pillow before he went to answer. When he opened the door, Thierry stood on the other side.

"*Salut*, Ben."

"Come in."

Thierry went to the room's only chair, a simple wooden piece of furniture with no pad, and sat down. "I hope you won't be surprised to learn that I expect more of you than any other man on this team."

Ben dropped onto the corner of the bed. "I expect it of myself."

Thierry slapped a hand on Ben's knee. "Good. Your first order is to get as much recuperation as you possibly can between now and tomorrow morning. I'm dedicating a soigneur entirely to your needs. Wait here for your massage."

"Thanks, Thierry."

"You wouldn't be thanking me if you had any idea how hard I plan to push you over the next week and a half." He stood and headed for the door.

"Don't you need the rings?"

Thierry turned. "The what?"

Ben reached under his pillow. He opened the box containing the one he'd chosen and showed it to Thierry. "Think she'll like this?"

Thierry whistled.

Ben showed Thierry the note on the lid and handed him the others.

"Robidoux hadn't told me about this. He's taking pretty good care of you."

Ben nodded. "I aim to repay him for believing in me, and then some."

Thierry paused, looking thoughtful. "This is business, Ben. If Robidoux gives you something I suggest you consider it payment for what you've already done. You're on a minimum contract. With the exposure you've gotten already you've made yourself into a better investment than he could have ever dreamed. Don't take that man lightly, and don't ever suggest to him that you're in his debt, *ça va?*"

Ben nodded. "*Oui. Naturellement.*"

Thierry left the room. Ben collapsed on the bed again, rolling onto his stomach. He set the jewelry box down next to the alarm clock. For a while he watched the second hand sweep around the face in endless circles, and then he fell asleep.

When he awoke, half an hour had passed. Bridgette stood above him. A bouquet of purple irises was arranged in a tall vase on the nightstand. Their fragrance filled the room. Orange and apple slices with cheese and crackers were laid out on a tray. A massage table was set up at the foot of the bed.

She patted the contraption. "Hop up."

"What are you doing here?" Ben asked.

She punched a button and the tones of Enya filled the room. "Didn't Thierry tell you? Monsieur Robidoux offered me a job. He wants me to pay special attention to your needs. How could I resist?"

The guy seemed to be everywhere. "That's great," Ben said.

He stood up. She stepped forward and put her arms around him. Ben watched his fingers disappear into the auburn veil of her hair. He closed his eyes as their lips met. Colors danced through his brain.

He opened his eyes and moved her slightly away. "You make my knees weak. One kiss like that is all I can afford."

She smiled. "That's my boy. Business before pleasure."

"I have something for you."

Her brow crinkled.

He grabbed the jewelry box and opened it.

"*Mon Dieu.* It's beautiful!" She removed the ring from the box and put it on her finger. It fit perfectly. She stared at her hand, moving it at various angles. When she looked at Ben again, tears tracked her cheeks.

"I'm glad you like it." He took Bridgette in his arms and held her. He'd never felt so filled with love. He wished he could thank Robidoux personally for making this moment possible.

"How did I get so lucky?" Bridgette asked.

"You're asking the wrong person. So many incredible things are happening to me that I can't even think straight. Maybe I can afford another kiss, after all."

"Just one," she laughed.

Exhausted as he'd been, now he felt weightless. Swaying to the music, he felt she was more than a part of him; she was the reason for his existence.

Eventually, she moved him toward the massage table. "Your self-control was so admirable earlier. We'd better maintain our focus."

Ben removed his hands from her hips and edged onto the table. "You're right." He lay face down and let out a sigh. "I've got to save my energy."

"I'm very proud of what you've accomplished so far, Ben."

He closed his eyes. "You're responsible for it. The best thing about my life is having you in it. I love you Bridgette."

"I love you too, Ben." Her fingers were alternately icy and sharp, and then smooth and hot. As always, Bridgette's skills were magical. He felt content.

She moved to the bottom of the table, focusing for the moment on his toes. Gradually, she transitioned to his feet, his ankles, and then his calves. Her kneading fingers increased his circulation, washing toxins from the muscles and speeding recuperation. The effect soothed his mind.

"Ben, I've been thinking about this drug thing."

He groaned.

She leaned into his right thigh, working it hard. "Kyle is going to get away with what he's doing."

"You're probably right." She poured warm oil onto his thighs and calves. It felt like a magic elixir. He could almost feel the liquid seeping into his pores.

"Have you thought any more about it?" she asked.

"It's crossed my mind. What can I do, though? I just have to beat him despite his methods." It stung when she touched the road rash on his left thigh, but he knew she couldn't treat the wound too tenderly. The muscles need attention.

"Do you feel strong enough?"

"Yes." He wondered if she doubted him, but it wasn't a thought he wanted to dwell on. He willed his mind to wander farther and farther from his present concerns.

"Robidoux knows about Kyle." She squeezed his thigh tight.

"Ouch." He tensed. "What did he say?"

"Ben, you need to relax."

"Okay. But what did Robidoux say?"

"A couple of things. He says that if you perform well enough tomorrow you can turn the decision into a non-issue."

"And if I don't?"

"First of all, you will." Her hands worked with unusual determination. "But he does have a contingency plan."

"Which is?"

"He wants you to take some pills."

His muscles tightened again. "What sort of pills?"

"Have I ever told you that you have the best gluteus maximi it has ever been my pleasure to massage?"

Ben felt impatient. "What sort of pills?" he repeated.

"They're harmless, Ben. You need to have them in your system because … because you just need to have them." Her voice had a warbling, nervous quality.

Ben turned his head toward her, alarmed. "Are you all right, Bridgette?"

She looked stressed. "Of course I am."

He tried to sit up so they could talk things through. She pushed him down, working his muscles harder than ever. "Please, trust me. It would be best to take the pills. They're nothing but masking agents."

"But I have nothing to mask."

"I know that. But you've got to agree that keeping Robidoux happy is in your best interests."

He thought for a moment. "He's nearby, isn't he. Have you seen him?"

"*Oui.*"

"And you spoke face to face about all of this."

Her knuckles bore into his spine, deftly checking the condition of each vertebra. "You can't be surprised."

She was right. When Bridgette tackled a problem she explored it from every angle. She collected information, made up her mind, and then brought the necessary people around to her way of thinking.

Two years ago, when Ben planned to retire from cycling, she decided it was the wrong decision. She recruited Coach and Thelma to her cause, and pretty soon Ben found himself back in the pro peloton. He was glad for her influence.

"You've decided performance enhancers are okay?" he asked.

"No. Only that at this particular moment we need to keep our options open. We owe it to ourselves to learn more. If Kyle is gaining an advantage over you, especially an advantage that improves his health, maybe you should consider using the same thing."

Ben inhaled and then blew his breath out slowly. It didn't calm him. "I've never heard you talk like this."

"I have to, Ben. Trust me on this. Take some harmless pills and don't dwell on it. You have enough to think about." Bridgette opened a bottle and spilled two yellow capsules into her hand. She extended a water bottle in the other hand.

He sat up. "You want me to take them now?"

She nodded.

In four days the race would reach the Pyrenees. It would travel those precipitous slopes for three, grueling stages. Toma would be on course for each of them. Spaniards always traveled in force to witness that portion of the race. Ben had already been imagining the boy's reaction to his success. The moment would be destroyed if he reached it by cheating. "I can't take them yet. I need time to think things through."

Bridgette dropped the pills into a plastic bag and handed them to him. "Promise me you'll keep them handy."

"Yeah. Okay." He stared at the clock. The second hand continued on as if this moment was no more significant than any other.

Bridgette leaned in front of him. "Time for me to go. Dinner's in fifteen minutes: Thelma's famous spaghetti. Frodie is fuming."

"That should make for an entertaining evening." Frodie, the team's chef, was an Austrian with a temper hotter than a boiling saucepan. The men loved to get under his skin. Ben hadn't thought about how he'd react to Thelma's presence.

He kissed Bridgette, but without the passion they'd shared before. He sat back down on the bed while she collapsed the massage table and left the room.

When she was gone, he stepped into the bathroom and locked the door. He opened his fist and examined the pills through the clear baggie. He didn't know what to make of the markings. Was it possible he didn't know Bridgette quite as well as he thought?

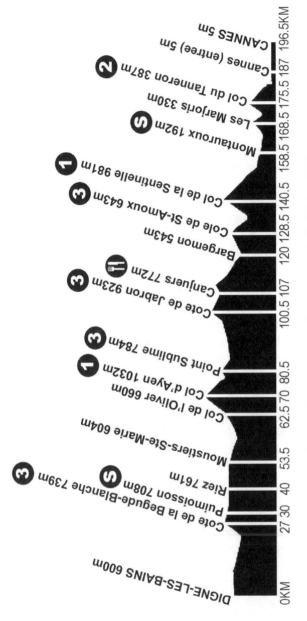

Tour de France Stage 12 Profile

Chapter Eight

Ben found the morning's copy of *au Fond* at his place when he sat down for breakfast in the hotel conference room. A front-page headline bragged of a witness who knew details of Ben's drug use. Ben ripped it in half and threw the pieces at Thierry.

Thierry laughed. "I knew that would motivate you."

"It pisses me off."

"Close enough." Thierry lifted a forkful of pasta. "This new cook you found is great, by the way. Much better than the old one. Don't you agree, Frodie?"

Frodie glared. "Oh yes. Ha ha. So funny."

Thierry looked at Ben and snickered.

Ben regarded his own heaping plate of spaghetti. He and the rest of the team were eating a meal similar to the one they had last night. Homemade noodles in a light olive-oil sauce, a little Parmesan cheese sprinkled over the top. Lots of carbs, no spices. Their internal organs were too taxed to deal with complex foods. The only big difference from dinner was that the evening meal always included a protein source for rebuilding muscles. At breakfast, highly accessible energy was the priority.

While tourists following the race were probably savoring the local cuisine, pro cyclists ate only the most energy-rich and easily digestible foods. Thelma had the perfect recipe. How she'd prepared so much, so quickly, he'd never know. She must be exhausted.

"Anybody ready to race?" Thierry asked.

"I can't wait," Albert said.

"Let's do it," Ben agreed.

Others followed with enthusiastic responses.

"Good. Here's the plan." Thierry moved a centerpiece out of the way so that the men on the opposite side of the table could see. "Megatronics fought hard for the maillot jaune yesterday. Let's let them wear themselves out defending it today. They'll assume we plan to attack, so they'll have to push the pace. For the first three quarters of the stage we'll tuck in behind and hitch a ride."

"What if Deutscher Aufbau takes the lead instead?" Albert asked.

"That's our silver lining. Ben didn't lose too much time, but our workload should decrease because we can let Gunter and Kyle fight things out for us. We'll wait to put the hammer down until the very end."

Ben glanced around the table. He met with numerous smiles. The team was in good spirits. Tomorrow was the second and last rest day of the tour. Since the following day was a time-trial where only the contenders had to go all out, the majority of the team was looking at a relatively easy stretch. After that, things would get tough in the Pyrenees.

Rikard looked at Thierry. "I'll work for Ben, but I need something in return. That's only fair." He was one of the most influential characters on the team. If he threw Ben to the dogs, several others would follow.

"What?" Thierry asked.

"Stage fourteen along the Mediterranean coast is my dream stage. The first seventy percent is flat along the Côte d'Azur. Then comes the Col de la Gineste, the very road where I fell in love with cycling. It's a tough little hill, but I know how to ride it. After that, a quick descent into my hometown of Marseille. The finish line is a kilometer from the house I grew up in. If you give me the support to win that stage, I'll lend everything I have to Ben's cause, all the way to Paris."

That was exactly the sort of help Ben needed. Rikard moved air like a truck, a drafter's dream on flat, windy stretches.

"I'll help you win it," Ben said.

Rikard smiled. "I know the run in like the curves of my wife's body."

"Remind me not to mess with your wife," Thierry said. "Marseille has no curves."

"*Ah, oui, oui.* None that you know of. You'll learn soon enough. In truth, Marseille has the most splendid curves in all of France."

"We'll see. I say it's the only city in this country where even an American couldn't get lost." Thierry winked at Ben. "I can understand why you've dreamed of that stage, though. The team will help however we can."

Rikard looked satisfied, and settled back into his chair.

"So," Thierry continued, "today we need to keep Kyle under control. I've got a trick to do just that. He's a powerhouse, but not skilled at accelerating multiple times on a climb. Let him build up a head of steam, and then interfere slightly at the critical moment. He'll get frustrated, and it will take him valuable time and energy to get back up to speed. His team will want to retaliate, so don't spring this on him until the last tough climb of the day."

"I'm your man for that," Albert said. "But how do we deal with Gunter?"

"We're going to take a risk. Gunter is capable of surging again and again. Ben's our only remaining team member with the skill to deal with that type of quick uphill acceleration, but he needs to preserve his strength for late in the day. The good news is that Megatronics has a couple of men capable of marking Gunter. We'll count on them keep him in check for us. It's a gamble but I think it's a good one. They probably see Gunter as their biggest threat to overall victory, so I expect them to react to any move he makes."

In theory, Thierry's plan made sense. As everyone in the room knew, though, practice could be a different matter. Today's route was another killer haul, crossing seven categorized climbs in the 196-kilometer journey from this little town of Digne-les-Bains to the Mediterranean festival city of Cannes. Today's route profile map looked like an alligator's dental x-rays—one sharp peak after another. Each cyclist carried a copy in his jersey pocket every day. He'd consult it by making comparisons to his odometer reading as the stage progressed. Today there were certain to be lots of last minute adjustments on the road. If the team failed to respond even a single time, it might cost them the race.

*   *   *

As the start time neared Ben headed to the staging area, the same spot as yesterday's finish. He straddled his bike, the starting line just in front of his tire. The pills lay in his jersey pocket. Tiny as they were, they seemed to weigh him down. He'd promised Bridgette he would keep them at hand. He'd meant to think through everything she'd said, but there hadn't been enough time. When it came down to it, after his massage and dinner, sleep was urgent. Most nights he couldn't think a coherent thought once his bedroom light went out. After breakfast there had been reporters, autograph seekers, and other obligations. Strangely, it felt relaxing to get the stage underway.

A politician on the announcer's platform bellowed to the crowd, informing them how fortunate they were that he'd convinced the Tour de France to visit their little town.

Ben hoped for a mild pace today, at least for the first half of the stage. He still felt the effects of his massive stage-ten effort and looked forward to tomorrow's rest day. It would do him wonders, giving him time to contemplate and recuperate. Under less stressful conditions it should be easier to make sense of everything—including the pills.

The crowd booed the politician. Ben clipped into both of his pedals and balanced in place, hopping the tightly braked wheels from side to side to maintain his stability.

"We're impressed," Gunter said in English. "You're the best I've ever seen at going nowhere on a bike."

Ben laughed, wondering if Gunter understood what he'd just said.

Finally, the speaker raised the starter's pistol and fired. Ben tucked in among his teammates and tried to stay as inconspicuous as possible. Even before they passed the steaming thermal baths in the third kilometer, he knew that hoping for a mild pace had been in vain.

Twenty-four kilometers later, on the arid slopes of the Côte de la Bégude-Blanche, he wondered if they could keep up the blistering pace. The stage had been miserable so far. Ben felt as under siege as the thorny, drought resistant vegetation eking a living from the chalky yellow soil beside the road. He unzipped his jersey and squirted a water bottle into his face, awed by the massive effort Megatronics was putting in at the front of the peloton. The work Kyle's domestiques were doing was called "riding tempo." The act was never as casual as the term made it sound, but today … Wow! Those men were animals.

Now that Kyle had the yellow jersey, his boys were drilling it. They guarded him like a fighter squadron escorting a dignitary. Nobody was going to escape off the front of this pack. Rikard and another of Ben's teammates had already been dropped due to the miserably rapid pace. The peloton had long ago shattered, and they still had miles and miles to go. How much longer could this go on?

The climb ended atop a plateau. Cultivated lavender stretched into the distance. Row upon row of perfectly aligned bushes were interrupted only by an occasional tree or small ruin. The domestiques were fried with fatigue. The men in the dwindling lead group fought to maintain contact.

"Stop shuttling food and water," Thierry said over the radio. "We'll resupply at the feed zone."

Ben removed the stage profile from his jersey pocket. He looked at the undulating terrain between their current position and the feed zone at the 107th kilometer. There was serious risk of bonking before then. A starved cyclist couldn't be expected to perform any better than a car with an empty gas tank. How long could he and his men hang on to this screaming train?

At one point the road headed straight toward the elegantly simple Riez Cathedral. Beneath a pair of horsechestnut trees framing its front door, a chamber orchestra entertained the crowd. The route turned sharply right, and the cyclists were forced to leave the celebration behind. Ben envied the partygoers with their wine and food.

The route dropped slightly downhill. Eventually they reached the bottom of the Grand Canyon du Verdun. It really did resemble its namesake in Arizona. At kilometer fifty-four the route kicked up the category-one Col d'Ayen on the canyon's northern flank. Megatronics slowed momentarily. Gunter's team moved to the front. Kyle must have been insulted, and the showdown was on between first and second place. The pace ratcheted higher and higher. Ben felt like a bit player as the powerhouses battled for position on the road. This strength couldn't be natural. Kyle must not be the only doped guy on his team. The Megatronics cyclists floated up the road as if they had helium in their veins. Ben clung to the group, wracked with pain. Weaker men fell off the pace, one by one.

The dwindling peloton hit village after village, far ahead of the fastest anticipated schedule. Roadside fans looked stunned as the group rushed past. Another of Ben's teammates lost touch with the lead pack. Every climb, even the category-three Point Sublime, took its toll. To the left side of the road a pair of royal eagles rose on an elevator of air. Ben wished he could climb so effortlessly.

After a short descent into a deep gorge came the long chug up the Côte de Jabron. At times the road was sheltered beneath overhanging rock. Ben had never dreamed France contained terrain so reminiscent of his home. These cliffs were paler and slightly more vegetated than those near Hanksville, Utah, but the similarities were unmistakable.

For the first portion of the ascent the athletes eyed Château de Trigance, strategically positioned to guard the entrance to a natural traffic funnel. As they rode, Ben's purple helmet collected heat like a solar powered cranium cooker. His mood continued to deteriorate. If conditions didn't improve quickly, Banque Fédérale would be in shambles.

The idea that Kyle was using drugs to inflict this punishment was unbearable. Ben wished he'd never heard the news. If he didn't believe

Megatronics had an unfair advantage, would he feel so near the edge? This overwhelming internal conflict was Kyle's fault. The rage distracted him from the race. He couldn't lead his team and hate at the same time. If reality was shaped by thoughts, this was one he'd be better off without.

But it wouldn't go away. Nor could he get rid of the ideas Bridgette had planted in his head. Drugs that might relieve his suffering were within his reach. She saw them as the healthy alternative. The thought was so enticing. The first step in the process lay in his jersey pocket.

Ben shook his head. He wouldn't do it. For all he knew, the other men in this group were enduring more than he was. He sank inside himself, shutting down every unnecessary system until only those critical to operating a bike remained functional. He watched his shadow, disembodied, a mere skeleton, fibrous muscle attached to his legs only. Some reptilian vestige of his brain, unable to comprehend pain in a human way, kept pushing, ordering the heart to throb, the legs to rotate, the arms to steer. The only things that mattered were turning the pedals, climbing the hill, ignoring the pain. Pain, after all, was an evolutionary invention, not merely useless to him in this moment, but an impediment.

By the summit of the Jabron only three of Ben's Banque Fédérale teammates remained in the lead group. The stage hadn't even reached its midway point. Fortunately, even with three categorized ascents still to come, the terrain over the last half appeared easier than the first. Maybe some of his men could catch back on.

It was an unrealistic hope. Ben gasped for air as he and the remaining cyclists darted down the backside of the slope. No one would be closing in on this group from behind.

They would soon reach the feed zone on the Canjuers plateau. The soigneurs would be positioned beside the road to hand off musettes, the simple cloth shoulder bags used to carry food. Eating would need to be rapid before the plummet resumed.

Ben's stomach rumbled. His odometer reading indicated that they were a kilometer past the feed zone, but he'd seen nothing.

Thierry spoke over the radio. "We just got word of a complication. The land we're crossing belongs to the military. The commander was so excited to have the feed zone on his base that he had his men erect grandstands and invite their families. The only problem is that he constructed everything where the highway passes his barracks, two kilometers beyond the spot marked on your profile. When the race officials came through this morning and set things up he threw a fit. He won the argument and the feed zone was moved."

"We'll make it," Ben said, though he wasn't happy.

"I'm glad to hear that, but the move created one other complication you need to be aware of," Thierry said. "The feed zone is now on a three percent downhill grade."

Ben and his teammates shared worried glances. Feed zones ought to be on slight climbs, not slight descents.

From the moment they crested the hill they heard the joyful oompa-loompa brass band ahead and slightly below them. Within a couple hundred meters the crowds came into view. No feed zone Ben had ever ridden through had been a tenth as popular. Tanks and other armored vehicles lined both sides of the road. Soldiers and civilians milled about. The temporary grandstands were full beyond capacity. The band belted out its music with vibrant enthusiasm.

Ben salivated, thankful his energy had held out. Mercilessly, Megatronics increased the pace, taking advantage of the gradient. The speed would make the upcoming food handoffs very dangerous.

"This is insane," Thierry called over the radio. "Drop behind the group and grab your supplies at a safe speed. If we aren't able to catch back up, so be it."

Ben didn't have the energy to answer, but felt thankful all the way to his marrow for the command to relent. He dropped back with his remaining team members. They approached, watching the mêlée of frenzied soigneurs and cyclists missing handoffs left and right. Dropped musette bags were crushed under an onslaught of bicycle tires.

One of Luigi's teammates plowed through a mess of bananas, sandwiches, energy bars, and drink bottles, losing control. He swerved toward the band.

The Canjeurs Color Guard stopped playing their tune as the musicians dove for cover. The man and his machine sliced into the band's formation like a bunker-busting missile. The rider toppled the cymbals and the bicycle's front tire sent the bass drum flying. As the drum rolled, an accordion emitted a final, pathetic call.

Ben passed the disaster, attention riveted on the road ahead. He squeezed his brakes, grabbed his musette at half the speed of the cyclists who'd failed in front of him, and accepted another from a rival team's soigneur who'd missed his handoffs. Each of Ben's teammates also grabbed an extra bag apiece. Every musette held two bottles of electrolyte drink plus lots of food, enough to feed two men.

Ben secured the backpacks, stood on his pedals, and chased the pack ahead. "Let's go earn some friends!"

The cyclists charged with renewed vigor, energized to have an immediate goal. It didn't take long to catch the peloton on the downhill slope. When Ben noticed three Megatronics cyclists carrying a couple of musettes apiece at the tail of his group he understood why. Their strategy had obviously been to deny meals to their rivals, and then have their own delivered. The extra food Ben's teammates carried foiled that plan.

This stage would require roughly 9000 calories to complete, even more given today's high pace. A cyclist's lean body could store only about 1500 readily burnable calories, so the math was simple. Eat or bonk. Denying food was a strategic decision on Megatronics part, but it hadn't been made by a genius. It would be tough to win this race without friends in the peloton. In Ben's opinion, Kyle's team had just made a mistake. If he could befriend the alienated men, he would gain a valuable asset down the road. He looked at his teammates. "The extra food is gold."

Gunter already had food, but two of his key lieutenants were empty-handed. Ben gave one of them a musette to share.

"*Ahhh. Für mich? Danke! Danke!*"

Ben noticed his Italian friend, Luigi, had also come away empty-handed. When crossing mountainous terrain, there was no better friendship to foster than with the best climber in pro cycling. Ben took a water bottle and a sandwich from his remaining bag. "Here you are, *amico mio.*"

"*Che Dio te bewidica.* You are a saint."

Music to Ben's ears. "This pace can't be maintained, right?"

Luigi shook his head. "Don't be so sure." He pulled his profile map out. He pointed at the Col de la Sentinelle. "Kyle will attack here." He gasped for breath. "Otherwise … why make us suffer?"

Ben nodded, surprised that his friend could think so clearly on a day like this. His theory made sense. Kyle needed to break away on a difficult section of road to build a gap. The final fifty kilometers weren't as hard. "Will you help us neutralize him?"

Luigi smiled.

Ben glanced around. Seeing so many men eating food delivered by his team made him happy. He ate as fast as his blood-starved digestive system would permit. The pace would return to overdrive at any moment. With legs aching for energy and oxygen, his body had a tough time diverting resources to break down even the simplest foods, but everything depended on it.

Gradually sensations returned. He heard the rhythmic chirp of insect hordes and smelled the fragrance of roadside wildflowers. Ben finished his meal just as they dropped into Bargemon. It was the quaintest village yet. In the central plaza the thick shadows of four-story buildings and hundred-year-old sycamores were further cooled by water burbling through an ancient fountain. Where the route turned left an inviting footpath led beneath a stone archway to a matrix of outdoor corridors straight ahead.

Spectators were sparse. One woman in a floral print dress threw open her shutters in surprise, calling her family to the window. How stunned the majority of fans would be to show up at the predicted arrival time only to learn that the cyclists had blown through town long before.

As the village slipped behind them, Megatronics stoked the furnace again. Just as Luigi had predicted, the train began to fly. Now they confronted the Col de St.-Amoux. With wicked rapidity the cyclists conquered the slope over a bone-jarring road. On the downhill Ben had to assume his tightest tuck just to maintain contact.

What had these guys eaten for lunch? Liquid victory? There were still seven Megatronics cyclists battering the peloton. Most of the rest of the field had been dropped. Their concern would be reaching the finish line before the cut-off time to avoid elimination.

Ben fought the bad pavement for control of his machine. He was down to just two teammates in the lead group, but that left him better off than some. Gunter was doing well with four team members still in play, but each man looked like he'd taken a trip to hell and back.

The route shifted onto the Col de la Sentinelle, and the tension increased. Electricity flowed through the pack.

"Get ready," Luigi said. This was the spot where he'd guessed Kyle would attack.

Albert looked at Ben with a pathetic expression. He was in no condition to run the planned interference.

Ben didn't feel capable, either. He needed all the help he could get countering the upcoming move. He pedaled beside Gunter. "Kyle might attack soon."

Conserving oxygen, Gunter nodded in agreement. The word was passed concisely to other sympathetic cyclists. Two of Gunter's domestiques made a charge for the front of the pack. The pair squeezed between Kyle and his lead-out man just ahead of him, but then slowed.

Kyle yelled at his teammate. "Dammit! Pay attention!"

Confused, the lead-out man stopped pedaling and looked back. The others soon caught him, but he didn't immediately resume. He shot Kyle an angry stare as cyclists passed on both sides. Kyle's men had busted a gut for him today. If he didn't show appreciation there might be trouble in the Megatronics camp.

Momentum shattered, Kyle looked like an eighth-grader blindsided by a biology pop quiz. For a moment, the gathering of athletes bore a stronger resemblance to a church picnic ride than to a pro peloton in the Tour de France. Ben and Gunter shared a grin.

"Beauty, mate," gasped an Aussie. "Those girly-men just got croc bit."

With the momentum lost at the foot of the steepest gradient, the revolutionaries littered themselves among the Megatronics cyclists. Kyle barked orders, fighting to regain control. His men reapplied the pressure in fits and starts, but Kyle had a hard time threading his way through scattered athletes to take advantage. Finally, his troops got organized for another attempt. This time Luigi sprinted into position and broke things up.

In the next moment, Gunter attacked up the right hand side of the road. Kyle's face reddened as he chased after the German. Ben poured all of his strength into the pursuit. Seeing his enemy's frustrations firsthand was all the motivation he needed to cling to the tail of the lead pack.

Albert wasn't able to respond. He fell off the pace, isolating Ben. With no teammates, he was at the mercy of his rivals.

Kyle and his men reeled Gunter back in and reorganized for another attempt. This time there was no one in the group still capable of blocking Kyle's progress, and in a moment eerily similar to the day before, he pedaled away from the strongest cyclists in the world. His big diesel engine merely revved higher and higher until no one could match his pace.

Ben sagged over his machine, frustrated that he couldn't keep up.

"Regroup, Ben," Thierry said. "This stage isn't over."

Ben corrected his form. He and the other chasers needed to hold the gap in check. They had to avoid the indignity of race officials allowing support vehicles, including the Megatronics team car, to move past them. Such a moment would be a big boost to Kyle's psyche. Cars were allowed only into substantial gaps, and this one had become substantial very quickly. Ben hoped that everybody in the group felt the same urgency he did.

The crowd screamed encouragement to the remaining contestants, but no one had the strength to increase the speed another increment. Only a half-dozen athletes remained in the chase group. Four of them, including

Ben and Gunter, took turns at the front. The other two were Megatronics men. They sat on the back of the pack, recuperating and strategizing. Eventually Kyle's support car was allowed to pass.

Thierry spoke over the radio. "Kyle used up three quarters of the mountain, plus a lot of energy he hadn't planned on, trying to get away. Now limit your losses and reel him in on the descent."

Race radio reported Kyle's lead at fifty-two seconds. Ben's heart thundered. He gulped oxygen as he fought for altitude.

His thoughts seemed mangled as a hollow sensation threatened to overwhelm him. He'd bonked in training many times before, and he knew he was on the verge now. Reaching into his back pocket he grabbed an energy gel. He ripped it open, squeezed the sweet contents into his mouth, and washed them down with a shot of water.

His vision had narrowed to a small sphere, sufficient only to focus on the wheel ahead of him. He lacked the mental strength to set tempo, or even to figure out who he was following. For the moment, his fate was in the hands of this unknown cyclist.

It would take all his concentration to survive the next couple of minutes, moving through blackness and guided only by the beam of a weak flashlight. As long as he maintained visual contact with the wheel in front of him he had hope of emerging from the other side.

"C'mon, Ben. Don't let them do this to you," Thierry said over the headset.

Only then did Ben recognize that the wheel ahead had slipped into the distance. He was fully cooked and being dropped.

He tried to reach deeper into his reserves.

"Dig, dig, dig!" Thierry commanded.

Ben meant to obey, but wasn't certain what sort of result he was producing.

Gradually, the pedaling became easier. He must be cresting the hill. He looked up and saw a regal fortress, surely built to command the ridgeline. Energy began to return, like ripples on a wind-blown lake. Life-giving sugar entered his bloodstream, but his brain was still deep in energy debt. Thoughts remained blurry and incoherent. He reached for another gel.

He put the tip of the packet between his teeth and tried to rip, but something was wrong. He removed it and took a look: a plastic bag containing two pills. Where had that come from?

Ben hid the capsules between his left palm and the handlebar while he tried to think. For the first time in what seemed like a long time he registered his surroundings. Terraced gardens tamed the hill on both sides. No fans were in sight. He wondered if anybody had seen the baggie. Legal or not, he didn't want to be spotted handling pills.

He entered a section lined with barriers, and then rode beneath the "King of the Mountains" banner. He crossed a short stretch of flat road leading to the descent. Now there were lots of fans on both sides of the road, but still no sign of Kyle.

"Okay, you did the hard part. Big gears and fast corners now, Ben. You need to catch back on quickly."

With his right index finger Ben tapped his gear lever several times. The chain dropped to a smaller cog on the rear cassette, and the resistance increased. He pushed the left brake lever to the side and watched his chain climb onto the fifty-three-tooth ring.

The wind in his face felt refreshing, but he still couldn't think clearly. He doubted he could catch Kyle on the coming slope. Not only was his enemy naturally gifted, he was competing with enhanced abilities. Ben needed help, real help; otherwise not only this stage would be lost, but the entire tour.

He was failing himself, and failing Thierry, too. He owed his sponsors and fans a better result than this.

He felt the two small lumps beneath his left palm. Could the pills save him? Suddenly they were his entire universe. They probably contained more than Bridgette thought they did. Was it possible they were more than a masking agent? It seemed likely.

An energy boost would be so welcome. After all, there were limits to the suffering a man could conquer. As deeply as he regretted it, the time had come to face reality.

Ben looked toward the road ahead. As on most descents, fans were sparse. The cameraman's motorcycle had sped ahead, probably wanting to be well positioned for photos of the leaders in the upcoming technical turns. Ben looked over his shoulder and verified that he was alone on the road. If he was going to take the medication, there wouldn't be a better time than this. He recalled Bridgette's words: "If Kyle is gaining an advantage over you, especially an advantage that improves his health, maybe you should consider using the same thing."

With his right thumb and index finger he removed the pills from the baggie, put them in his mouth, and grabbed his water bottle. A quick squirt, and the medication slid irretrievably down his throat.

Chapter Nine

Working in the Cannes finish area with the other domestiques, Bridgette could hardly bring herself to watch the monitor. Her stomach had tied itself in knots. Ben was having a bad day on the bike and winning this stage now looked out of the question. She shut her eyes and prayed for a miracle.

When she opened them, Robidoux's diminutive valet stood in front of her. Wordlessly, he turned and headed toward the marina. She followed, her eyes searching for his likely destination. Sailboats rocked on the shining waters, the thousands of masts swaying lazily like a contented porcupine's quills. Her footsteps echoed hollowly as she walked down the floating, wooden dock. Ahead the valet faced her again. He stood beside a gorgeous sailboat. Its sweeping triple-tiered roofline made it look fast, even when moored. The sleek lines and inlaid wood accents resulted in an intoxicating combination of old and new.

As she approached, the valet tilted his head toward the boat. He lent a supporting hand so she could step atop the transom wall. Then she descended two stairs to the aft deck. Rich light emanated from the cabin below. She glanced back at the valet, and he nodded. Time to speak with the boss.

Taking in a deep breath, she went below deck. She paused at the bottom stair, awed by the teak interior before her. She'd never dreamed a boat could be so luxurious. The quarters seemed cavernous, possibly the result of the way the space widened from bottom to top, or maybe because of the tinted windows surrounding the entire space at eye level.

She'd been expecting to stoop as she entered, but the ceiling was seven feet high. Curved half-walls created intimate nooks, but rather than compartmentalizing the space, the result was a feeling of easy access. Beneath her feet a Persian runner softened the slatted wood floor. It led down another three stairs, through the galley, and into a comfortable looking bedroom tucked beneath the prow.

"*Bonjour*, my little flower."

Bridgette's heart skipped a beat at Robidoux's voice. She looked left. He sat in another of the curved spaces, this one apparently custom-made for him.

"*Bonjour, monsieur*," she answered.

"Sit." He opened his palm toward the seat opposite his.

She sat down quickly, before her legs gave way on their own. A glass of ice water awaited her. Lifting it from the cup holder, she took a sip.

"You look stunning."

"*Merci*." She knew it wasn't true. Her stress level had never been higher.

"Have you given thought to what it would mean if Ben won this race?"

She had. His words stoked her competitive fire. "Nothing would mean more."

"I like you, Bridgette. Your vision is clear. Does Ben understand what we're facing?"

"Partly."

"Partly … Well, that's a start." Robidoux opened a small drawer and extracted a cigar. "Do you mind?" Without waiting for an answer he produced a cutter and snipped off the end. Then, almost magically, a tiny flame spurted from the bulkhead wall. Robidoux puffed on the stogie while positioning the other end over the fire. The flame shut off, and his aromatic smoke curled toward the ceiling. The white air disappeared obediently into an overhead vent.

"Let's get to business. It's clear Ben is going to lose time today. Fortunately, we already have plans in place." The corners of his mouth lifted in a subtle grin.

She was silent until he looked straight into her eyes. "Yes, fortunately."

He tilted his head. "You convinced Ben to take the masking agent, didn't you?"

"I … I'm not certain. He refused to swallow them while I was there, but he promised to keep them with him and think it over."

"Hmmm. Well, that's not the answer I'd hoped to hear. You do recognize the importance, don't you? Today's results should make it clear that Ben has no shot at victory unless he adopts his rival's techniques."

She nodded. His opinion seemed valid. Either way, she'd given her word and now she had to live with it.

"You're quite a friend to do these things for him, Bridgette. Because of the taboo nature of the subject, most athletes find themselves facing these decisions alone, or at least without the consultation of those they love. I wonder if Ben recognizes how lucky he is."

She pondered the suggestion, but just as she was getting her mind around it Robidoux spoke again.

"Did you follow the French Open this year?"

She nodded. She'd had a difficult time taking her eyes off the television. It had been the most fiercely fought version in years. The gladiator nature of the competition enticed her like a drug.

"The gentlemen's final," Robidoux said. "What a match! I could watch that sort of a display twenty-four hours a day, every day, and never tire."

She took a bigger drink of water. "Me too."

"You know, the winner just purchased a sailboat exactly like this. He even accepted an invitation to rendezvous with my primary yacht not more than a week ago."

Primary yacht? That must be the one she'd heard about, complete with helipad.

"I arrived there in this boat. It was quite a sight, that big powerful vessel with two agile sister ships tethered to either side." His eyes rose dreamily to the ceiling. "Wouldn't it be spectacular if I could eventually invite you and Ben to join me there as well? Of course, we'll have to get you a proper boat."

Bridgette felt her eyes go wide. This sort of lifestyle could be theirs? She'd never even imagined anything so luxurious

"Let's do it, then," Robidoux said. "I shouldn't keep you any longer, though. I'm sure Ben will be anxious to see you at the finish line."

She stood, wondering if she'd actually agreed to anything or not.

"If only I'd had someone like you to assist me in my cycling career. Unfortunately, that opportunity is forever lost for me. The prime years slide by quicker than you expect. I lacked the necessary support system when my big chance presented itself. All the lucky breaks in the world couldn't make up for it. In retrospect, it's fascinating to analyze the moments that differentiate the winners from the losers."

"Ben is one of the winners," Bridgette said.

Robidoux raised his eyebrows. "He could reach that level. There's no doubt the stars have momentarily aligned; it's unlikely that such an opportune moment will ever present itself again. With the right management Ben stands to be very fortunate indeed."

His words rang true. "Thanks Laurent. I'm sorry, but I really do need to go."

"I understand." He extended a sealed envelope. "Read this document on your walk back. It contains everything you need to know."

Chapter Ten

Ben tossed his empty water bottle aside and returned his concentration to the road ahead. This descent plummeted 769 meters, more than 2400 feet. The pavement was a dangerous assemblage of patched and deteriorating base. Taking big risks, he powered forward and finally caught the group ahead. He took the lead for long pulls, dragging the men with him and willing them back into contention. He punished the pedals, flying faster and faster, ripping through the corners, feeling powerful. The others had strength only for short turns at the front, and then Ben charged through again.

Even though his chase group had the advantage of riding in a pack, it wasn't until they cruised into Montauroux at the base of the slope that Ben finally recaptured Kyle. He couldn't resist glancing back as he rolled by. Kyle looked angry enough to take a bite out of someone's bicycle frame.

With no shock absorption, descents were often rough. On this hill, the vibrating ride had put Ben's arms to sleep. He could hardly feel his handlebars. Only the sight of his hands on the brake levers told him they were where they should be. He flexed his shoulders, elbows, wrists, and fingers, working to restore the blood flow.

The two Megatronics men, who had been hitching a ride since Kyle's attack, moved forward and paced their leader. Kyle's scowl didn't vary. He looked determined, his spirit unbroken. There were two upcoming hills, albeit small, where he could still do damage. The thought of having to reel him in again made Ben dizzy. He just might have the strength to do it, though. What had those pills contained?

On the first of the hills, a 150-meter high bump called Les Marjoris, Ben rose to match the pace of the group, but his lack of power surprised him. How had the medication lost effect so quickly? He couldn't keep pace. Luigi looked back, concern in his eyes, but there was no way he could help.

Thirty kilometers to go, and suddenly Ben was alone, his earlier confidence gone. High atop a switchback in front of him he saw large crowds cheering the approach of his former companions. He struggled toward that spot. Once he reached it he passed a parked limousine so deluxe it had a separate door near the middle of the body. He couldn't believe how long it took him to travel the length of a single car. Finally, he rounded a corner and the last few wicked switchbacks to the Col du Tanneron's summit became visible. God, have mercy.

He spotted the leaders again, well on their way to the top. Kyle went off the front once more, and Gunter chased. Ben was the seventh man on the road. He had to close the gap, but within a few more revolutions he knew he was still losing ground. It took him a long time to haul himself into the hilltop village. It seemed he'd been climbing for hours. Fans crowded thickly. As soon as there was a break in the humanity, support vehicles whipped past him, one after another.

He gained speed on the descent, a modern but sandpapery oil-and-gravel road base. He rounded a bend, and the beauty of Cannes and the ocean beyond revealed themselves. In the commercial sector, high-rise crescent shaped resorts stretched their concrete arms toward the sea, but the majority of the city consisted of single-family estates. From afar, these elegant homes looked like some bizarre variety of sun-loving moss. Their clay-tiled roofs dominated the seaward side of every hill, while the landward side exploded with untouched greenery.

On the cobalt Mediterranean a myriad of white wake trails pointed like confused directional arrows to a thousand scattered destinations. Jets launched, one after another, from a runway near the beach. The many roads were filled with cars going this way and that. A train screamed along the coastline. People sure kept busy moving around.

How far behind the leaders was he? He needed to risk disaster to stay in contention. He slid his hands side by side near the fulcrum of his handlebars. He rested his chin on their backs and peered beneath the top rim of his sunglasses. The goal was to minimize his wind profile. He tucked his body forward of the seat, flat along the top tube, with his feet in mid-stroke. This was the same precarious riding posture that had once resulted in a horrendous crash on Boulder Mountain near his boyhood home. More recently he'd used it to produce one of the fastest descents in cycling history, on the slopes of the Col de la Croix de Fer. The wind sound raised an octave. He was going very fast, but in this position, steering was all but impossible. He fought for control of the bike as he screamed down the slope amidst a tempest of his own creation.

Over the headset Thierry begged, "Faster, faster!"

With ten kilometers to go, Ben had reached sea level. The route turned onto the Boulevard du Midi, along the Mediterranean shore. Colorful umbrellas dotted the beach to his right. The sand wasn't visible because of the sea wall, but many sun worshipers had climbed to the road. A smokin' hot babe, topless of course, was smoking. It seemed that in France everyone did. There was the usual French mixture of topless women, young and old, heavyset men in Speedos, and children. Laughter pervaded everything. These people were "fun oriented."

Now Ben rested his elbows on his handlebars, dangling his hands over his front wheel. In this position steering was even more difficult than when he'd been descending, but the slower speed and straight roads required little navigation. The aerodynamics were better than any alternative, but the aluminum bar beneath his elbows amplified the numbness in his arms. He couldn't feel his fingers at all, and his feet weren't much better, yet he drove the cranks with everything he had. His thighs pounded against his abdomen at every revolution. Cheering fans disappeared behind him as he charged forward.

The electrical scream of a passenger train startled him as it blew past on his left. He wished he could hitch a ride. He passed snow cone huts, lifeguard towers, palm trees, rock jetties, sidewalk restaurants, kids wearing blow-up toy duckie floats, and countless people enjoying the day.

Mercifully, as he reached a crowded sailboat harbor, the final straightaway opened before him. As Ben passed beneath the finishing arch the timer showed his deficit at nearly two minutes. The number felt enormous—far bigger than he'd imagined. He had finished the stage in seventh place. Exhausted at a level he'd never before dreamed of, he rolled across the line. Thank God, the rest day was now upon him. No more racing for almost forty-three hours. Oh man, did he need the break!

He wobbled through the finish area, looking for a place to stop. Regal old-money hotels bordered the course on his left, while a raucous midway separated the road from the sea to the right. Merry-go-round riders strained to catch glimpses of the race between revolutions. Commotion behind him caught his attention, and he realized he'd rolled right past Bridgette and Fritz. With his narrowed vision and muddled brain he had a difficult time thinking coherently. He wanted to lie down and vomit.

"Aren't you glad you use Dial. Don't you wish everybody did?" Fritz said.

Ben put a foot on the ground. Someone grabbed his bike, and he stepped off. Bridgette's arm wrapped around his waist. He stumbled along with her.

"Reporters are waiting to hear from you," Bridgette said.

"Can't," he heard himself reply.

"Okay. I'll take care of it."

She guided him along and eventually laid him in a bed, possibly the one in the back of the team bus.

A gentle hand tickled his arm as consciousness slipped away.

Chapter Eleven

Ben woke to Bridgette caressing his face. Behind her, a bald man in an Italian suit worked on something hidden by his open briefcase.

"Where are we?" Ben asked.

"This is Doctor Peraza's camping car," Bridgette said.

"Doctor Peraza?"

The man peered over his briefcase, reading glasses balanced on his long nose and concern in his eyes. "The world's premier human performance specialist, at your service."

He was pretty arrogant. "Why am I here?"

"Precautionary," said the doctor. His voice had an unhurried quality. "Your friends were concerned."

Bridgette's eyes showed fear. Had she been crying? "Maybe you shouldn't continue."

Was she kidding? Bridgette knew better than to suggest something like that. "No! This is war." Ben searched the room. His jersey lay across a seat back. His feet were bare. A pint size bag of clear fluid hung from the ceiling. A small gauge hose disappeared beneath several pieces of tape halfway up his left forearm.

The doctor approached with a syringe. He stuck the needle into the port on the IV line and pressed the plunger. "What are you giving me?"

"Don't worry," Bridgette said. "You need it."

Ben noticed a small regulator on the vertical portion of the line. Drip, drip, drip, drip. It ran fast.

The doctor looked at the regulator. "Normal saline, plus five cc's of B-12 from the syringe."

Vitamin B-12 kept red blood cells healthy, extending their life. Amino acids were also commonly administered this way. Ben watched the drip. Now it felt refreshing to see this legal liquid entering his vein. He'd been running on empty. Drip, drip, drip.

"Do you still have the pills I gave you?" Bridgette asked.

Sweat rose on Ben's brow. He shook his head, indicating the doctor with his eyebrows.

Bridgette dabbed his forehead with a handkerchief. "No secrets. We're here because I'm concerned about you. That's all that matters. What happened to the pills?"

Ben dropped his gaze. "I swallowed them on the descent of the Sentinelle. I had to." He looked up again.

Bridgette and the doctor glanced at one another.

The doctor smiled. His teeth were straight and shiny. "You've made a wise decision."

"What did they contain?" Ben asked. "They brought me quick strength."

The doctor chuckled. "Those pills didn't make you stronger. You're about to know what real strength feels like." He opened the refrigerator and selected some of the contents.

"If you felt better after taking them," Bridgette said, "it was purely placebo effect."

"Really?" Ben had heard how powerfully the body could be influenced when the mind thought medication was real, but he'd never experienced it before. "Damn."

"That's what you'll be saying once this stuff is flowing in your veins." The doctor arranged a group of ampoules and vials on a tray.

What was he doing? "I haven't decided to use performance enhancers."

"You believed you doped when you prepared with the masking agent. That speaks of your inner desire. Don't complicate things." Peraza enunciated, as if he believed Ben lacked intelligence. "The correct path is obvious."

"Not to me." He hadn't been thinking clearly when he swallowed the pills. He shouldn't even have been carrying drugs under those circumstances. For the first time he understood how some people could turn to medication under severe stress and regret it later. At least he had the chance to rethink the decision.

An exasperated sigh escaped the doctor's lips. "It's time for you to adopt a more professional approach."

Peraza had an unusual definition of 'professional.'

Bridgette took Ben's hand. "I can't bear to see you suffer like this, *Minet*. You're running yourself into the ground."

Ben stared at her. Something wasn't right. She normally supported him by overestimating his abilities, but now she doubted him. How could she do this when he needed her encouragement more than ever? What was going on? "Let me get some food and rest. I promise, I'll think this through. We have some time now, don't we? Tomorrow's a rest day."

The doctor spoke calmly. "You're losing ground at the rate of two minutes a stage, Ben. Do you know what your deficit is now?"

"No."

"With bonuses figured in, three minutes and eleven seconds, my friend. Soon you won't even be a contender."

He felt his throat constricting. He needed fresh air. Could it be true that he was falling out of contention? That had to be an exaggeration. Sure, he'd lost time, but he remained one of only three men who still had a legitimate shot at winning, especially because two of the remaining stages were time trials, a discipline where each cyclist battled the clock on his own. Having grown up as the only cyclist in a tiny town, pushing himself to ride hard when there was no one else to set the pace had always been one of Ben's strengths. Yes, he'd like to be closer to the lead, but he could accomplish that in the next stage … or could he?

Ben closed his eyes. He'd designed his entire life around cycling. In the last twelve months he'd ridden his bike twenty thousand miles. He'd trained four to seven hours a day, six or seven days a week for years, spending more time than he could recall hooked up to monitors, undergoing physical therapy, adjusting his position in wind tunnels, and reading books about everything from strategy to championship mindsets. Every calorie he'd consumed in the previous six months had been accounted for, logged into a computer, and analyzed. Yet, it wasn't enough.

"I can't give any more than I already am."

"The key is working smarter, not harder," the doctor said. "The sooner we begin treatment, the better shape I'll have you in when the race resumes."

Ben looked at Bridgette. He couldn't read any answers in her expression. Was this the woman he thought he knew so well?

"I've seen many athletes face this dilemma, but the problem is really only one of interpretation," Peraza said. "If you were to use appropriate medication to restore some of your endurance and recuperative abilities, who would be the victim?"

"Are you serious? How about the athletes who don't dope?"

"The only athletes who might beat you, whether you dope or not, are Kyle and Gunter. We know that Kyle is using PEDs. It wouldn't surprise me to learn that Gunter is too."

"It would surprise me. And even if he is, I would be deceiving the fans."

The doctor shook his head. "They don't care whether they are deceived or not. Spectators tune in to watch you deliver an incredible performance. In reality, they get more of what they want if you perform at a higher level."

Ben rubbed his face in his hands, eventually steepling his fingers against his lips. "How about the way I cheat myself? I'm not some lab rat. Drug use has repercussions. People die sometimes."

"My therapies aren't experimental. The medication I administer will make you healthier."

Bridgette took Ben's hand. "You know it's the truth, *Minet*. Your blood system is depleted. Why is it wrong for you to address that condition?"

Ben glared at her. "You're not helping."

She touched his cheek with her free hand. "I'm discussing these things because I care about you, Ben. I'm crazy for you. You don't have to win this race to prove anything to me."

He looked at her skeptically, but her eyes were on the doctor.

She continued speaking. "Since I know you won't stop, I want you to continue in the safest and fairest way possible, and that is by allowing Doctor Peraza to help."

The doctor sat down, putting himself closer to Ben's level. "Listen, my friend. I'm extending the maillot jaune within your grasp. I suggest you take it, that you seize the opportunity to become a cycling immortal. You can accept your place in the history books, or you can finish with the pack and never be heard from again. The choice is yours."

Bridgette cleared her throat. The sound echoed inside the RV. Ben stared into her eyes, always caring, now pleading with him. He cherished her advice, depended on her to keep his best interests in mind when the toils of the race clouded his judgment.

"It is said that a man who wins a single Tour stage will never again have to pay for his drinks in France." The doctor would have made a great hypnotist. His tone and manner were captivating.

Bridgette nodded agreement. She seemed to hang on every word the man spoke. Ben returned his gaze to the doctor as well. The attention brought an arrogant smile to the scholarly face. He continued speaking.

"Just imagine what it will mean to be the overall winner, not just what it will earn you in France, but everywhere. You'll be a hero, Ben. Can you dream that big?"

Ben closed his eyes, shutting out the doctor's image but unable to block his words.

"The others are using. You're at a disadvantage. This is the equalizer."

"You've worked so hard." Bridgette squeezed his hand. "You've given so much and come so far. Don't sabotage yourself now."

Chapter Twelve

Was Ben throwing sand in his own sprockets? Of course there was a level at which he'd always been tempted by drugs. What pro athlete wasn't? The gauntlet necessary to reach this point automatically eliminated non-competitive people. Those who made it to the pros were, by definition, hard-wired to give everything for the win. They were the sort who'd go to nearly any length to gain an edge. After all, at the height of any vocation, tiny improvements could result in massive moves up the rankings. The best athletes were often only fractions of a percentage point superior to the men they regularly beat. Those tiny differences meant results, and with results came success, prestige, and cash.

Drugs, illegal or not, could be oh, so tempting. That was why Ben considered them forbidden fruit. He'd always feared that if he got too close he wouldn't be able to control himself.

It was also why Bridgette was pushing them. The race had set her already hot competitive instincts on fire. That explained her behavior. She wanted him to use drugs because she knew that second place would ultimately result in a stronger sense of regret than accomplishment. She recognized that winning was everything. Bridgette had accepted reality, and he ought to as well. It wasn't unfair of him to use drugs; it was simply a necessary step toward a goal he'd committed himself to long ago.

"What is your decision, Monsieur Barnes?" The doctor stood again and returned to his workspace. Tiny bottles jingled as he made preparations. "Will children be singing your name? Here comes Ben Barnes! Conqueror of the Tour de France!"

Children. Ben recalled Toma's admiring face and thought about the boy's cycling aspirations. Toma would be on course at each of the Pyrenean climbs next week. Then Ben pictured the expression of the small boy on the big bike. The smiles of countless other young people he'd spoken to over the years flashed through his mind. He yanked the needle from his arm and pushed himself to his feet. Crimson blood trickled onto his tan skin. "Thanks for putting things back in perspective, Doctor."

Ben's head spun with the sudden exertion, but he maintained his balance as he exited the RV. He stepped onto a spiny cactus. His foot recoiled involuntarily, and he looked for better placement. This wasn't the finish line staging area. He gripped the vehicle for support as he looked around. Where was he?

The sun was low and hot, an hour at the most until it set. He stood on a rugged mountainside. Red boulders, some the size of cars, had been stacked by natural forces like a child's abandoned building blocks. Far below town lights were twinkling, but the dirt road he stood on didn't go in that direction at all. Was he hallucinating?

"Bridgette!" he called. "What the hell is going on?"

"Don't overreact, Ben."

"Are you kidding me? This isn't an overreaction."

Bridgette stepped from the RV and tried to take his hand. "The doctor prefers to stay out of the public eye."

Ben stepped away. This was too much. He spoke through clenched teeth. "Why did you bring me here?"

"A decision had to be made."

An engine roared to life, and the camping car jolted forward. Ben pulled Bridgette away from the road. They watched in astonishment as the vehicle jounced into the distance, trailed by a cloud of dust. It disappeared over the ridge.

"He's stranded us. I can't believe it." Bridgette sounded stunned.

"I can't believe you put us in the position to become stranded. What were you thinking? I'm living a nightmare!" Ben looked at the town. It would be insane to leave the road to cross such terrain in encroaching darkness.

A rumbling sound caught his attention, and he looked down the road. Here came the RV. Peraza's eyes didn't stray from the road as he blew by, abandoning them for a second time. A flock of starlings cackled as if amused by the joke.

"At least now we know the way out," Ben said. His legs felt too exhausted to walk even a short distance, but there wasn't another choice. His throat was parched. Hunger pangs stabbed his gut.

"Sorry," Bridgette said.

"Thierry's going to be furious when I turn up missing. It doesn't look like we'll find help soon."

"I'll explain things to him."

Ben started down the road, the setting sun at his back. "The excuse won't matter, Bridgette. He'll be mad because he's single-minded in his determination to help me win. I ought to make that as easy as possible for him. Taking unscheduled strolls in the wilderness is an unnecessary complication."

Bridgette matched his stride. "What are we going to do?"

"I'm going to find help. You can do whatever you'd like." He avoided the sharp stones by walking in the tire tracks. Chalky dust softened his steps.

"Please don't take this out on me, Ben."

He turned to face her. "That's laughable. I can't afford any more of your help, Bridgette. I'm exhausted, and my nerves are fried. You kidnapped me and nearly convinced me to take a step I couldn't have lived with. Right now I should be eating dinner with the team, but I don't have even the slightest clue where I am. Who knows what'll crop up next. It's the wrong time for this sort of garbage."

"I'm sorry, Ben. I want what's best for you."

"Bridgette, I thrive on clear goals. I depended on you to handle the details while I concentrate on the job at hand. I trusted you to keep my convictions in mind. Apparently I can't do that anymore." He felt so thirsty. Dust seemed to coat his throat and lungs.

"I'm sorry for letting you down." She looked so vulnerable.

He was furious, and he had a right to be, but it was impossible to stay mad at her while looking at her face and hearing her voice. There were too many positive emotions attached. Without a word, he looked away and strode down the road again.

"Sorry," Bridgette cried. "You wouldn't be here if not for me."

He stopped dead in his tracks. He'd thought that thought a million times, except it had been in appreciation. He began seeing the absurdity of this situation, and he realized that he'd rather patch things up than humiliate the woman he loved. She couldn't have meant to put him in this fix. Bridgette would never do that.

He turned toward her. "Just to clarify, do you mean that I wouldn't be riding in the Tour de France, or that I wouldn't be standing barefoot on a French mountainside wearing nothing but a pair of purple tights?"

She laughed her intoxicating laugh, the embodiment of joy. Then she ran to him and threw her arms around his neck. "Your life wouldn't be as rich without me, and mine would be empty without you."

They kissed.

"For the rest of my life, when I look at the leader's jersey I wore yesterday it will remind me of a day where I exceeded my highest expectations. I could never have imagined that moment could lead to this."

Bridgette dropped her gaze. "It's my fault. I saw drugs as the last chance for victory. I became convinced that it was in my hands to save your opportunity. I was so mistaken."

"It's a lesson I'm glad I learned in time. If I won another jersey by cheating, can you imagine what that would symbolize? I came so close to making a huge mistake, but it was the doctor who reminded me what matters. He, of all people, clarified my thoughts."

He looped his arm around Bridgette's waist and began walking. "What would I have told people about my victory? Should I have made up some lie about capturing my dreams through perseverance? Do I encourage kids to ride bicycles, knowing that, if they decide to race, I've set them on the path that led me to illegal drugs? What could be worse than reciting those sorts of lies over and over and over; telling people that the jersey symbolized victory when, in fact, it was my private scarlet letter. My permanent reminder of having taken the easy way out."

"I hadn't thought about it that way." A tear ran down Bridgette's cheek.

Ben caught it with a fingertip and pretended to deposit it on his tongue. "The first rule you learn growing up in the desert is, don't waste water. You can never tell know how long it will be until you find more. Now, it's time to make the best of the situation. Without you, my career as a pro would have ended a couple of years ago. I owe you so much and I love you so much."

"Thank you for saying that, *Minet*." She seemed lost in thought, as if measuring out the correct words, taking care not to further complicate things. "I promise that from now on I'll do everything in my power to support your decision to win clean."

"I know you will," Ben said.

They rounded a shoulder of the mountain. Sunlight danced on towering rock formations atop the opposite canyon wall, a petrified inferno. Near the canyon bottom a car sped along on an asphalt highway.

"Look," Bridgette said. "All roads lead to Paris." To the far right an enormous high-voltage transmission structure, its latticework silhouetted against the darkening sky, resembled the Eiffel Tower.

Ben walked on with more conviction, relieved by the potential for rescue. The road dropped steeply now. This side of the mountain was cooler and supported more and more vegetation the lower they got. He noticed deer hair clinging to the low branches of trees and also to the gravel below them. He bent down and rubbed the hair between his fingers. The texture and color told him a story. A doe and her fawn had bedded down here not long ago.

Bridgette found some tiny wild raspberries to share. She handed him a few along with a small bouquet of fern, angels-breath, and delicate pink flowers. "See. This isn't such a bad side trip."

Squinting into the dark shadows ahead Ben made out the silhouette of a manmade object. It was a water tank, similar to the sort mounted on semi-trailers. He started to jog.

Reaching the big green cylinder he climbed the wrought iron ladder welded to its side. He unclasped the top hatch and lifted the cover. It howled a rusty protest, but then dropped open with a clang. It was too dark to see inside. He reached down. He felt cool liquid. Oh, let it be water. He repositioned himself and scooped both hands into the tank. The splashing echoes were almost life giving in and of themselves. It was water!

He slurped handful after handful. Finally he slowed down. "Are you thirsty, Bridgette? There's only about 2000 gallons here so you better get some before I drink it all."

She didn't answer.

He propped himself up and looked around. He couldn't see her anywhere. "Bridgette!"

Confused, he climbed down from the tank and searched the vicinity. Beside the road a directional sign he hadn't noticed earlier pointed down a pathway to a location called Gorges du Blavet.

He followed the trail into thick woods. Within fifty meters he noticed a narrow opening to a huge, square clearing, twenty acres of clear-cut pines. Bridgette sat atop a tractor parked in the corner of the lot. She appeared to be fiddling with the controls. His mouth dropped open as the 1960's vintage green and yellow paint job brought memories charging back. The pile of stumps nearby told him why this machine was here. About half the clearing still awaited de-stumping.

Bridgette noticed him. "Look at this, Ben! If only we could get it started. I've searched everywhere. There's no key."

"It will be a cinch to hotwire."

She stared at him in surprise.

He banged a hand against the fender. "This baby's the spitting image of the tractor I raced against outside of Hanksville, when I was fourteen. The reason I believed I could beat the old beast over that mountain is that I knew exactly how fast it could go. My buddies and I used to take it for a spin from time to time."

Bridgette's eyes lit up. "Could we write the owner a note?"

"With what? We're just going to have to take it." Ben climbed aboard and put it into neutral. Everything was exactly the same as old man Glick's machine.

He reached beneath the dash and detached wires from the ignition switch without even having to look. Then he twisted the exposed ends together. Next he detached the starter motor wire. He pumped the gas pedal.

"Un … deux."

On the second stroke he touched the starter motor wire to a live wire on the opposite side of the switch.

The tractor coughed once, twice, three times, and then settled into a constant grumble. He pulled the starter motor wire away from the power and wedged it into a niche so that the bared end couldn't come into contact with anything.

Atop the exhaust pipe the hinged lid now bounced energetically. Even sitting still, the clattering of loose parts had to be louder than the engine itself.

"Are we ready to go?"

Ben nodded, removing a t-shirt from the seat back that had been serving as upholstery. He pulled it on, put the tractor in gear, and headed back past the water tank. Another kilometer of dirt road brought them to an asphalt highway.

The paved road ran downhill to the right, and the dirt from Peraza's tires seemed to trail off in that direction as well. Ben flipped a switch, and the fender-mounted headlights popped on. What a relief that they worked. He hadn't considered the danger of driving along a highway at dusk until just then.

He turned in the same direction that Peraza had. As the road reached level ground large cultivated fields and ranches began to appear, many of them featuring rusted cars on blocks. Ben decided to continue on until he found a town. A guard emu strutted along one fence line. They climbed a long, gradual hill.

Finally they crested it and descended into an ancient settlement with a surprising dose of neon. The colorful modern signs gave the main corridor a brilliant and captivating feel.

There shouldn't have been anything unusual about an old tractor clattering down a rural road in southern France, but something attracted a lot of stares as they rolled into the village square. Maybe they looked like an unlikely pair to be cruising the Mediterranean by tractor, Ben so oddly dressed and Bridgette resembling a supermodel with her hair blowing in the breeze. Then Ben realized that the residents recognized the machine, but not the driver. He disconnected his hotwires. Before the engine stopped a crowd had already gathered.

Ben hopped to the ground.

A burly man in overalls shuffled forward. He poked around inside of his left ear with the blunt end of a wheat shaft. "*Pardon.* What the hell are you doing wearing my t-shirt? I won that in a pie eating contest."

Ben stepped backward, clearing his personal space. "I can explain."

"*Bon.* While you're at it you might want to let us know how you were able to start my tractor without the aid of keys." He dangled a loaded key chain in front of Ben's face.

"We were stranded. I —"

"You expect me to believe that?" The man looked at Ben's shorts. "Your bicycle broke down so you hiked into the hills looking for a tractor?"

"Not exactly."

The man puffed out his chest and moved forward again. "I'll bet if you spent a night in our local jail you could figure out what happened." He turned to the crowd. "*Agent de police!*"

Bridgette climbed down and stepped between the men. "*S'il vous plait,* Monsieur. This is Ben Barnes. He's racing in the Tour de France."

The logger's eyes widened. "You're Ben Barnes?"

Ben nodded. "*Oui.* I'll be happy to pay for the use of your tractor."

A policeman elbowed his way into the center of the crowd.

"Your ride the other day was stunning," said an olive-skinned woman toting a child on her hip.

Ben nodded. "*Merci beaucoup.*"

"Are you here checking out the course?" asked the policeman.

Ben traded a curious glance with Bridgette. "Sunday's time trial comes through here? Where are we?"

"Bagnols-en-Forêt," said the olive-skinned woman.

"You don't even know where you are?" The logger asked.

Ben shook his head. "Which way will the bikes be traveling through here?" Thierry and the other contenders would have scoped out the course a month or more ago, but Ben had been only a domestique back then. At the time, most observers hadn't even expected him to be included on the nine-man Tour squad. Nobody had been surprised when Banque Fédérale failed to include him on Tour de France recognizance trips.

The logger used his wheat shaft as a pointer. "The course enters from the northeast on that highway you just traveled."

"So we pass straight through here?" Ben asked.

"That was the original plan, said the policeman. One of the photographers talked the organizers into a small change, though. You'll make a tight turn here around the water fountain, then there are two quick switchbacks on a one-lane corridor. At the bottom you rejoin the main highway, and it will take you straight back to Fréjus where the time trial begins and ends."

Ben smiled. "St. Raphaël is adjacent, right? That's where our hotel is."

The policeman nodded.

"Can we get a taxi from here? I should already be in bed, and I haven't even eaten dinner."

"I can get something to tide you over," said the olive-skinned woman. "My husband runs the restaurant across the street. He could fix you some dinner."

Ben patted his cycling shorts. "I can't pay you now, but I'll be sending money back for the tractor rental."

"It's on the house."

"A baguette and butter would be great," Bridgette said. "We'll get a full meal later."

The woman nodded, turned toward the restaurant, and then disappeared.

"I'm glad I got a chance to do some course recon," Ben said. "I look forward to visiting again, though I hope to be moving pretty quickly my next time through."

"Forecast is for rain," the policeman said. "Let's go take a look at those switchbacks so you'll be prepared."

"I really appreciate it." Ben took Bridgette's hand, and they followed the policeman across the street to the alley he'd indicated earlier. It led into a passage barely wide enough for an automobile.

The policeman pointed above them. "Notice how much roof area slopes toward this one street."

Ben looked at the buildings and nodded.

"When it rains the left half of this road becomes a river, but down there is where it can get really tricky." He pointed to the corner, cobbled in sandpapery stones.

"Yikes," Bridgette said. "Whose idea was it to ride over those?"

The policeman shrugged. "The photographer plans to sit in this alcove while the mayor's wife—you might say she looks like a stereotypical French grandmother—will be stepping from that stoop with a load of laundry. They're going to remove the satellite dishes from that wall in the background beforehand, and *voila*, add a cyclist leaning into the corner like so," he pantomimed a rider tilted into a turn, his eyes intently focused on what came next, "and you'll have a postcard-perfect shot."

Ben walked the corner. "No doubt it will make a great looking photo, but that's a sketchy piece of road we've got to cross."

"I think that's why the photographer likes it. Great textures. Here's the important part, though. When the water is really coming down the alley it shoots across the cobbles clear to here." He stood three quarters of the way across the road. "It's safest to ride as close to this wall as you can get where the base is highest."

"Wow. You probably just saved me a layer of skin," Ben said. He looked downhill toward the highway. "The outlet looks fairly routine."

The policeman nodded as he signaled the others to follow him back up the hill. "The intersection down there is dangerous, but only because of the through traffic. Drivers gather speed coming off the hill and ignore the limit. It's a non-issue because the road will be barricaded when you come through, but earlier this very evening I ticketed some fool in a camping car blowing through at almost double the posted limit."

Ben looked at Bridgette. Her eyes were wide. "Was it white with a wide blue stripe?"

"That's the guy," the officer said as they re-entered the plaza. "You saw him too?"

Ben chuckled. "Yeah. He nearly blew us off the road."

"People need to slow down." The policeman looked at the logger. "Now, was there trouble of some sort here?"

The logger waved it off. "These people are hungry," he said as the olive-skinned woman handed Ben two baguettes plus a pair of bottled drinks, "and they need a ride to St. Raphaël center."

The policeman pulled a set of car keys from his pocket. "I can solve that. I need to go there, anyway." He leveled a look at Ben. "Perhaps along the way I can find out why these two are wandering around out here without transportation."

Chapter Thirteen

Ben sat in the front passenger seat of the patrol car. A Plexiglas barrier separated him from the back seat where Bridgette sat. The policeman opened a pass-through portal so communication would be easier. He spoke loudly so she could hear. "This road outside of town is fairly straight. Like I said, I think it will be raining, but you won't have to worry about any corners for a couple of kilometers."

Ben took in everything he could, despite the darkness. France never ceased to stun him with its beauty. The setting seemed unreal. Cozy cottages dotted the landscape, adding to the charm. Back where he'd been raised the homes often subtracted from the view.

"I'm a big Banque Fédérale fan," said the officer. "Any chance you could sign a water bottle for my son?"

"I'd be happy to."

The policeman reached beneath his seat and produced a bottle with the Banque Fédérale cycling team logo on it. He hadn't been kidding when he claimed to be a fan. "There's a pen in the glove compartment."

Ben found the pen and personalized the water bottle with a brief message.

"So, how did you end up stranded out there?" the policeman asked.

"We were preparing for the time trial, when we got into an argument with the man who had driven us," Bridgette said. "We were stunned when he drove away without us."

The officer turned toward her. "I can imagine. Oh, Ben, pay close attention to this section of road. See the ditch at the bottom of this swale? They put that in because heavy rains kept eroding the pavement. Hit it hard and you could blow a tire. You'd do well to slow down."

"Or bunny-hop it," Ben said, handing the water bottle back.

"*Oui.* That would work." He looked at the signature. "*Tien*, thanks for this. My son will treasure it."

The policeman became increasingly animated, describing the

nuances of the course and the local history. They passed through a wide swath of fire-scorched trees before dropping into the city. He pointed out the ruins of a Roman coliseum. "The crowds will be enormous through here." Then he flipped on his emergency lights and drove the wrong way up a narrow, one-way street. An oncoming car turned onto a side alley to let him pass. "Save something for this last little, climb and you'll finish between the aqueduct ruins, right there."

Golden lanterns lighted the ancient architecture. The crumbling brick towers looked resplendent in the rich light.

It took another five minutes to reach Hotel Excelsior. "Here we are."

"How can I repay you?" Ben asked.

"Win the time-trial. That will be enough."

Bridgette took a business card from the officer, and they headed into the hotel. The lobby was compact. A door on the right led to a bustling, ocean-side restaurant. At the center, beside a staircase and an elevator, a single chair was tucked beneath a grandfather clock.

Bridgette stepped to the reception desk on the left and gave their names. While the clerk handed over their keys Ben pushed the *Appel* button to call the elevator. Cyclists never used stairs during competition if there was an alternative. Ideally, everything they did between stages was geared to rebuild energy for their time on the bike.

They stepped into the lift and Bridgette hit the button labeled "2," the highest floor in what Americans would call a three-story building. Street level in France was referred to as "zero." Just before the door shut Frodie appeared and squeezed in as well. It was a tight fit.

"You're just getting here?" Frodie asked. "Why so late?"

"Wrong turn," Ben said. He had no reason to confide in the chef.

Bridgette handed Ben his key. "You're a floor above me. I'll make sure everything is okay with your room before going to mine."

When the lift stopped Ben pushed open the elevator door and walked across the hall. Frodie stepped out and lingered a moment, before he walked down the hall and knocked on a door. It opened, and he disappeared inside.

Ben shrugged. "I've never trusted that guy." He inserted his key and opened the door. Inside the phone was ringing. He hurried to the nightstand and picked up the receiver while Bridgette stood in the doorway, watching.

"*Bonjour.*"

"*Pardon,* Monsieur Barnes. Would you be willing to tell me what in the hell you are doing?"

Ben's gut clenched. He'd heard these exact words before. This time he didn't need to ask who the speaker was. The scratchy tobacco residue voice was all too familiar. "Are you angry with me, Monsieur Robidoux?"

Bridgette put a hand over her mouth.

"Of course I am," Robidoux snarled.

"Why?"

"Because I sent you help, Benjamin, and you turned him away."

Peraza was his doing? Reflected light from the stunning ring on Bridgette's finger caught Ben's eye and tweaked his memory. He'd assumed a debt came with the gift, and now he understood that accepting treatment was one of the ways Robidoux expected Ben to pay him back.

"Doctor Peraza was stunned by your lack of professionalism. That's very insulting to me," Robidoux continued. "You obviously don't understand what's at stake."

Ben swallowed hard. "*Non.* I do. If I win, it would result in big publicity for your company."

"If? Would? Young man, I deal in absolutes. If you're not ready to say '*When* I win, it *will* result in big publicity' then we need to figure out what's wrong and fix it."

"When I win, it will result in big —"

"Nonsense! If you want to know what my wrath feels like, go ahead and tell me what you think I want to hear; otherwise, take the necessary steps to remove the uncertainty. I always win, but I don't gamble. There's power in knowing the outcome in advance. Am I clear?"

Ben grappled for an answer he felt comfortable with, but he couldn't find one. He had to say something. "*Oui.*"

"You'd be staggered if you knew the costs that go into supporting the cycling team. Since I've personally reorganized things, including eliminating the director you couldn't get along with, and since all of our resources are now focused on getting you to the finish line first, I should think you would appreciate the support you receive."

"I do."

"Good," Robidoux said. "Then you will, in return, do everything within your power to win this race."

Ben had to answer or risk losing the team's support. He'd made his drug decision already, and it wasn't negotiable. As far as he was concerned, that strategy wasn't within his power. Robidoux didn't need to know that. "I will."

"Excellent. I'll send Doctor Peraza to your room at eleven, tomorrow morning."

Ben swallowed hard.

"Though it's not public yet," Robidoux continued, "Banque Fédérale has tendered an offer to purchase North American Bank Corporation. We will become the fourth largest banking concern in the world. Believe it or not, your rise to prominence has been a factor in cementing this deal. I demonstrated to them how cycling has impacted our bottom line, and they were thrilled to see an American star emerging on our squad. Assuming you can make good on the promise you showed a few days ago, you will remain a leader on this team for the remainder of your career. In addition, I will make certain your efforts assist in introducing cycling to your country."

"What are you saying?"

"How would you like to ride in a World Championships race in Salt Lake City within five years?"

Ben's stomach tingled at the suggestion. What a dream it would be to bring his home state the taste of such an event. "I know the perfect course."

"When you win the Tour you can consider it done. I'll sponsor the best bicycle race America has ever seen, and I'll do it right in your own back yard. Now, think that over."

"I will." Ben had lost some time in the last two days of racing, but nowhere near the amount he'd made up on the leaders the day before that. He could come back again. The two time trials were looming increasingly important. In those stages Ben was determined to beat Kyle, no matter what medication his rival took.

Attempting to win the Tour de France had defined Ben's life. Now that he was within reach of his goal, he planned to make the most of it. The thought of a World Championship race in Salt Lake City made that dream even more exciting. As discouraging as it was to be pressured by his team owner to cheat, it wouldn't stop him from giving this race everything he had.

"I wish I hadn't had to make this call. Bridgette promised me that everything would be handled. I'll assume it now is."

The line went dead.

Ben stared at the receiver and then collapsed onto the bed. Bridgette had promised what?

Bridgette came to his side and took his hand. "What did he say?"

Ben looked into his pillow as he spoke. "I think you and I need to take a break."

"Ben! What did he say?"

He rolled onto his back and stared at her. "Did you guarantee Robidoux that you could get me to dope?"

Her eyes told the story. They were simultaneously desperate and resigned. She looked like she'd lost something irreplaceable. Then she started to cry. "It's not the way it seems."

Ben's body tensed. "You convinced me you were looking out for my best interests. I took you at your word when you said you involved Peraza out of concern for my health. How could you lie?"

"I didn't lie. There were just things I didn't know how to tell you." Mascara streaked her cheeks.

"I can't imagine what Robidoux offered you to do this." He rolled to his side, facing away from her. "We need to take a step back. Our lives are too intertwined. Let me finish this race; then we can reassess things."

"Ben, let me explain. Robidoux forced me —"

"No, Bridgette!"

"He threatened that if I didn't get you to take his medication he'd pull the team's support. It's not possible to win if he decides to prevent —"

"I'm not willing to allow these sorts of distractions right now. Robidoux won't pull support if I continue to bring him publicity. That's a fact. You've allowed him to control you using empty threats."

She looked confused. "I have?"

He nodded. "You say you're here to simplify things, but you keep complicating them instead. This story sounds like more of the same."

"But, Ben. Please listen."

He held up a hand. "It's too late for that. This competition has changed you. You need perspective and I need space."

When she finally spoke, her voice sounded foreign. "I've been trying to help because I love you. Now I'm going to step away for the same reason. It kills me to do it." It was obvious she wanted to say much more, but she turned toward the door.

"*Au revoir*, Ben."

He didn't respond.

The door closed to a crack, but didn't shut. Ben watched it, wondering if their relationship was over. Could it really end like this? He'd halfway convinced himself to go to her when suddenly it clicked closed. The sound had a finality that reverberated in his head.

Chapter Fourteen

Bridgette wiped her eyes as she left Ben's room, her hand still on the doorknob. Was she stepping out of his life? Everything had crumbled, and she was to blame. She had been so blinded by the opportunity to help him win the world's biggest race that she'd sacrificed her ethics. She couldn't believe what she'd done; yet she had done it. Ben had been right to throw her out. She felt dirty and confused by her actions. He needed to know that she meant the best for him, that she supported him unconditionally. She needed to let him know about her past with Christoff DuPont. It had been wrong to conceal that. He deserved to know everything. If she didn't tell him now she might never have another chance. She should go back in and talk to him.

The door down the hall where Frodie had disappeared opened again. The chef stepped into the hall. The moment he saw Bridgette a pleased smile spread across his face. No reason to allow him to see or overhear anything. Robidoux obviously had at least one set of eyes and ears within the team. In her opinion, and apparently Ben's as well, Frodie's were a likely suspect. She couldn't allow him to suspect anything had changed between them. Regretfully, she pulled the door shut.

"*Salut*, Bridgette. How is Ben's preparation coming?"

"He's feeling strong and making great strides. I think he'll win."

Frodie moved close. "Do you really believe that? I don't see the killer instinct."

"Why don't you go flip your crepes, Frodie! You might think of him as just a nice guy, but mark my words: Ben is focused and ready. He'll do whatever is necessary. He's proven to me that he's willing to make tough decisions when the race is at stake."

"Tough decisions, huh?" Frodie regarded her skeptically. "Is that why you've been crying?"

"*Oui*," she said. "Tears of pride."

Chapter Fifteen

Ben shivered. Sweat soaked his body. How had everything gone so wrong? He was trapped on a Tilt-A-Whirl that wouldn't stop. He was getting dizzier and dizzier. The thought of his life without Bridgette was too much to bear, yet he couldn't fathom her actions. He'd considered her completely truthful, yet she'd lied to his face more coolly than if she were reporting the weather. He'd thought she supported him, but instead she'd tried to control him. How had she fooled him for so long?

After awhile he got to his feet. He went into the bathroom, splashed water on his face, and stared into the mirror. Was continuing with this race worth the cost? In his gut he believed it was, but the loss of Bridgette … what a price to pay.

His stomach ached. The baguette he'd eaten hadn't been nearly enough to satisfy him. He looked at the alarm clock: 21:13. He should never have allowed his schedule to get so out of whack. He opened the door and stepped into the hall. He looked at the room list posted in its usual spot beside the elevator. Two rooms down the hall he knocked on Thierry's door.

It opened. "I'd begun to think Bridgette was going to keep you out all night," Thierry said.

"You knew I was with her?"

"Sure. She said she needed to help you get your head straight. I agreed."

Ben's stomach growled. "I haven't eaten yet."

Thierry's expression darkened. "That's irresponsible of you, Ben. If you don't take proper care of yourself you're letting the whole team down. Don't you realize that?"

Ben nodded. Stress, whether brought on by excessive exercise, hunger, or worry, killed red blood cells. He'd been experiencing too much of all three. "I haven't had a massage either. I'm exhausted, and I only just got back to the hotel."

"Where's Bridgette?"

"We broke up."

Thierry looked like he'd been clubbed with a baseball bat.

"I think she's trying to sabotage me," Ben said. "She's been feeding me one lie after another."

"Ridiculous. Did you come here to ask me to referee a lover's quarrel? Okay, here's my advice. Whatever's wrong, fix it now!"

Ben stretched out a calming hand, but didn't dare touch Thierry. "*Non.* That's not it. I'm not asking you to arbitrate anything. I'm just telling you that Bridgette and I can't work together anymore."

Thierry's face was red with rage. "You know better than to do this right now. I'm stunned that you would put your personal life ahead of the team. Your focus needs to be entirely on this race. Do you think you're the first man who has been asked to adjust priorities to succeed?"

"*Non.*"

Thierry hit the wall with a fist. "You're damn right, Ben! I'm speaking from experience. It's impossible to win any other way. You'd better get your head straight, and quick."

"That's what I'm trying to do. Stuff just got out of control."

Thierry's eyes were fiery. He grabbed his crutches and hobbled into the hall, slamming the door behind him. "I've got enough to do without babysitting athletes. Let's go down to the hotel restaurant and find something for you to eat. Then we'll try to come up with another plan to see to your needs. It's a damn good thing tomorrow is a rest day."

Ben followed but kept his mouth shut. He wanted to simplify the situation just as much as Thierry did.

They took the elevator to the lobby and headed toward the restaurant. Coach entered the hotel and crossed just in front of them.

Thierry blocked his progress with a crutch. "Do you have a moment, Bill?"

"Sure."

"That's good. Not only are you the perfect man for the job, you just saved Ben's life because I was considering strangling him. Please get him some food and see to his immediate needs. I have urgent phone calls to take care of." He spun back toward the elevator, recognized that it was full beyond capacity, and started hopping up the stairs grasping the brass railing with one hand and his crutches with the other. Pity the next guy Thierry met.

Ben breathed easier. What a stroke of luck to run into Coach.

"I saved your life?" Coach asked.

"Yeah. I think he was trying to decide the best way to dispose of my body."

Coach's brow furrowed. "Food first. Then we can talk."

They took seats at the bar. In the mirrored backsplash behind colorful and shapely liquor bottles they could see droves of partiers strolling along the beach boulevard, nowhere near ready to call it a night. Ben took a quick glance at the menu. He ordered pasta primavera with chicken and a glass of cranberry juice. Coach asked for a beer.

"What's the matter, son?" Coach asked.

Ben dropped his gaze. "Everything." He laid out all that had gone on, including the pressures to dope and the possibility of bringing a world-class race to Salt Lake City. He told Coach Bill about Doctor Peraza's scheduled visit tomorrow. Then he explained the promise Bridgette had made to Robidoux.

The bartender slid their drinks in front of them.

Coach picked up his glass. "Maybe you misunderstood."

Ben shook his head. "I kept giving her the benefit of the doubt when stuff didn't add up, but each time I tried to straighten things out, they took another turn. Now everything is in knots. I don't want to see Bridgette get hurt. I can't quit loving her, but I can't try to figure out what's going on with her in the middle of this race, either."

"I understand."

"Could you talk to her?"

Coach swallowed and set the glass on the table. "If I can find her. I'll let you know what happens."

Ben shook his head. "I don't want a report. My emotions are too intense. I've got to concentrate on the race."

Coach chewed his lip. "Okay. Don't think of her for the moment, but once we reach Paris do me a favor."

"What?"

"Give her the benefit of the doubt." He patted Ben's forearm. "Don't forget what made you two so great together."

Ben looked at the ground. "I think we're history."

"Do yourself a favor. Wait until this race is over to make that decision," Coach said. "Now, it's time to look forward. Clear your mind and fill your belly. What are your goals?"

The question ignited within him like a flame hitting tinder. Ben put a hand on each of Coach's shoulders and stared into his eyes. "I want to win. I want to win more than ever. I need this victory so badly that I'm consumed by it. It's the only way I can make things right."

"What do you mean?"

"I've built my life around this goal. Now that I'm approaching it, some people are telling me it doesn't stand for what I always believed it did. They're saying that to accomplish my dream I need to compromise my values. I have to prove them wrong."

Plates clattered in the kitchen.

Coach grabbed a fistful of peanuts. "Can you?"

"Yes. I know I can, but since I'm unwilling to play by the owner's rules, he might cut me off. If Robidoux chose, he could prevent me from reaching the finish line. Not only that, he's influential enough to keep me from ever landing another job with a top pro team."

Coach looked curious. "Do you think he wants to stop you?"

Ben shook his head. "Not if I represent his company well. He covets airtime. Every time the broadcasters mention Banque Fédérale, his bank account grows larger."

"Some powerful men are accustomed to obedience. If you don't do what he asks in private, he might worry that you won't say what he wants in public."

Ben turned the idea over in his mind. It seemed to fit Robidoux, but Ben couldn't do what the team owner had asked him to. Taking illegal drugs was out of the question.

Coach Bill stared into Ben's eyes. It felt like the man could see all the way into his soul. "Unless he thinks you are doing what he wants, Robidoux might stop you before you reach the staging area for the time trial. What happens when Peraza shows up tomorrow to start his treatment and you say, 'No thanks'?"

"Yeah, I've been worrying about that."

Coach took another swallow of beer. "Let me worry about it instead. I'll come up with something."

Ben felt enormous relief. If anybody could solve this, Coach could.

"I'm with you, all the way," Coach said. "We need to think everything through carefully."

Ben's food arrived. He spoke while swirling a bite onto his fork. "What Thierry said was right. You're the perfect man for this job, but it's a bigger job than he had in mind. Thierry assigned Bridgette to care for my needs throughout the rest of the race, but you're the best choice. You've got to convince him of that. There's a week and a half of racing left.

I need your help like never before. You've got to take charge of everything."

"Done."

Ben laughed. "Try not to be so bullheaded."

Coach smiled. "You just focus on the results you're chasing. Nothing else matters, okay?"

Ben nodded. He noticed that his muscles were finally relaxed. "Tonight, when you speak to Thierry, tell him that I guarantee a win in Sunday's time trial."

"Can you deliver? He's not Thelma. He'll hold you to your word."

"I'll win, but I'm sure Thierry's wouldn't tear my bib number off if some disaster prevented it. He has reason to be mad right now, but he's really a good guy."

Coach shook his head. "I know you love him like a big brother, but don't be naïve. He's under pressure to produce results, too. How do you think he'd react if he knew you plan to defy his boss? Would he tell Robidoux?"

"If he did, I'd be cut down at the knees."

Coach pointed the rim of his glass at Ben. "Then be careful what you say."

"Okay."

"Tomorrow morning I'm going to try to scrounge up a copy of one of my favorite books," Coach said. "If I can find it, will you give it a read?"

"I'll do whatever you ask."

Coach grinned. "Okay then, trade me rooms."

"Huh?"

"You'll sleep in my room tonight. Thelma and I will sleep in yours. Leave your luggage where it is. I'll deliver your toothbrush."

"You and Thelma are sleeping in the same bed?"

"Of course not? Why would you ask that?"

Ben laughed. "Because my room has a queen bed."

The sprockets turning in Coach's head were almost visible. "Okay. Thelma will sleep in your room. I'll find another spot. Now, give me your key. I'll go grab a massage table and be waiting in your new room for you."

Ben handed over his key. "Whatever you say, Romeo."

Chapter Sixteen

An hour later, after finishing Ben's massage, Bill put away the equipment. He stepped into the hall carrying the folded massage table in one hand and dragging his luggage with the other. He'd previously moved Thelma and her luggage to Ben's old room.

Thierry's door was open a crack. He could hear the directeur talking. Bill walked to the door and knocked softly.

"*Entrez.*"

Bill pushed the door open.

"*Bon*, come in, Bill," Thierry held the phone between his ear and shoulder. His bed was strewn with maps and charts. More documents covered the dresser. He spoke into the receiver. "*Oui.* I have a guest now, but I look forward to continuing this conversation. It will be to our mutual benefit ... *Merci* ... *Allez salut.*"

Bill left his luggage in the hall and carried the table inside. He leaned it against the wall.

Thierry reached out and shook his hand. "Sorry about my rudeness earlier."

"I understand what happened," Bill said.

"How's Ben?"

"Intense. I've never seen him so determined. The stuff with Bridgette won't distract him. Bad timing I realize, but he's focusing on the race now. He asked me to tell you he promises to win the time trial."

"Excellent! That's the sort of confidence I needed to hear." Thierry pumped a fist. "He can do it, you know. This course plays to his strengths."

"I know."

Thierry nodded. "I'd like to make you a proposal, Bill. I can't pay —"

"You don't have to pay me. I'd love to look after Ben."

Thierry chuckled. "So, you're a mind reader as well as an expert motivator. Good to have you on the team."

Bill slapped Thierry on the shoulder. "It's great to be here."

"So, what's your first move?"

"I want to do something kind of radical." Bill rubbed his hands together. "If you're okay with it, I think we should sequester Ben from now until the start of the time trial in two days. I don't want him to read newspapers or watch television. I don't want him to talk to teammates, the media, or any outsiders, just you and me. He needs to eat, sleep, and breathe this time trial."

"I already planned to keep him away from reporters. Ben's got a thing or two to learn about talking to them. He's in a unique situation because he has a lot to absorb with his new role as leader and almost no time to do it. Your plan's a good one."

Bill hesitated before making his next request. "Let's keep the breakup quiet for now. It's likely just a passing thing, so there's no reason to bring the team, the media, or even Robidoux into it yet."

"Team and media I agree with. They're both Robidoux's employees, though, and he would want to know."

"Just give it a couple of days, okay?"

"No promises," Thierry said.

Bill hadn't expected any.

Thierry handed Bill a copy of the Race Bible. Every major cycling race in the world had its own version of a book known by this same nickname. It was packed with detailed information about the event: everything from exhaustive diagrams of the finishing stretch to detailed instructions on finding each evening's hotel.

Bill returned to the hallway, picked up his luggage, and carried it down the stairs. The grandfather clock chimed twice as he stepped into the lobby. He looked toward it and noticed Bridgette, head in hands, in the lone chair.

As he stopped beside her she looked up. Their eyes met. Her's were bloodshot and her hair hadn't been combed. She fought for control but started crying. "I've let him down completely." She stood and held out her arms.

He returned the embrace. "Ben told me what happened."

"Can you convince him to let me explain myself?"

"Let's give it some time, Bridgette. He asked me to find you, but he doesn't even want to hear about our discussion. He has to concentrate on his job right now, but there will be time for this later."

She looked up hopefully. "Do you think he'll eventually listen to my side?"

Coach nodded.

"Okay. That's good." She dabbed at her eyes with a handkerchief. "My old college roommate lives in St. Lary-Soulan. Stage sixteen finishes near there. She'll help me get my head straight."

"That sounds like a good idea."

She pursed her lips as she composed herself. "Can you let Ben know that someone from the village we visited the other night must have contacted the press? A journalist just asked me how we ended up out in the countryside riding a stolen tractor."

"Ben mentioned that. What did you tell the reporter?"

"That it was a big mix up. I didn't know what else to say."

Bill nodded, thinking. "He'll drop it. What could he possibly make of it?"

"I hope you're right. I'm just concerned. I want Ben to reach his goals, but I can't stand to lose him as a result."

"Everything will be fine. You'll see."

She pulled the ring from her finger as she backed away. "I should return this to him, for now."

Bill shook his head. "No. Don't do that."

She didn't look convinced, but nodded. "All right." She found a piece of paper and pen in her purse and wrote down a number. "Will you hold on to this in case he decides he's ready to talk?"

"Of course."

Bridgette turned and wandered away. At the door she looked back. "One more thing. He's been craving watermelon."

Bill snapped his fingers and pointed at her. "Now that's a hell of an idea."

Bridgette didn't see or hear him. She'd already stepped into the night. It took Bill awhile to refocus. Eventually he decided there were better places to work than the cramped lobby. He found a quiet spot near the beach where a streetlight illuminated the area around a lounge chair. He spread out his materials. For Ben to win he would need a cohesive plan. Bill had to figure out where his young friend might be able to gain time, and where he was likely to lose it. He knew a wide variety of strategies for maximizing gains and minimizing losses, but employing the right one at the right time required understanding everything he possibly could about the terrain, the conditions, and the competition. In no time he was consumed with his work, determined to relieve Ben of every decision he possibly could.

*   *   *

As a shaft of sunlight shone through a gap between buildings, Bill looked at his watch. He gathered his things and returned to the hotel. Thierry stood in the lobby making arrangements with the desk clerk. Because of the rest day and the time trial, which didn't move the race forward, they would stay here for three nights.

When Thierry finished he turned to Bill. "I just got a call from a journalist wanting to speak to Ben. He wasn't happy when I told him he'd have to wait until after the time trial."

"No surprise there."

"He asked me if I'd rather he made something up.'"

Bill wondered if this had anything to do with the tractor story. "I hope he's kidding."

"It really doesn't matter. I don't want Ben talking to him," Thierry said.

At eight a.m. Bill slipped into Ben's room with breakfast. Ben's snores echoed off the walls. Bill placed the food on the dresser and left. He returned hourly. By nine the pancakes and sausage had been devoured. At ten he replaced them with two chicken sandwiches and a salad. Even though he'd obviously been awake at some point, Ben slept so soundly he was nearly comatose. This sort of rest was exactly what Bill had hoped for.

At ten thirty, Bill went to the lobby to watch for a man matching Peraza's description. Thelma took a seat out front in the sidewalk café, as he'd asked her to. From time to time they made eye contact. Peraza had to be diverted, and Bill needed her help to do it.

At eleven o'clock sharp, a baldheaded gentleman in an Italian suit entered the hotel. He carried a briefcase. Bill looked at Thelma and nodded. She pointed up the street, which meant she'd seen where he came from. Then she hurried off in that direction. So far, so good.

Bill intercepted the man as he reached the staircase. "You're Doctor Peraza, aren't you?"

The man squirmed slightly. "Have we met?"

"No. I've heard about you, though. I admire your work."

Peraza nodded, apparently flattered. "I'm pleased to meet you. Regrettably, though, I'm short on time. Please excuse me."

"No."

"*Pardon?*"

"I can't let you go without an autograph." Bill held out a pen and paper.

Peraza looked annoyed as he tried to sweep Bill aside with his arm. Bill kept himself planted in front of the stairway, but the elevator door opened at the same moment. A pair of Banque Fédérale clad fans stepped out and Peraza stepped in. He turned around but avoided eye contact with Bill.

The elevator door closed. Bill swore under his breath. He'd hoped to delay the doctor a lot longer than that. He ran through the lobby and out the door. Looking down the street he spotted the camping car facing the hotel and hurried toward it. Thelma was on the ground beside the front bumper, struggling with a screwdriver.

"How's it coming?"

"They're too tight. I've only gotten one screw out."

Fortunately, only two screws held the license plate to the vehicle. Bill took the screwdriver from her hands and twisted the other free. The aluminum tag fell to the ground. "Pick that up. I'll go around back."

He ran to the rear of the vehicle, too rushed to check if anybody was watching. At least he couldn't see the hotel entrance from here, which meant that people leaving the hotel couldn't see him. That's where the real danger lay.

Two more screws on this plate. He struggled to free them. Time ticked away. As he extracted the first he sensed Thelma standing at his side.

"Quick! Break the tail light," Bill said.

By now Peraza would have discovered that Ben wasn't in his room. With luck he'd run into a Banque Fédérale team member and ask questions or at least go to the front desk and be delayed, but there were no guarantees. He might be furious and head straight back to his vehicle.

Bill hadn't heard the plastic break yet. "Thelma! Do it."

He twisted the screw with all his strength. His grip failed and his knuckles smashed into the license plate bracket, ripping open. Blood covered his hand but the screw wouldn't budge.

The vehicle rocked slightly to the side. Peraza was back! The door slammed shut.

"Thelma, hurry! Now!"

Desperately, Bill twisted the plate. The aluminum ripped and the tag came free, minus one torn piece still screwed to the bumper.

The vehicle rolled forward, and Bill clambered to his feet. He'd have to do the job Thelma refused to, though it was probably too late.

Something shattered. He covered his face from the shards of red plastic; then he looked up.

The vehicle paused. Had Peraza heard Thelma break the light, or was he waiting for traffic to clear?

Thelma stood motionless, staring at the adjustable wrench in her hands, shaken by her act of vandalism. Bill jumped to his feet and pulled her behind the vehicle where she couldn't be seen in the side mirror. He grabbed the wrench from her and tossed it with the screwdriver beneath the car parked behind them. Then he picked up the license plate Thelma must have dropped and held it with the other in his bleeding hand.

The camping car started to move again. Bill took Thelma's hand and pulled her into a group of people walking down the sidewalk. They scurried away from the hotel and darted down the first alley they reached. He dropped the license plates into a trashcan.

"You did well, Thelma."

"I hardly did anything."

"I wouldn't have finished in time without your help. You broke the tail light, plus you got a screw loose."

"You can say that again. I must have a couple of bolts loose too, getting myself tangled up in doings like these."

Bill hugged her. "Sorry you had to be involved."

"I wish you'd tell me why we did it."

Bill left an arm draped around her as they turned back toward the hotel. "If you happen to see a headline about a drug dealer being busted in a routine traffic stop, give yourself a pat on the back. The French authorities aren't too keen on traffickers. I bet they'll lock him up and throw away the key."

Chapter Seventeen

Ben opened his eyes. Sunlight illuminated the fringe around the thick curtains. He looked at his alarm clock: awake at the crack of noon.

He'd slept soundly and dreamt vividly. The images had been of coaching Toma.

He noticed sandwiches on the dresser where breakfast had been earlier. Flicking on the light, he sat up in bed and reached for the tray. He thought of Bridgette. Had she left these? Of course not. He'd asked her to leave and she'd said she would. Coach must have delivered the food.

Within a few minutes, Coach entered the room. He smiled when he saw Ben. "Feeling better?"

Ben sat on the corner of the bed, eating his sandwich. "Like a new man. Thanks for the food. What happened to your hand?"

Coach looked at the bandage on his knuckles. "Just clumsiness."

"Any sign of Peraza?"

"That's no concern of yours."

Was Coach stifling a grin? Ben wanted to know more but knew he wouldn't get a straight answer. Coach was serious about controlling the distractions.

"By the way, I sent Thelma out cruising used bookstores this morning. She found this for you." Coach tossed him a small book.

"*Man's Search for Meaning* by Viktor E. Frankl," Ben read. "Sounds deep."

"It's written by a Holocaust survivor."

"Did he escape on a bicycle?"

Coach smiled. "Nope. No connection to cycling at all, but there is a connection to the traits that separate great performers from good ones."

Ben looked at the cover, a little puzzled.

"Frankl was quite a guy," Coach said. "Instead of dwelling on the hell he was living through, he focused on figuring out why some people made it out alive and some didn't. He discovered that physical strength wasn't the important difference."

Toma's frail body flashed in Ben's mind. "What was?"

Coach tapped his forehead with an index finger.

Ben tightened his grip on the little book. "I'll read it."

"Good. Try to finish part one at least. As you do, underline anything that strikes you as interesting. Now, ready for your massage and supplements?" Coach asked as he set up the table.

Ben climbed aboard and lay down.

"In two hours I'll have a car parked in front. Let's meet there and head out for a bike ride in the country."

"We're not going to ride the time trial course?"

Coach's hands were rough and muscular, nothing at all like Bridgette's. His technique was equally effective, but not nearly as enjoyable. "Too much media nosing around there. If there's time we'll drive it this evening, with the windows rolled up."

Ben chuckled. "You're the boss." His tractor and police car reconnaissance from the previous evening might be all he'd get.

It often surprised observers that cyclists rode on their days off, but it would be just as reasonable to ask a scientist not to think. Muscles accustomed to exercise begged for more. In addition, Ben's brain craved the endorphins physical labor produced.

When Coach left, Ben found himself dreaming of Bridgette. This was no time to go down that road. He needed to get his mind in the right place. He noticed the book and opened it.

As he read he used a pen to highlight various passages. When the time to meet Coach arrived he strode from the hotel, nose in his book and pen behind his ear. He'd love to escape without being noticed by reporters. He climbed into the car and Coach shifted into gear.

"This book isn't bad. Listen here: *In the concentration camp every circumstance conspires to make the prisoner lose his hold. All the familiar goals in life are snatched away. What alone remains is the last of human freedoms—the ability to choose one's attitude in a given set of circumstances.*"

Coach Bill merged onto the coast highway. "Uh-hmm."

Ben underlined the words. Then he looked out the window at the glorious day. He'd never seen such a blue ocean. The sky was equally pure, not a cloud in it. "My obstacles are nothing beside what this guy went through."

"It's easy to let worries get out of perspective, isn't it?"

Ben nodded. "The author says success and happiness are byproducts of pursuing a cause greater than oneself. Running after those things actually chases them away, while dedicating your life to a meaningful purpose outside yourself attracts them."

Coach nodded. "Poetic justice."

"Yeah."

"So, are you happy and successful?"

Ben recalled pushing toward the summit of 'l Alpe d'Huez three days before, convinced at the time that he owed victory to the memories of his father and Thierry's brother. "One of the best feelings in my life came on stage ten when it seemed that my suffering benefited others. The last two days I've been more concerned about defending my sudden reputation. That hasn't been much fun."

Coach entered a roundabout and circled it twice, reading the many directional signs, before exiting onto a lesser-used highway. "So, who can benefit from the suffering you're going to go through over the next several days?"

Ben closed the book over his index finger. Doctor Peraza's suggestion that kids would admire him if he used drugs to assure victory wouldn't leave his mind. At every turn lately, people seem to justify cheating. "I'd like to prove to young people that it's possible to win while playing by the rules."

"How are you going to do that?"

"If I win I'll let the world know that I competed clean."

"Are you sure that's a good idea? It seems the cause should be to compete well, hopefully win, and be able to hold your head up. If accused, deny using with a clear conscience, and show yourself as a model to kids without having to hide anything or fear drug use will be revealed later on. There's no need to stand on a podium and say I did this drug-free."

"Very stoic. But the problem is, I'm going to be accused. Hell, that's already happened. If I don't respond forcefully it will look like I'm avoiding the questions. It's time someone put his neck on the line for this. It's important."

Coach shook his head. "Do you plan to accuse anyone of breaking the rules?"

"Of course not."

"And you realize that proclaiming innocence will make some people suspect the opposite."

Ben leaned back against the headrest. "It's a good message, the one

I want to make. If I win, people will listen."

"Why do you have to win to speak up?"

"Who listens to the second place finisher? I'd sound like a sore loser."

Coach Bill pulled off the road and into a grassy field. He stopped beneath a gnarled oak tree and shut off the engine. "Be careful what you say, Ben. You could make enemies. I've been thinking about the way Bridgette put it. Different people have different definitions of cheating. She made a lot of sense."

"The definition is crystal clear. Cheating is not obeying the rules. The rules state no PEDs."

Coach nodded. "Not everybody sees the world so black and white, that's all I'm saying. Never forget, whenever things change, somebody stands to lose. That somebody will fight to maintain the status quo, and they might not play fair. I'm proud of your dedication to ride clean, but that doesn't mean you need to turn yourself into a lightning rod. Be careful that you don't risk more than you're willing to lose."

Should he stay quiet out of fear? Ben owed so much to the sport, but corrupt forces had hijacked the driving ideals at the pro level, not just in cycling. Somebody had to stand up for what was right. That could only be done by confronting the problem head on.

He recalled last night's dreams. No way would he send Toma down a road that led to drug use.

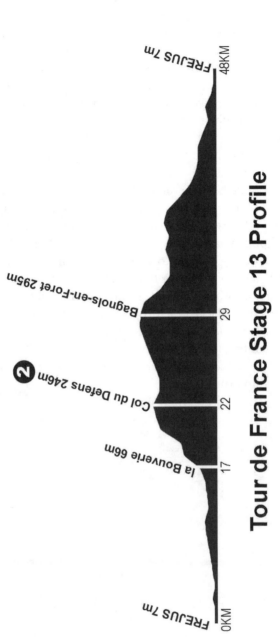

Tour de France Stage 13 Profile

FREJUS 7m
48KM

Bagnols-en-Foret 295m
29

Col du Defens 246m
22

la Bouverie 66m
17

FREJUS 7m
0KM

Chapter Eighteen

Ben arrived at the start for the stage thirteen time trial as relaxed as he'd ever been before a race. Coach's efforts had allowed him to focus purely on this moment. Somehow Coach had even gotten Doctor Peraza out of the way. Ben felt grateful not to have to deal with those complications. This was the most important event he'd ever lined up for. If he didn't win, Robidoux was certain to take steps to end his career.

Time trials were often called "the race of truth." Whoever came up with that description must have equated truth with pain, for in the time trial it's one man, alone, battling the course. There's no place to seek shelter. Mile after heart-bursting mile Ben would need to push himself to his limit. Average speeds today should be around fifty kilometers per hour over an unforgiving, forty-eight kilometer route. The fleetest horse couldn't come anywhere near maintaining such a pace—an hour of pure suffering.

Thierry walked into the Banque Fédérale staging area. Ben pedaled on his stationary setup. The rear wheel spun on rollers, allowing him to loosen his muscles and warm his heart without having to head off onto the roads where the crowds were likely to make exercise difficult. The bicycle he'd use today had aerodynamic alterations—disc wheels, frame modifications, and handlebar extensions—that weren't allowed on regular stages.

"You ready?" Thierry asked.

Ben nodded.

Thierry slapped him on the shoulder. "I want you to think about something."

Ben focused on the team directeur's face.

"Producing a perfect time-trial is similar to rolling out a red carpet. The center rotates faster and faster until, at the last moment, the trailing fibers snap. Keep that image in your mind today, because that's what I want you to do. Build throughout the race, push with everything you have, then cross the line with nothing left in the tank."

Ben nodded, but again his thoughts drifted to Bridgette. He had to get her out of his mind. Each time he'd read the book that had worked. What had the parts he'd underlined said? He couldn't recall any of them clearly.

Despite the forecast, the weather in Fréjus had been overcast, but dry. Most of the competitors were either on course, or already finished. Start times had been assigned at two-minute intervals in reverse order of the current General Classification. The three leading cyclists were the only ones remaining. Kyle, as the wearer of the yellow jersey, would go last. He'd have the advantage of knowing how his time compared to everyone's as he passed through the intermediate checkpoints.

Coach approached.

"Can you grab that book out of my bag?" Ben asked. "It's in the bus. I'd like to read a few lines just to get my mind back in the right place."

"Why should you need the book? *Pleasure is, and must remain, a side-effect or by-product, and is destroyed and spoiled to the degree which it is made a goal in itself,*" Coach said.

Ben gaped at him. It was one of the passages he'd highlighted.

Coach winked. "You're on now. Just relax."

Ben dismounted his bike while Fritz removed it from the rollers. Then he got back on and, with Coach and Fritz at his sides, rode across the staging area. He reached the start house and pedaled up the ramp. An official held his bike stationary so he could keep both feet clipped into the pedals.

Ben inspected his sunglasses and put them on. Closing his eyes, he inhaled. Then he opened his eyes as he expelled air through his nose.

The starter extended the five fingers on his right hand as he began the count down. "*Cinq, quatre, trois, deux, un, partez!*" He pointed to the road ahead.

Ben leaned onto his uplifted pedal. He charged past a graceful fountain and into a narrow, one-way passage through the heart of town. If he couldn't prove it was possible to win within the rules, then no one would care what he had to say.

Coach's voice came over the headset. "*To live is to suffer, to survive is to find meaning in the suffering.*"

Another of Ben's underlined passages. Coach had tricked him into perfecting his own motivational tool. Ben's thought patterns changed. His discomfort would be non-existent compared to what those prisoners had gone through, especially because his pain was self-inflicted. They'd been fighting for their lives.

Coach read a quote describing the initial phase of shock as the prisoners entered the camp. The idea of one man so robbing another of dignity infuriated Ben. Rage drove him harder. Leaning into his most aerodynamic tuck, this time with the aid of the ergonomically designed handlebars, he punished his pedals.

Instead of calling out time checks, Thierry would oversee Ben's race by managing his workload, driving him to build intensity at just the right rate to produce his best possible result.

"Give me more, Ben. C'mon, push," Thierry said.

Ben looked at his cyclometer readout: 48.3 kilometers per hour. He increased his effort, and the readout climbed to 48.6. Tiny adjustments, if they could be sustained, made big differences. Milliseconds became seconds, and seconds meant victory.

Thierry would be consulting the chart he'd built as the stage progressed. It showed him how fast the preceding cyclists had covered each section of the course. He'd also challenged Banque Fédérale cyclists to ride various pieces of the route at specific speeds to measure the results. Using his chart, Thierry knew how fast Ben needed to cover each piece of road to beat the men who had finished ahead of him.

The directeur would also be looking at the split times that Gunter and Kyle were posting behind Ben. If either man handled the challenge quicker than anticipated, Thierry would demand more speed. All Ben had to do was obey instructions and hold whatever effort level the voice in his ear dictated. The only problem was, these were going to be instructions that only the most elite cyclists in history could possibly obey, and even then, on only their very best days. Was he good enough?

"Suffering completely fills the human soul and conscious mind, no matter whether the suffering is great or little. Therefore the 'size' of human suffering is absolutely relative."

For most of the first fifteen kilometers the road had inclined upward. Despite that, Ben cruised at fifty kilometers per hour. He flew past the man who had left the start two minutes ahead of him. He had to do better, though. He needed to destroy the competition.

"I'm strong today," Ben said.

"*D'accord.* Give me another increment. Show me what you've got."

Ben hit the shift lever, causing the chain to slip onto a smaller rear cog. He slowed his cadence slightly, but the cyclometer readout verified that his speed increased.

"Faster?" Ben asked as he rode through a modern housing development built to resemble an ancient town.

"*Non.* Save it. Here's where the toughest climb of the day begins. You're going great. Keep it up."

Ben pushed for kilometer after kilometer over a boulder-strewn slope, alternately listening to Coach Bill's motivational passages, then to Thierry's instruction. Gnarled oak trees gripped the hillside. Dry wheat grass, hearty green thistle, and low bushes grew at wide intervals. Microburst winds buffeted him, first from one side and then from the other. His rear disk wheel acted like a sail each time a crosswind hit. Ben fought to keep his machine on the road.

As he approached the top of the toughest climb, lightning flashed. The bolt struck on a distant hill, near the structure Bridgette had compared to the Eifel Tower. Ben noticed the rock formation that, two evenings before, had looked so fiery in the sun. Today the stone flames had been extinguished.

He crested the Col du Defens, then flew downhill. He passed the dirt road where he'd entered the highway on the tractor. At that same moment he felt a single raindrop, two drops. Then the heavens opened. Water came down in buckets. The sheer weight of it bogged down the bike. Fans ignored his passing as they scrambled to open umbrellas or climb into cars. The road became a blur. Ben was thankful for the freshly painted yellow line down the center of the highway which kept him from cruising off the shoulder.

"*Everything can be taken from a man but one thing: the last of the human freedoms—to choose one's attitude in a given set of circumstances, to choose one's own way.*"

Ben could overlook this weather. He could focus on the positive. He had to. Even in this race format designed to equalize the challenge for all competitors, weather had changed everything.

Nearing the midway point he felt strong, and having the major climb behind him was a bonus, but he wouldn't be coasting to the finish. He'd better pour even more energy into the second half of the course than he had the first.

Could he do it? How could there be any doubt? Unlike Frankl, he knew where his suffering ended. All he needed to do was cross an arbitrary line. In that moment, he'd go from pure effort to pure ecstasy. The harder he pushed, the sooner his pain would end. In comparison, no prisoner of war had ever known when his trial would be over.

"There is only one thing that I dread: not to be worthy of my sufferings."

"Slow for safety if you must," Thierry said.

Ben didn't need to. He'd traveled this section of road aboard the tractor. He recognized the outline of various cottages through the rain. He even thought he saw the burly tractor owner scrambling for cover. Farther on, the emu he'd seen guarding the fence line two days before sat like an enormous chicken, enduring the downpour.

"Suffering is an ineradicable part of life, even as fate and death. Without suffering and death human life cannot be complete."

Ben reached Bagnols-en-Forêt, his favorite little town. There was no time to stop for a baguette this time, though. Feeling like an honorary resident, he recognized half a dozen faces in the maniacal crowd as they willed him through their little corner of the world.

The olive-skinned woman, still with a child on her hip, stood dead ahead. She screamed at the top of her lungs. "Go, Ben Barnes! You're my hero!" Beside her, a man in a chef's hat was holding an umbrella over the three of them.

The policeman Ben had met stood near the water fountain where the photographer's scenic detour began. He pointed insistently at the right-hand side of the road.

"Merci." Ben squeezed his brakes. Rubber pads barely bit into the slippery rim but he slowed just enough to enter the side road in the preferred spot.

"Soigneux Ben, use caution!" the policeman shouted.

Ben shot down the right edge of the alley. To his left, flood waters raged. The policeman hadn't been kidding when he said this road became a river in the rain. Curtains of water sheeted off each building and added to the flow. Ben took the next corner extra wide just as the policeman had instructed. The machine shuddered over the sharp cobbles, but it kept its traction. From the corner of his eye he noticed the mayor's wife posed just as the policeman had said she'd be, although considerably soggier than the image in Ben's imagination.

He couldn't afford to look in the other direction to see which photographer had dreamt up this obstacle. As soon as he regained a straight road Ben lay into his pedals.

The rest of this route he'd traveled in the policeman's car, absorbing secrets the officer had shared. From here on he would go all out, exceeding whatever speed Thierry requested. Ben had enough strength left to push for the line relentlessly, even from so far out. He gritted his teeth and hammered the pedals until he thought the crank arms might bend.

"Men who allowed their inner hold on their moral and spiritual selves to subside eventually fell victim to the camps' degenerating influences."

Ben might be at a disadvantage battling moral codes that caused Kyle no qualms, but in being true to himself he felt his power regenerating. Today he was the sort of man he would never want to compete against. As he reeled in the road, faster and faster, he imagined Toma's reaction. The boy would be cheering for all he was worth.

In the road ahead Ben saw a second cyclist who had begun before he had. Luigi. Pain might wrack Ben's body and mind, but it was being exchanged for great results on the road. Ben bent as low as he could to cheat the wind. He pummeled the pedals. The road here was pancake flat. His odometer read 56.1 kilometers per hour. In the rain? Insane!

"Emotion, which is suffering, ceases to be suffering as soon as we form a clear and precise picture of it."

Was this Toma's secret? For a teen he had unusually sharp focus, as if he knew exactly what he meant to accomplish in life, even if he had no idea how.

Ben kept his eyes on Luigi, battling the road ahead. As skilled a climber as he was, the Italian's time-trialing skills weren't good enough to contend in a tough all-around competition like the Tour de France. Still, Luigi shouldn't lose more than four minutes to the stage winner. Ben must be laying down the time trial of his life. He hated to demoralize his friend by blowing by so quickly, but this wasn't the time for good manners. He had to shorten his journey by every second possible.

"Life ultimately means taking the responsibility to find the right answer to its problems and to fulfill the tasks which it constantly sets for each individual."

Ben shot past the Italian. A moment later he bunny hopped the ditch the policeman had pointed out.

"No man and no destiny can be compared to any other man or any other destiny."

Nothing was more important than this moment on the bike, and shortening it to the minimum time was of utmost importance.

"The immediate influence of behavior is always more effective than that of words."

Ben carried his supporters on his back, but instead of increasing his load, they lightened it. He had to win for those who believed in him. He'd put years of hard work into this effort already. What was a little bit more?

"*Whatever we had gone through could still be an asset to us in the future.*"

He passed the two-kilometer-to-go marker. He snarled and drove with every last ounce of strength.

"*What you have experienced, no power on earth can take from you.*"

All the years of training and building up aerobic capacity would be for naught if he didn't capitalize on the opportunity at hand in this moment.

"*There are two races of men in this world, but only these two—the 'race' of the decent man and the 'race' of the indecent man.*"

The raucous crowd beside the Roman coliseum drove Ben to a maniacal level of effort. He had to give these people what they had come to see.

"*A man who for years had thought he had reached the absolute limit of all possible suffering now found that suffering has no limits, and that he could still suffer more, and still more intensely.*"

Searing agony tore holes in Ben's body. He charged forward with viciousness he'd never dreamed himself capable of.

"*Man's search for meaning is the primary motivation in his life.*"

Ahead, where the road kicked up, he spotted the flamme rouge. One kilometer to go! A brutal little climb.

"*In the Nazi concentration camps one could have witnessed that those who knew there was a task waiting for them to fulfill were most apt to survive. My deep desire to write this manuscript anew helped me to survive the rigors of the camps I was in.*"

Ben's suffering had meaning, too. People were counting on him. He owed it to children. So many people had supported him. He'd promised the team. He'd keep his word no matter the cost.

"*Mental health is based on a certain degree of tension, the tension between what one has already achieved and what one still ought to accomplish. We should not, then, be hesitant about challenging man with a potential meaning for him to fulfill.*"

Thierry shouted out the window from the car behind. "Go harder Ben! Go harder! Give it all you have!"

"*If architects want to strengthen a decrepit arch, they increase the load that is laid upon it, for thereby the parts are joined more firmly together.*"

He could give even more, another increment at least.

"Each man is questioned by life; and he can only answer to life by answering for his own life; to life he can only respond by being responsible."

Responsibility had new meaning today. Greater causes than himself needed him to seal this deal.

"In some way suffering ceases to be suffering at the moment it finds meaning."

In this moment Ben craved pain precisely because his suffering had meaning. He was only tangentially aware of the delirious crowd.

"Man does not simply exist but always decides what his existence will be, what he will become in the next moment."

He broke the plane and the clock timing his effort stopped. He looked up at the scoreboard and saw his bib number light up in first position on the display. Never before had the digit 9 looked so beautiful. Every other result on the board moved down one spot to make room. As he squeezed the brakes he noted his finishing time. The next best man was a minute and fifty-four seconds back, but his two main rivals were yet to finish.

He felt overwhelmed by love as he never had before. He loved Dad. He loved Coach and Thelma, Fritz, and Thierry. He even loved Bridgette—or at least the woman he'd believed she was for so long. He could express that love all the more by sacrificing for kids like Toma, by doing his part to ensure their dreams didn't become steppingstones to a nightmare.

Fritz took Ben's bike, and a soigneur handed him a drink and towel. Thierry approached on his crutches. Coach walked beside him, an umbrella in one hand and the book in the other.

"Those passages were great," Thierry said. "I've never heard anybody speak of suffering so optimistically, and this guy has endured misery we couldn't even dream of. It's heroic."

"Yeah, I couldn't feel sorry for myself with messages like those flowing through my brain." Ben wiped sweat from his brow. Slowly, he began feeling human again. He leaned forward, drinking in oxygen as he watched Luigi finish.

Thierry pointed toward the giant television screen.

Ben turned toward the monitor. It showed Kyle nearing an intermediate time check, six kilometers away from the finish line. Watered-down blood made swirling patterns on his right leg. He'd crashed, likely in the corner the policeman had foreseen. His face was a mask of torture. He passed through the checkpoint, and the result flashed on the screen: nearly two minutes down, almost certainly out of contention for the stage win.

"If you beat Gunter you'll win this stage," Thierry said.

"And you'll have done it the right way." Coach flipped open the book. "*Our generation is realistic, for we have come to know man as he really is. After all, man is a being who invented the gas chambers of Auschwitz; however, he is also that being who entered those gas chambers upright, with the Lord's Prayer or the Shema Yisrael on his lips.*"

Ben's gaze settled on the church spire beyond the cheering crowd, but below it something else caught his attention. Gunter charged for the line. The German dug deep, all the way up the finishing straight. He crossed the tape and crumpled onto his handlebars. The clock showed a time thirty-two seconds slower than Ben's, a big gap over a great time-trialist.

By the time Kyle struggled up the finishing straight, Ben felt relaxed.

"He looks like a damp rat to me," Coach said.

"Really?" Thierry asked. "I see a man who knows how to suffer."

"Yeah," Ben said. "That's what I see, too."

Kyle crossed the line a minute and forty-eight seconds behind Ben's time. Somehow he'd closed the gap by nearly a dozen seconds in the last several kilometers. Blood oozed from an open wound on his right leg.

Coach threw his arms around Ben. "Congratulations! I knew you could do it."

Thierry hugged both of them. "Tough as he is, you're tougher. This is a worthy contest. You blew my mind out there."

"Thanks, Thierry."

"The quotes from that book were great too. I plan to steal that strategy for myself one day."

"Yeah? Well there's one in particular I can't get out of my mind."

"What is it?" Thierry asked.

"I didn't underline it. I almost wish I'd never read it."

Thierry's eyes widened. "Now you have to show me."

Ben took the paperback from Coach and flipped to the page. He pointed to the passage and handed the book to Thierry.

Thierry read: "*On the average, only those prisoners could keep alive who, after years of trekking from camp to camp, had lost all scruples in their fight for existence; they were prepared to use every means, honest and otherwise, even brutal force, theft, and betrayal of their friends, in order to save themselves. We who have come back, by the aid of many lucky chances and miracles—whatever one may choose to call them—we know: the best of us did not return."*

Accompanied by the storm, the words weighed even heavier than the first time Ben had read them. He knew that good people had survived, but the quote reminded him that rule breakers had certain advantages, particularly if they disguised themselves well.

Thierry closed the book and handed it back. "Wow. There's a statement that takes guts."

Chapter Nineteen

Ben listened to Tour de France theme music blare from the loudspeakers as technicians readied the finish area for post-race festivities. A modified flatbed truck served as a stage. The press would normally fill the fenced area just in front of it, but the weather had driven most of them elsewhere. A smattering of dignitaries sat in bleachers to the right. The fans were cordoned off behind these areas, scattered around the ruins of the ancient aqueduct. They peered from beneath a sea of umbrellas.

Thierry found a race official who handed him a stapled results list. Limping across the finish area on his crutches, he flipped through the pages until he reached the General Classification. He stopped beside Ben and held the paper out so they could read together.

Kyle Smith's name was still on top. He'd maintained his advantage over Gunter, but only by four seconds. The third name was Ben Barnes, a minute and twenty-three seconds off the lead. He'd grabbed back a satisfying hunk of clock today. Below Ben's name, the remaining competitors were increasingly distant. Even the fourth place cyclist stood more than six minutes down. There was little doubt the eventual winner would emerge from among the first three.

A race official asked Ben to follow him to an interview area adjacent to the press corral. Ben turned to Thierry. "What do I tell them?"

"Answer their questions. Don't respond to rumors."

Soon Ben faced the reporters, though there were fewer than before.

"How did you keep your focus through all the distractions?" asked Simone Sardou, the journalist Ben admired most.

"What distractions?"

The reporters laughed.

Ben smiled, relieved at the lighthearted tone. "Our coaching staff allowed me to concentrate on my job. They deserve the credit."

Ben became increasingly comfortable as he fielded questions, but his nerves tightened when he noticed the *au Fond* journalist join the group.

"Do you know a veterinarian by the name of Ermenegildo Peraziglio?" the *au Fond* man asked.

"No." Ben had never heard that name in his life, and he didn't know any veterinarians, anyway.

"He's the man who was pulled over yesterday for a broken tail light, and ended up being taken into custody for transporting a laundry list of banned products."

Ben shrugged. "I haven't been following the news."

Atop the stage, the race announcer called to the crowd, "*Mesdames et messieurs*, thank you for enduring the storm. Three Sundays down and one left to go. Only seven days of racing remain. Shall we get underway with today's awards?"

The fans cheered.

The race official that had led Ben to the reporters tapped him on the shoulder. "Time to go on stage. In addition to the regular prize money, you've won a huge pig."

"*Superbe*. I've been needing one of those."

Most finishing towns put together a local prize like this. The winning cyclist's weight in wine was one of the most common. Usually the item was sold and the proceeds put into the pot with the other prize money. The cash would be divided among the team members after the race.

Ben turned to follow. Local newspapers were certain to want lots of photos of him mugging beside his new pig.

Behind him the *au Fond* reporter yelled. "It turns out that the evening before his arrest Dr. Peraziglio received a speeding ticket near one of the towns on yesterday's time trial course, so we know he's been traveling near The Tour, at least for a while."

Ben stumbled. Was he talking about Doctor Peraza? The world's premier human performance specialist had been demoted to jailed veterinarian for a broken light bulb? Ben suppressed a grin, resisting the temptation to look back as he rounded the corner of the stage. Coach Bill had to be behind Peraza's troubles. That crafty old coot!

"Any comment?" the journalist yelled after him.

Chapter Twenty

Yesterday's storm was a distant memory as the cyclists milled about the St. Raphaël starting line. Today was Bureau de Tourisme weather. The church bell of the Englise Notre Dame de la Paix clanged. A monkey ran back and forth along a decorative railing, collecting coins from amused passers-by. Today the athletes would take a 173-kilometer cruise of the Mediterranean coast, eventually finishing in Marseille. Music boomed from the massive speaker system surrounding the announcer's platform. An enormous crowd had already gathered. The spectators were edgy with anticipation of another day's racing.

The Banque Fédérale team had been in a jovial mood ever since Ben's time-trial victory yesterday afternoon. Success worked amazing magic as a tension reliever. The only unhappy team member was Rikard.

Today's stage was the one he'd begged for a few days earlier. Thierry had surprised everyone at the morning meeting by assigning only two men to work for Rikard. One of them was Philippe, Rikard's best friend and traditional lead-out man. The two worked together with legendary precision.

The disappointment on the big sprinter's face was obvious. The same team decisions that put Ben in a position to win the overall race had derailed Rikard's dream of sprint victories. Despite that, Rikard responded with dignity. He didn't like Ben, but he'd been there when needed, breaking a trail through the wind, and even shuttling food and water. He'd been a stud the whole race.

Ben thought about the growing team camaraderie. A victory for Rikard could only help matters, and the big sprinter couldn't be more deserving. Despite the risks, he'd do what he could to help. He rolled alongside Rikard and set his left foot on the ground. "I made a promise to help you the other day. I'll keep it."

"I'm frustrated with Thierry, not you. You're not even a bad guy, for a Yankee. Sorry I doubted you." Rikard put out a hand.

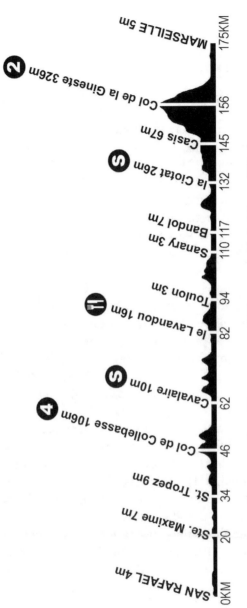

Tour de France Stage 14 Profile

MARSEILLE 5m
Col de la Gineste 326m
Casis 67m
la Ciotat 26m
Bandol 7m
Sanary 3m
Toulon 3m
le Lavandou 16m
Cavalaire 10m
Col de Collebasse 106m
St. Tropez 9m
Ste. Maxime 7m
SAN RAFAEL 4m

0KM 20 34 46 62 82 94 110 117 132 145 156 175KM

Ben slapped the open palm. "Thanks. You're not too bad yourself, for a Frenchie."

They both laughed. Cultural stereotypes crumbled, as usual, now that they had gotten to know one another.

The stage left St. Raphaël center on palm-lined roads. Attacks began immediately, but each time a handful of cyclists established a gap, one team or another decided the composition didn't suit them, so they chased the escapists down. Only when every team strong enough to control the peloton was satisfied with the breakaway's composition, could it succeed. At the ten-kilometer mark, where waves exploded in rocky coves, a group of nine cyclists built a substantial gap at the front. Some of the squads were happy because they had teammates in the lead group. Many of the other team directeurs probably believed the athletes in the break weren't strong enough to outrun the peloton for the entire day. For a variety of reasons, no one chased them down. Finally, with an acceptable breakaway up the road, life in the peloton calmed down.

As always, the men in the break would face a hard slog. The nine men would have to share the workload of well over a hundred riders in the peloton. But for some men there was a very different motivation to be in a breakaway. Not everybody could hope to win the race, but winning wasn't necessary to gain valuable exposure. Leading the race, no matter how briefly, meant camera time. Getting a sponsor's jersey on television was critical to pleasing the men who signed the checks. For athletes who had little hope of leading the race late in the day, audiences sometimes estimated at more than a billion people gave them ample motivation to burn rubber early. They quickly built a three-minute advantage.

The peloton seemed as relaxed as the vacationers soaking in sunshine along the route. The men rode comfortably, periodically shaded by the expansive branches of exotic terraced evergreens. They looked like bonsai trees on some sort of ultra-growth hormone.

As the day progressed the cyclists passed through some of the hottest holiday spots in the world: St. Aygulf, Ste. Maxime, St. Tropez. Even at this pace the peloton crossed these roads far faster than any tourist in a car could. Traffic congestion brought this road to a standstill every summer day.

The cyclists climbed the category four Col de la Collebasse then passed through Cavalaire, Rayol Candel, St Clair, le Lavandou, and Heyres. They pushed kilometer after kilometer of asphalt behind them

Thierry came over the headsets as they navigated by Toulon Beach.

"Eighty five kilometers to go. The break has a six-minute gap. Play it cool, guys. Save your energy for the finish."

Rikard's hopes hinged on the gamble that one of the sprinters' teams would get nervous and drive the chase to bring the escapists back, setting up the win for the fastest finishers. Ben eyed Rikard. The big man looked twitchy. He badly wanted this win.

The men stayed tucked within the peloton as it wasted road that might be better spent closing the gap. Within the dockyards of Toulon they saw clearly that not everybody on the southern French coast was rich. Sailors, prostitutes, wharf men, and beggars mingled beneath the shadows of run-down modular apartments. By the time the peloton reached the seventy-kilometers-to-go mark, the gap had widened to eight minutes, but the pack was still at only about eighty percent effort.

"This pace is killing my chances," Rikard said.

Ben wanted to help, but it would be unprofessional to call Thierry over the radio and question his strategy. A conversation like that had to be kept private. That meant dropping back to the car, a risky move for a leader, but he owed Rikard.

Ben slowed his pedaling and allowed the peloton to flow around him. Commissar's cars and motorbikes came next. Fortunately, because of Ben's placement in the overall, Banque Fédérale was near the front of the team caravan.

Thierry shook his head as Ben pulled up to the window. "What are you doing here?"

"Someone needs to shuttle water."

"It shouldn't be you," Thierry said, handing out a bottle. "If the terrain wasn't so flat your rivals would dig a hole you could never climb out of."

Ben looked across the sands of Sanary and thought of San Diego's Ocean Beach. This was a similar surf bum's paradise, minus the big waves. He slid the water container into his cage. "Rikard wants to win today. He deserves it."

Thierry handed out another bottle. "So, that's why you're here. Tell him I wish him luck. You'd better get back up front, or you'll be hating it once the chase starts. Each time you speak I'm going to hand you another bottle as punishment."

Ben put the water into his back pocket. "What if the chase doesn't start?"

Thierry held out another container. "It will."

As if on cue, the car accelerated to keep up with the peloton. Ben tucked the new bottle into his pocket, and then pushed hard to catch up. Thierry laughed. "Now do you see my point? All we had to do was sit it out. The sprinters' teams can't afford to gamble any longer that we'll join the chase. Rikard gets the opportunity he wants, and our men get to hitch a ride so they'll be fresh to protect you in the mountains tomorrow. Trust me next time."

Ben didn't have the spare breath to reply. Besides, he couldn't afford the risk of another water bottle. Thierry had read the race correctly once again, assuming they caught the escapists.

Ben up shifted and fought to regain the tail of the peloton. It was a brutal slog, even though he didn't have far to go. The cyclists were tearing up the road. Men were peeling off the back like skin flying from a potato over a mess-hall garbage can. The last cyclist in the line gave up the chase just as Ben tucked in behind. He veered wide, but then he had to fight his way through several more fried domestiques and up to the group again. He caught the peloton just as it screamed past the scenic rock-walled harbor in Bandol.

He paused to catch his breath, but quickly resumed his trek through the pack. He needed to return to the front as quickly as possible. If this group fractured, those caught in the rear peloton would lose time to the leaders.

Flatter stages rarely had a significant impact on the General Classification because the peloton was likely to finish in one big mass with the sprint specialists fighting out the victory. For safety, each cyclist in a continuous group was awarded the same time. That prevented mayhem throughout the pack on tight finishing straights. Today's race had the potential to end in fragmented bunches or possibly a mass sprint. It all depended on how many men had the strength to get over the top of the Col de la Bineste, a category two rise, only twenty kilometers from the finish.

Ben picked his way through the group, struggling to return to his team. This sensation had been so familiar in his days as a domestique, but already it felt quite foreign. He was gasping by the time he moved beside Rikard. He handed off his spare water bottles and watched his dehydrated teammates empty them.

"*Oh la la!*"

"On the … rivet now?" Albert panted.

Ben didn't bother nodding. A cyclist on the rivet is surviving by the narrowest of margins. The expression refers to the studs that secured the leather upholstery to old-time bicycle saddles. Maxed out athletes were known to sit so far forward that only the rivet at the nose of their saddle held them aboard.

The spear shaped peloton pierced the wind. The men up front took short turns, drilling it with everything they had.

"Hang on guys," Thierry said over the radio. "You've taken a minute thirty out of the chase group in just over five kilometers. You're smoking! My right foot is winded just holding down the gas pedal."

The pace slackened as the riders in the lead got the word. The break was doomed, and everybody knew it. The peloton had proven it had the horsepower to devour any man who dared test its resolve. There was no reason to kill themselves bringing the escapists back too early. None of the sprinters wanted to see a fresh attack launched ten kilometers out, so having those exhausted men up front as a preventive measure was ideal. Catching the current group with around seven kilometers to go would be just about perfect. This scenario couldn't be better for sprinters who needed to get over a climb.

The gap to the lead group continued to fall like a carefully constructed timetable, one minute per ten kilometers. The peloton reached the vineyard-covered base of the Col de la Gineste two and a half minutes behind the leaders. This climb consisted of three steps connected by two wide terraces. Rikard and the other sprinters were able to get up front in preparation for each climbing section, and then drift back through the pack as the going got tough. They'd catch back on and repeat the process when the road flattened again. Most of the sprinters crossed the summit only twenty seconds behind the climbers and just over a minute behind the exhausted breakaway.

The riders looked down on the stunning whiteness of Marseille. Surely, no paler settlement existed in the entire world. White cliffs loomed high above white buildings, apparently built out of disassembled cliffs.

The descent was much more abrupt than the ascent had been. Soon, the cyclists hit flat land and screamed across the city limits. There were only twelve kilometers of level streets to go. Now they rode among the pale buildings. Even the air had a dusty, white feel. Everything seemed coated with talcum powder.

Three of the nine lead men gave up, and the peloton devoured them beside a monument called the Obelisque de Mazargues. The snack whetted the beast's appetite, and the speed increased. They were now on the most unusual of French roads, Boulevard Michelet, an avenue so perfectly plotted they could literally see out the other side of the city. Thierry hadn't been exaggerating when he teased Rikard about a lack of curves. Even strait-laced Salt Lake City didn't have roads this wide and long. The remaining breakaway men where forced to dangle in the wind within permanent view of their pursuers. The beast teased them with false hope.

The capture came just before the Rond-Point du Prado where the course turned sharp left onto another straight-as-an-arrow road. Just like that, the escapists were once again the property of the peloton.

Ben's skin tingled as they passed beneath the five-kilometer marker. Next came the part of cycling the sprinters lived for. These guys would prefer never to climb a mountain again, and most of them despised time trials; however, give them a sprint finish and watch them thrive.

Thierry called out the names of the two men tabbed to help Rikard. "Philippe, give Rikard the most perfect lead out he's ever had. The rest of you, keep Ben out of trouble."

Ben thought Rikard deserved four men, but he couldn't spare the breath to mention it. Thierry wouldn't change his mind, even if Ben could have spoken. Besides, Thierry had just reminded him not to second guess. The peloton streamed toward an enormous statue of David in a thin ribbon, undulating like the tail of a colorful kite. Cyclists buried themselves past redline, like engines revved beyond manufacturer's recommendations, as they fought to maintain position for their respective leaders. Ben felt the strength to lead out Rikard's train. General Classification contenders normally avoided the risks inherent at the front of a sprinting pack, but he couldn't resist doing it. Rikard would gain a third helper without fighting for one.

Cyclists made lightning quick choices as they threaded their way between asphalt islands, past roundabouts, beside directional signs, and through a myriad of other mid-road obstacles. Again and again the peloton shattered into fragments as the men rushed around traffic furniture. Ben felt his machine in his bones, every pebble in the road, and every gust of wind. They dove into another ninety-degree right-hander where the road abutted the ocean. As on most occasions, the anarchy reshuffled itself into something resembling order.

Another straight road! Somehow they even had geometric beaches in Marseille. Ben's machine jolted when someone quacked his rear wheel. "My bad," an unseen cyclist yelled. The interruption knocked Ben off his line, and he bounced shoulder-to-shoulder into another athlete. Both men rebounded and held their balance.

Contact was nothing new to sprinters. Rikard wouldn't have cared whom he'd ricocheted off or who had jolted him from behind, but Ben felt nervous. It was time to peel off. He veered wide but kept all the speed he could.

The sprinters roared past as the road suddenly got interesting with the most beautiful curves imaginable, suggestive of the most desirable of women. Rikard had been right after all. Built upon concrete arms, the Corniche du John Fitzgerald Kennedy cantilevered from cliffs and hung over the ocean.

Rikard rode pedal-to-pedal with the man wearing the green jersey. The color designated him the most consistent sprinter in this year's Tour so far. Every fast cyclist in the world coveted that shirt.

Fans went wild as the leaders streamed through a dodgy corner. An instant of poor judgment sent another Banque Fédérale man wide and out of contention, but Philippe's line was perfect. Rikard stayed glued to his wheel. Two thirds of the sprinter's assistance had disappeared in the span of a hundred meters, but everyone had remained upright and Rikard's position looked good.

The men blasted beneath the two-kilometer banner. Philippe sputtered and peeled wide to leave a path for the strong men. The pack took another corner, and Rikard dove into the pace line that had formed to his right, gluing himself in sixth position, right on the wheel of the green jersey wearer. It was the perfect spot to slingshot himself to victory.

Ben's adrenaline rushed as the battle unfolded. Fifteen hundred meters to go, right on schedule, legs churning with the bike in the biggest gear, fully alive. No wonder the sprinters loved this!

A finger of cyclists surged on the left. Rikard glanced at them but seemed to dismiss the threat. Those men were pretenders. The race surrounded him, Rikard, the two men immediately in front of him, and the two men behind him. Those were the five fastest closers left in this event.

Under the flamme rouge with one kilometer to go, the group on the left imploded and disappeared. Two of the lead-out men also fell off the pace. Rikard now held fourth position.

The leaders swept through a smooth right-hand bend and onto the finishing straight. Ben hurried around the corner as well. With the finish near, he and the other men who weren't fighting for the win finally relaxed. It was obvious they'd be awarded the same time as the winner. At this moment, Rikard's concentration would be shifting to an even higher level.

The spectators seemed stacked on one another at the sides of the road. To the left, frothy white waves beat at pale rocks. On the right, geometric white buildings appeared to grow from the cliffs, each structure alive with humanity. People leaned from every window, covered the roofs, and stood on the porches. The racket they were making began to register in Ben's ears as his focus turned from his role in the race.

He looked up at the giant television mounted abreast the finish line. Pixilated sprinters images seemed to be charging directly toward him. At three hundred meters the man in the green jersey opened his sprint full blast, diving to the right of the athlete in front of him as the cyclists ahead drifted left. A thousand similar experiences must have combined to tell Rikard to plunge left into the narrow hole between the three riders still ahead of him and the spectator barriers. He stood on the pedals and threw his machine back and forth as he pumped, wheels swaying within centimeters of the spectator-fences. Ben clenched his teeth, fearing an impact. Rikard had better judge the available pavement exactly. Contact between a bicycle wheel and the aluminum foot of a spectator fence always led to disaster.

The spot Rikard picked narrowed, but he redoubled his effort. He charged through, dinging the man on his right with every stroke. He gained ground with each revolution as well. An instant later, he shot clear, still slightly behind the green jersey whose wearer was charging up the opposite side of the road.

Three meters from the line the man in the green jersey threw his arms skyward in victory. In the same instant Rikard thrust his machine toward the line. Though the margin couldn't have been more than hundredths of a second, Ben knew his teammate had won. The stunned expression of the green jersey wearer proved that he also knew his fate. Rikard spread his arms to the sky, and then rose from the saddle in an amazing feat of balance. He stood in contact with his bicycle only at the toe clips, his head two feet higher than the other cyclists as he coasted through the finish area.

For the sprinters, winning a race with the peloton intact was as good as it got. These specialists had no hope of winning the whole tour, but they would risk everything for the prestige of a single stage. The other men drooped forward on their handlebars in exhaustion and defeat. Rikard looked good, damned good.

Ben hurried through the finish area, anxious to congratulate his teammate. As he approached, other athletes were already praising Rikard for his perfect sprint.

"Incredible work!" Ben said as he pulled alongside.

Rikard nodded generously. "There'll be partying tonight!"

Ben clasped his hand. "What a team! Three stages in the bag and a shot at the overall, even though we lost the defending champ. We can't be stopped."

"I wouldn't have made it without you, Ben. Nice work," Rikard said.

Thierry's voice emerged from the radio. "Well done, Rikard."

"Thanks, Thierry."

"Ben, I need a word with you. Leaders who take the sorts of foolish risks you just did never lead for long."

Chapter Twenty-One

Ben tensed at Thierry's reprimand. Within moments, the rest of the Banque Fédérale cyclists surrounded Rikard, laughing and bragging. Ben relaxed and allowed the celebration to overtake him. The teammates dismounted their bikes and threw arms about one another. Rikard began singing "Knights of the Round Table," and the rest joined in:

Chevaliers de la table ronde,
Goûtons voir si le vin est bon.
Chevaliers de la table ronde,
Goûtons voir si le vin est bon.
Goûtons voir, oui oui oui,
Goûtons voir, non non non,
Goûtons voir si le vin est bon.

Hard work and the resulting success had fused the men into a team. For the second day in a row they celebrated victory. Not long ago, Ben had been the outsider in this group, separated by citizenship and culture. Now, common purpose made all that irrelevant. The acceptance he'd ached for was finally his. Enveloped by their fellowship, he felt powerful.

Coach Bill split a watermelon and handed Ben a slice. Then he handed out slices to the rest of the team members.

Ben bit into it. Fresh, and unmistakably Green River! It must have been flown from Utah today. They ought to make a habit of this. From the smiles on his teammates' faces he knew they agreed.

The press gathered, shooting pictures and asking questions. Ben blended into the team, preferring that the moment belong to others. In the distance, through the arched Monument du Moyen Orient he spotted the unmistakable outline of the Château d'If, the island castle turned prison from which the fictional Edmond Dantès, hero of Alexandre Dumas' *The Count of Monte Cristo*, had made his spectacular escape. At age twelve Ben had watched the first of at least a dozen versions of the movie he'd seen since, and he'd read the book many times. The story was his first exposure to France. He dreamed of it often, but now his first sighting of the citadel reminded him of Peraza.

Might the veterinarian be locked in its musty bowels? Ben didn't wish him any harm; still he prayed Peraza was somewhere beyond Robidoux's reach. Ideally, Robidoux wouldn't learn that Ben's scheduled appointment with the doctor had never occurred. The thought calmed his mind. Would Robidoux drop the doping efforts now that his facilitator sat in jail? Ben hoped so.

Eventually a reporter looked his way. "Are you acquainted with a logger who lives in Bagnols-en-Forêt?"

Ben looked at him, surprised. How had the press gotten a whiff of this?

"His name is…" The reporter scanned his notes.

Rikard waved a dismissive hand. "What kind of a stupid question is that? Ask him something relevant, like how did he ride so well today, or why did he risk his safety for me?"

"It's a team sport, and I'm a member of the greatest cycling team in the world," Ben said.

"I noticed you shuttling water late in the race, Ben. What was that all about?" Simone Sardou asked.

The cyclists laughed.

"Force of habit," Ben said. "I got it out of my system, though. I nearly coughed up a lung trying to catch back on."

An hour later the cyclists were together on a chartered train ride to Perpignan, 320 kilometers away where the Pyrenean foothills fell into the Mediterranean. Three days in the high mountains would follow. Most of the crew, including Coach Bill, would travel in the team vehicles.

The rail transfer was much faster than the road the support staff would take, but it would still be a couple of hours before they reached their destination. To minimize the discomfort, Banque Fédérale had the club car to themselves. It was a glitzy two-story restaurant on wheels. Purple neon railings accentuated the stainless steel walls and ceiling. Monsieur Robidoux had arranged the luxury.

Thierry steadied himself with one hand on the bar. "I'm very proud of you men today. I'm not speaking so much of Rikard's victory, though that's a great accomplishment. The thing that makes me happy is that you have become a team. A round of champagne's on me!"

The athletes cheered.

Thierry took the first two glasses from the bartender. He limped across the car, his crutches abandoned. "Ben, come this way."

Ben's gut clenched as he stood. Thierry led him to the end of the train car. He pushed a button and the passageway to the next car opened. Through the far window he could see the Megatronics team having some sort of meeting. Surely Thierry wasn't going to barge in there.

Thierry stepped into the breezeway and Ben followed. Steel wheels clattered, uncomfortably loudly, against steel tracks. Through the gaps in the pivoting floor a trestle whizzed by. Thierry turned to face him. He must really need privacy to choose a spot like this.

Thierry extended a glass of champagne, but when Ben reached for it the directeur pulled it back. "Only if you promise to behave like a leader the rest of the way. Today worked out well, I admit. You're not likely to be so lucky next time. No more shuttling water, no more sprint lead outs."

"I was trying to help morale." Ben shouted over the noise.

"How committed are you to winning this race? What if the peloton had split when you dropped back, or what if you'd gone down in the sprint?"

"Rikard deserved the win."

"Not at the price of knocking you from contention. Your generosity might be admirable under ordinary circumstances, but if it continues in this race it will be your downfall. Things are going to become increasingly difficult. Soon you'll have a tough time dragging yourself from bed. If you overextend, it will come back to haunt you. That's a guarantee. You'll pay sooner or later for every ounce of energy you use, so I can't allow you to expend any you don't have to. Understand?"

Ben nodded.

Thierry stared at him long and hard. "This is about my brother, isn't it? You're still stung over what happened and the aftermath. I've forgiven you, Ben. Everybody who matters got over it a long time ago. You've got to as well."

"I thought I had."

"Then why are you so obsessed with acceptance? It only matters if you allow it to. You shouldn't even have time to worry about it. Now that you're the team leader, your job is to selfishly pursue the win. If you're unwilling to do that, I need to know. It's unfair to ask these men to support you if you aren't fully committed to the task. They're well paid to take care of you, and as you know, whatever prize money you earn will be divided among them."

Wind tickled Ben's stubbly scalp. A week ago it would have been tousling his long hair, but he'd had it all cut off the night before the Alpe d'Huez stage. Since that moment, he'd become a different man in many ways. Thinking back, it seemed like a lifetime ago. Here he stood, balanced on the unsteady floor above a clattering coupler knuckle. He was within sight of the two pro squads he'd raced for, but isolated from teammates old and new. As France rushed beneath his feet in a darkening blur he admitted to himself that Thierry was right. He still hadn't changed quite enough. His desire for acceptance was interfering with his goal of winning. "*Oui*, Theirry. I understand."

"*Bon.*" Thierry handed Ben the champagne.

Ben watched the bubbles rise, considering the irony. To bring glory to the team he had to hog it for himself. "Do you really expect selfishness to decide the overall winner?"

Thierry shook his head. "Generosity is only a symptom of weakness. I've noticed that when a cyclist begins to doubt his ability to deliver, he'll often justify his coming failure by giving gifts. Don't do that, for your teammates or anyone else. Determination is the key. The man who refuses to allow anything to get in his way will be the victor."

"I want to win."

"Will you sacrifice everything for it?"

What more could he be expected to give up? His relationship with the woman of his dreams was over. His unconditional trust of those closest to him was shattered. He'd sequestered himself and focused as he never had before on the time-trial. His universe was centered on this race. Then he thought about the points he meant to prove by winning, and he understood why the decisions he'd made today angered Thierry so much. Any slight misfortune and his opportunity could have been squandered. He wouldn't risk that again.

Thierry hit another button and the door slid open.

Soigneurs had set up massage tables as if they were already in their hotel. Thierry pointed Ben to one of them. He walked over and lay down on his back.

Directly above him, Rikard leaned over the second floor catwalk, wearing nothing but briefs and flexing his biceps. He looked exceptionally fit, yet comical. Sinewy muscles rippled beneath dark bronze arms. The coloring abruptly switched to white six inches below the shoulder. His torso was the same pasty tone, except for a bronze triangle below his neck that gradually blended to his deeply tanned face.

"You look like a crazed cattle rancher I once knew," Ben said, aware that his own farmer's tan and starved physique cut a similar profile. "*Proche.* I'm a crazed Tour de France stage winner! The fastest of them all!" He vaulted atop the half wall and sat with his legs dangling. A million powerful fibers twitched beneath the taut flesh. The transition between sun-drenched and sun-starved skin was even sharper here than on the arm. It almost looked like he wore a flesh toned pair of cycling shorts.

The soigneur began oiling Ben's legs, but using methods so different from those of Bridgette or Bill. Ben put them both out of his mind, closing his eyes to focus on the moment, enjoying recovery. The miles melted away.

Ben's thoughts turned to tomorrow's course. The hills were going to hurt, and since Pyraneean roads were generally lower quality than those in the Alps, the flats might too. Chipped pavement, potholes, and rough asphalt abounded.

"To Ben Barnes, the next Tour de France champion!"

Ben lifted his head. Rikard held his glass high in a toast. The other men cheered Rikard's surprising optimism. It wasn't characteristic of him to ever say anything so positive.

Rikard took a drink. "I've never finished the Tour before, even though this is my fifth start, but I'm going to do it this year. I'm going to do it for Ben."

Chapter Twenty-Two

Bridgette glanced out the window down a narrow St. Lary Soulan alley as she brewed a pot of coffee. Pyraneean peaks rose at the edge of town. It was the perfect setting for getting back to basics. Her former college roommate, who owned the home, had left for groceries an hour ago and should be back any moment.

The phone rang. Maybe it was her.

"*Bonjour,*" Bridgette said.

"Bridgette?" A man's voice.

"*Oui.* Who is this?"

"Frodie told Robidoux he hasn't seen you around lately. It worried me."

A chill raced up her spine. "Who is this?"

"I told Robidoux your schedule is probably hectic. I suggested the loss of Peraza must have you scrambling."

For a moment she thought the speaker might be a reporter fishing for information, but then she placed the voice. "You're Robidoux's valet, aren't you? What's your name? How did you get this number?"

"I found it in Robidoux's files and played a hunch. He has information on everybody. He knows my habits, and he knows yours as well. We aren't the only people he's in a position to blackmail."

Was this a trick? Was Robidoux listening in? "Why did you call?"

"I want you to be safe. Ben too. He's a nice kid, one of the best I've met. I'm still hopeful he'll win."

"Is he in danger?"

"Robidoux is concerned that Ben's appointment with Peraza may have been missed … and missed on purpose. He thinks that Ben might be behind Peraza's arrest. I've been researching that for him. I must admit,—the circumstances look strange."

She didn't even know the circumstances, but she couldn't tell him that. "I won't say anything against Ben."

"I wouldn't ask you to. I'm calling from a phone booth on my own time. Telephone calls over Robidoux's lines are recorded. I can't lie to him about what I discover."

"Who asked you to?"

"I'm hoping I'll come across something that suggests you are carrying out Robidoux's wishes."

"*Pardonnez-moi?*"

"Like any man, if Robidoux sees evidence that supports the conclusions he prefers, he's prone to jumping to them."

The line went dead. She stared at the handset, baffled. Could she trust him? Which conclusions did he believe Robidoux would prefer? The valet had said many strange things. She couldn't completely make sense of them. What was he asking her to do? She wasn't about to push Ben to use drugs, if that's what he meant.

She'd had lots of time over the last several days to come to grips with her errors. She felt better about things. Ben wouldn't have had the same sort of time himself, though. There was no reason to think he'd be ready to hear from her. Losing the race, if it came to that, wouldn't be the end of the world. Losing Ben would.

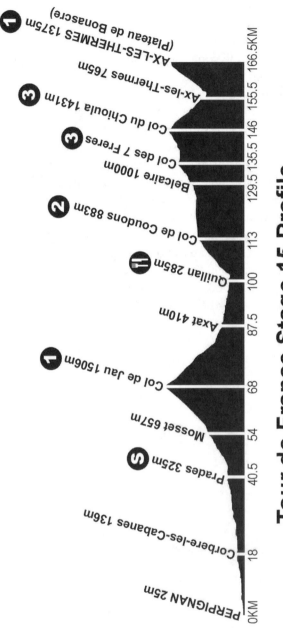

PERPIGNAN 25m

Corbere-les-Cabanes 136m

Prades 325m ⑤

Mosset 657m

Col de Jau 1506m ①

Axat 410m

Quillan 285m 🍴

Col de Coudons 883m ②

Belcaire 1000m
Col des 7 Freres 883m ③
Col du Chioula 1431m ③

Ax-les-Thermes 765m

AX-LES-THERMES 1375m ①
(Plateau de Bonascre)

0KM 18 40.5 54 68 87.5 100 113 129.5 135.5 146 155.5 166.5KM

Tour de France Stage 15 Profile

Chapter Twenty-Three

Ben strolled down a glistening marble-paved alley, the click of his cycling cleats echoing between five-story Perpignan buildings. Much of this city's core was permanently closed to automobile traffic which created a vibrant space for people to mingle.

A dress shop owner drew water from a public well, added soap, and then squeegeed her portion of the red-veined walkway in preparation for the day's crowds. Throughout the neighborhood others performed similar rituals.

Ben took a bite of his millefeuille. The flaky cream-filled pastries had become his favorite pre-race snack. He watched a woman in stilettos pass through an intersection a block ahead, her shoes tapping out a catchy tempo.

It made him think of Bridgette. He struggled with feelings of betrayal. How could he have been so misled? How could he have been so blind? His attention returned to the passing lady. Watching her made him realize he'd have opportunities to meet other women. Hopefully he could eventually find one who was as understanding and supportive as he'd once believed Bridgette was.

He reached the staging area and got his bicycle from Fritz. Although he had the utmost respect for the mechanic's skill, he stooped beside his machine and double-checked each component, just as he did every day. It was impossible to be too prepared.

An hour later the race was underway. Ben tucked in behind Rikard, and the breeze disappeared. He felt like a sports car sheltered by a semi. Having such a wheel to follow was going to be a deluxe lead up to the mountains, though Rikard would be left behind once the road became steep.

Today's route began within a hundred kilometers of Ben's European home of Gerona. He had cycled these roads often and had many friends in the area. Maybe he'd see some of them today.

"How are you boys doing?" The voice over their headsets was Monsieur Robidoux. He enjoyed calling from the deck of his yacht, or wherever he might be, and being patched through to the racing cyclists. At least he'd chosen to contact them early in the day, before things became too intense.

Rikard looked back at Ben. "You do the talking."

Ben tensed as he activated his radio. "Couldn't be better."

"Ah, Benjamin. Nice time trial."

"*Merci beaucoup.*"

"But it was impolite of you to leave your room so early the day before. You missed the appointment we talked about."

Ben's throat caught. Peraza wasn't out of Robidoux's reach, after all. The man could walk through walls.

"I was thrilled by Rikard's performance yesterday as well," Robidoux said. "Can he hear me?"

"I can. *Merci,*" Rikard said.

Robidoux coughed. "*Bon.* I have good news for you."

"*Oui?*" Rikard asked.

"You aren't going to have to haul your carcass over these big mountains. I'm sending you to Hamburg to prepare for the HEW Cyclassics. You can pull out right this moment."

Rikard looked at Ben. "I'd prefer to stay here."

"*Non, non.* Of course you wouldn't." Robidoux sounded upset. "It isn't polite to ignore my gifts. Right, Benjamin?"

The message couldn't have come through any clearer. Robidoux needed to speak in code, and he did it well. Losing Rikard's help was Ben's belated punishment for dodging Peraza, a reminder that the road could be pulled from beneath him at any time. Robidoux must have learned only recently about the missed appointment. It was no surprise that Peraza's access to the outside world was limited. The French authorities would use whatever means necessary to wring information out of him. Some people might not be anxious to crack down on drugs, but the French government sure was.

"HEW is a perfect race for you, Rikard. I want you to win it. You're not going to be useful in the Pyrenees anyway. You've already fulfilled your role in this race."

"That's not true. I can still help out for at least a couple more days."

"Must I spell it out?" Robidoux's voice sounded more like a growl. "The mountains aren't going to do your legs any good. In fact, you've just

convinced me to pull Philippe as well. This isn't a request. It's an order!"
Rikard snarled. "*D'accord*. Okay, okay, I've got it!"

"*Bon*. I'll see you in Hamburg. *Au revoir*." A dial tone sounded.

A pit had opened in Ben's stomach. Why would Robidoux hobble his own team when things were going so well? He must have figured he could make a point by stealing men who were going to drop out anyway. He probably hadn't known of Rikard's commitment. He'd been surprised to learn that Rikard didn't want to go, but by then it was too late. The owner wasn't in the habit of allowing underlings to change his mind, so he got angry and took Philippe as well.

Philippe looked at Ben. "I wish this hadn't happened. You've earned my respect. *Bonne chance*."

Rikard spoke through gritted teeth. "We're not leaving without a hammer fest. Let's see how your rivals like this."

The two men accelerated and Ben eased in behind them. The pace got hot, but he rolled along, numb and flabbergasted. It felt like he'd been told his left arm was about to be amputated and they were taking his right foot as well, just for kicks. He kept waiting to hear something over the radio. He wished Thierry would say that the misunderstanding with Robidoux had been cleared up. But nothing ever came.

Thierry had predicted in their morning planning session that the first summit, the Col de Jau, would prove uneventful. He was wrong, but only because of the determination of his own team. Rikard and Philippe hadn't quit pulling the peloton once they reached the hills.

"If I have to lose you two today, I'm glad you're inflicting all the damage you can beforehand," Thierry said over the radio.

The stage had started near sea level. They'd spent most of the day skirting the foothills of mountains to their right. Benign clouds gathered overhead. Forty-one kilometers into the stage they went through Prades at 325 meters in elevation. Five kilometers later the serious climbing started. Sparkling granite retaining walls held the road to the hillside. They rounded a corner to meet a stunning view of the Grand Hotel Thermal, set in a mountain notch between a waterfall and an enormous arched bridge. Wide strips of rough granite cobbles accented the road. But Rikard didn't slow to take any of it in.

In another eight kilometers at 675 meters above sea level they reached Mosset. The village lay draped over a fertile ridgeline, like a care-worn blanket tossed onto the arm of a favorite chair. Once the cyclists passed the town's church spire, the road bent even more sharply toward the heavens. Rikard and Philippe kept forcing a pace that had climbing specialists gasping for breath.

The clouds seemed propped atop the pine trees. Beside the road, fresh-shorn sheep wearing numbers on their flanks, just like the athletes, looked up from munching sweet ferns. A course official in motorcycle leathers knelt beside the great white Pyreneean sheep dog that guarded the flock. The man's right arm was looped firmly around the animal's neck. With his left hand he offered the dog a distracting patty of ground beef. These officials were responsible for keeping the event racing across the French countryside, and they would go to whatever lengths necessary to clear the inevitable obstructions.

The big hound blew out three plaintive woofs as the cyclists passed. The road snaked back and forth up the slope. Eventually the riders reached the level of the fog. It rolled over the men in pillow-like waves. Soon, everybody was drenched. The pace had remained hot when suddenly Rikard and Philippe both pulled to the side of the road and dismounted. The peloton passed them, curious and confused.

Without its tandem of crazed engineers, the group slowed, allowing four cyclists to escape. Ben imagined his two teammates, suffering the indignity of having their jersey numbers removed while photographers snapped shots. The farther a man rode in the Tour de France, the more he valued the accomplishment of crossing the finish line with his race bib intact. Such intense emotion flowed upon abandonment of the race that cyclists frequently cried as they climbed into the broom wagon. In their exhausted state, they rarely had the strength to deal with this ceremony that seemed to celebrate their failure.

A minute later the radio crackled. Ben pricked up his ears, still hopeful the dilemma had been solved.

"Scratch bib number 2, Rikard," Thierry said. "Scratch bib number 5, Philippe." Then there was silence.

With the loss of these two men, 154 remained in the race. Ben had five teammates left. He hoped they wouldn't need to chase anybody down across the flats because none of his remaining comrades had the horsepower Rikard and Philippe could provide.

The summit came almost by surprise, its location evident only by increasing numbers of fans. The cyclists crested the mountain and poured onto the downhill slope. Ben strained to make out the route through the fog as the road swayed this way and that beneath towering pines. On the downhill side of a rock archway they finally found clear air.

Colorful flowers overflowed their pots on the walls of Ste. Colombe. Below the town, smokehouse fumes teased Ben's nose. Soon afterward the road dropped into the tight Gorges de St. Georges and then entered the even more spectacular Aude River Gorge. In places, thousands of tons of rock overhung their heads. A cool breeze rose off the rapids as they followed the water into town.

After the feed zone came a forty-five kilometer climb. This long, gradual hill was categorized by the race organizers as three lesser-category ascents connected by two hanging valleys. Within them, succulent flowers and sweet crops pleased the nose as well as the eyes. Long-maned ponies frolicked in the sun.

Two-and-a-half minutes behind the breakaway, now only three cyclists strong, Ben entered the fog again. They must be nearing the 1431-meter summit of the Col du Chioula. He rode past a long, black limousine. Ben could swear he'd seen this car before. He'd become accustomed to encountering many of the same fans day after day, but none of the people in the immediate area looked like the type that would own a car like that.

"Ben!"

He looked to the other side of the street. Toma's dark eyes glowed as he sprinted beside the cyclists, fist extended thumb up. He was dressed in the Banque Fédérale kit Ben had given him, complete with jersey and shorts, plus matching socks, gloves, and cap.

As the strength in Toma's legs gave out he yelled, "Fifty-three minutes!" That must have been his time climbing the slope the peloton was about to descend.

Ben looked over his shoulder. "You're my hero!"

The boy's beaming expression warmed Ben's heart. He had to gain more time somewhere to retake the yellow jersey, and now he felt a surge of energy he may as well exploit. With the available road diminishing, testing the competition was worth a shot. He worked his way to the front, and then accelerated.

The fog sat so thick that the top of the climb appeared from nowhere. He charged across the flat, thankful for the tall elms and firs that lent dimension to the whiteness. Then the bottom dropped out. Ben winged through the plummeting descent, taking big risks on the sharp hairpins and charging with his full strength whenever the route straightened. He judged how hard he'd need to brake in the turns by watching the red taillight on the cameraman's motorcycle ahead of him.

Soon he dropped below the cloud deck.

"Good move, Ben," Thierry said over the radio. "Let's see who has the *cojones* to take risks alongside you."

For two kilometers Ben lay into the pedals, hoping he was inflicting damage. On a descent like this every sense had to be on high alert. Disaster lurked around every corner.

When the road straightened, Ben slowed and let Albert pull even. Ben set a hand on his teammate's shoulder for guidance so he could look back and study the faces of the riders who had followed. It took a lot of trust in a man's skill and his intentions to attempt this maneuver. Ben trusted Albert completely.

Gunter and a dozen other men, including two domestiques each from Banque Fédérale and Duetscher Aufbau, were on his wheel. One cyclist from Megatronics joined in, but Kyle had missed the move. Whether he'd made a tactical error or had lacked the strength to follow didn't matter for the moment. Ben's experimental acceleration had suddenly become meaningful.

The other cyclists would also be surveying the group's composition. As they charged forward, their reactions didn't surprise Ben. With a major competitor left behind, the atmosphere became urgent. Both Ben and Gunter had a big stake in distancing themselves from Kyle. No words needed to be spoken to form an alliance. The six Aufbau and Fédérale riders went to the front and pulled furiously. The Megatronics man made several attempts at interference, but the group strength overwhelmed him and soon he gave up. He drifted to the back of the line to strategize over the radio.

Ben followed Albert in the draft. His first lieutenant breezed down the hill, risking everything on the rapid switchbacks and pedaling full speed in his highest gear whenever there was the slightest opportunity to lend momentum through leg power. On a long straightaway Ben flew past, bringing the following train with him. The bunch dove through more turns and undulations. On the opposite side of the valley to their right, Ben could see the day's final climb. Fans packed the steep hillside.

"Kyle's group is half a minute back," Thierry said.

"Thirty second gap!" Ben yelled. He wanted to make sure the men on the other teams were aware of the good news. The measure of success reenergized the breakaway. This move just might stick, and everybody knew it.

Gunter charged ahead, obviously aware that if he kept Kyle at bay while matching Ben he'd wear yellow tomorrow. The road hit the valley, and then rebounded onto the Bonascre. Men shed their helmets, anxious for every advantage the cooling air could deliver. Gunter and his teammates took the lead, content to ride a high tempo but take everyone along with them for the time being. They passed the three breakaway cyclists as if they were standing still. Now this group was first on the road.

"How badly do you want this?" Thierry asked over the headset.

"Badly."

"Leaving Kyle behind isn't enough. You've got to put time into Gunter as well."

Chapter Twenty-Four

Laurent Robidoux listened to the fans chattering outside the partially open limousine window. He enjoyed mingling with them like this from time to time. His car sat near the summit of the Col du Chioula, and the leading cyclists had just passed.

The conversations outside his window amused him. Most of the opinions he overheard were ridiculous, but the words made him smile. One young boy, dressed head to toe in Banque Fédérale gear, went on and on as if Benjamin Barnes was a deity. Apparently they'd met.

"Do you hear that?" Robidoux asked his valet. "Benjamin's fan base is exploding. It's due to our efforts. He should show proper gratitude."

The valet nodded. "He's been impressive. That young woman you hired, Bridgette, is obviously quite skilled."

"Why do you say that?"

The valet pointed at the television. "Ben has played a dominant role in the last two stages, and look at him now."

Robidoux looked at the screen. Benjamin was drilling it, leading what just might be the decisive break. Kyle had fallen behind, and didn't seem to have the strength to catch back up. "Benjamin is strong, isn't he?"

"Unnaturally so."

Robidoux studied his cyclist more closely. Benjamin looked good. "But Frodie swears that Bridgette hasn't been with the team."

"Who can blame her for trying to stay hidden?"

Benjamin had turned in three spectacular performances in a row. His form had improved dramatically since the disastrous twelfth stage. Robidoux snipped off the end of a cigar and set it between his teeth. The valet extended a flame and Robidoux inhaled, building the ember to a satisfying glow.

There was reason for hope. Benjamin appeared determined. If he was using performance enhancers, that indicated strengthened commitment. Still, Robidoux wanted proof that drugs were in use for two reasons. First, they improved his man's prospects of winning. Second, and more important, if Robidoux held evidence that doping had occurred, it increased the chance that Benjamin would behave as instructed in the future.

Robidoux felt proud of his instincts. It appeared that Bridgette had come through. What a piece of luck, considering the nightmare surrounding Peraza. She'd probably taken a good look at the documents she'd signed and realized that attending to Benjamin's needs was in both their best interest. He congratulated himself for devising a way to get the message across.

Looking at the ceiling, he blew a perfect smoke ring. He'd spent the last two days pulling strings, trying to get word from Doctor Peraza. When he finally did he learned that Monsieur Barnes hadn't been available for his appointment. "My temper got the best of me earlier."

"Understandably," said the valet. "How were you to know he'd taken matters into his own hands? Even an easygoing man would have snapped."

"*Oui*, and I am not an easygoing man. The race looked lost." Robidoux held his index finger and thumb a fraction of a millimeter apart. "I was a hair's breadth away from gutting the whole team. I'm still not sure what to make of Ben. I waver over whether or not he's the right sort of man to build a team around."

"The answer ought to become clear soon enough." The valet handed Robidoux a vodka on the rocks. "Your decisions so far have been justified. The men you pulled aren't the sort who can finish this event. If anything, you earned extra publicity for the way you handled it this time. It was brilliant."

Robidoux tapped the ash from his cigar. At times the valet seemed to read his mind better than he could read it himself. Had it been he or his valet who figured out what Benjamin was up to? After a moment of contemplation he realized it hardly mattered, because the valet's ideas belonged to him as well.

"Phone the Residence Armazan and tell them we'll be arriving a day early," Robidoux said.

"You want to check in tonight?" the valet asked. "You hate that place."

"*Oui*. Whose idea was it to blow that awful textured treatment onto all the walls and ceilings? It reminds me of dried cottage cheese. I hate everything built in the 60's, and I especially despise hotels without a concierge. But the Armazan is the place to stay if you want to watch a Tour de France stage ending at Pla d'Adet for three critical reasons. Location, location, and location. Now, do as I say."

The valet shrugged, and then instructed the driver over the intercom. Next, he picked up the phone and dialed. After the broom wagon passed, carrying a couple of wasted cyclists and in close pursuit of a couple more, the limousine merged into traffic and headed up the hill.

Even though it was just a two-star establishment, Robidoux didn't really mind the pair of apartments he had on the top floor. The balcony of one commanded the ultimate view of the last several kilometers of the climb. From the deck of the other room, across the hall, he could look straight down on the finish area.

Whenever the Banque Fédérale team visited Pla d'Adet they were lodged one floor below him. Tomorrow night Robidoux's men would be where he preferred them. Right beneath his nose.

The valet, phone to his ear, looked up. Robidoux stared into his eyes. Did they hold a hint of panic? The valet looked away.

Robidoux turned his attention back to the television screen. Benjamin was now on his own in the lead, pounding his way up the Plateau de Bonsacre. He just might win.

"Everything has been arranged," the valet said.

"*Bon.*"

"The manager looks forward to hosting you again."

"Of course he does."

"He mentioned that the atmosphere in town is incredible. There are more people camped on the mountainside than he's ever seen before."

"I'm not interested in what a bunch of freeloaders are up to." Robidoux glared into the valet's eyes. "Now, quit your delaying tactics and tell me what he said that upset you?"

The valet looked down, swallowing hard. "Right now, Bridgette LeBlanc is watching the bicycle race from that pizzeria next door to his hotel."

Strange. She ought to be more than 200 kilometers from there right now, atop Plateau de Bonascre where today's stage would end. "He was certain?"

The valet nodded.

"Call back and ask him to delay her until we arrive. We'll need a few hours," Robidoux said.

The valet bowed slightly. "Already done. She's with another woman. Once the race broadcast ends, an hour or so from now, the restaurant's proprietor will offer her and her companion dinner. The wait staff will take their time getting it to the table."

"Excellent," Robidoux said. "She should remain unaware that I'm on my way."

"But, of course."

Chapter Twenty-Five

These intense moments, where the race moved full bore and decisions must be made with lightning rapidity, intoxicated Ben. He felt powerful as his breakaway group drove their way up the Plateau de Bonascre.

"You must drop Gunter, too," Thierry reminded him over the headset. "He leads you by a minute nineteen in the General Classification, just four seconds less than Kyle."

Albert nodded. Ben nodded back. The Frenchman threw it into overdrive, blasting the Germans and everyone else off his back wheel. Ben hit redline in the effort to keep up. It nearly brought tears to his eyes to see Albert sacrifice so much for him.

From time to time Albert glanced under his arm. Ben wished he could have smiled or thanked his lieutenant, but he couldn't afford the energy. He peeked beneath his own armpit. No sign of the chasers.

"The gap to Gunter is eleven seconds," Thierry said.

Ben had expected much more. He looked around the opposite side of his body. Gunter and two other men approached. The cyclists passed beneath the four-kilometer banner.

"Where's the beef?" Fritz said.

Ben summoned everything and willed his bike to move faster. He passed Albert. In that same moment he sensed the Frenchman turning off the afterburner. No point spending fuel chasing down his team leader. As Ben crossed under the three-kilometer marker, cheers rained down like molten lava, the din giving voice to his tortured muscles.

Ben strained to make out the time gaps. "… Kyle is forty-three seconds back …" He couldn't process it completely, but knew the news was good. He caught a bit more of Thierry's message. "… six seconds to Gunter …"

How could that be?

Ben looked back. The German was alone, devouring the road like a runaway rototiller. Now the crowd's pandemonium made even more sense. Gunter was strong today. Ben reassessed the situation.

The two of them could do more damage to Kyle together than either on his own. Ben wasn't going to shake Gunter on the remainder of this hill, anyway. The German had him pegged. Gunter had been cooperative back on stage eleven. Now was the time to pay him back.

Ben slowed slightly, permitting Gunter to cross the gap. "Truce?"

"*Ja.*"

Ben wound up his cadence. He pulled for five hundred meters. Then he moved aside and let Gunter come through. Holding the German's wheel tested him, but it was easier than leading. When the speed lagged Ben came by for another pull. Gunter led out for the second time just as the finish line came into view. Then the Deutscher Aufbau rider stomped on his pedals and pulled away.

Hadn't they made an agreement? Ben watched in frustration as, ten meters ahead, Gunter raised his arms in victory. Ben crossed the line, fuming.

Gunter's bike stopped quickly because of the uphill finish.

Ben pulled beside him. "What the hell?" He'd been robbed of a time bonus and several seconds finishing margin.

Gunter's forehead creased, obviously confused.

"I slowed for you. I did most of the pulling," Ben said.

"Someone has to win. If you're so strong, why didn't you beat us?"

"And give time back to Kyle by slowing to position for a sprint?"

Gunter shrugged. "Kyle might be your only focus. He's not ours. We need to beat both of you."

Media surrounded Gunter and the two separated. As Ben's pulse slowed he realized he'd been too focused on Kyle. With the finish line in reach, all agreements were out the window. Alliances can only exist so far. Spending so much time in the grupetto, crossing the line with the other domestiques well after the stage was decided, had eroded his competitive instinct.

Ben looked down the road. Other cyclists trickled across, Albert among them. Where was Kyle?

Just then he came into view. He crossed the line in sixth place, forty-nine seconds back of Gunter. His face revealed pure misery. Not a good day for the yellow jersey wearer. Kyle's discomfort strengthened Ben. His posture improved, and so did his outlook. Performance enhancing drugs might be enough to elevate Kyle's game on some days, but Ben still had what it took to beat his rival when it mattered.

"What a treacherous hit you took today."

Ben turned to see Thierry. "Why do you say that?"

Thierry handed him a paper. "Do you need to see my calculations to understand what happened to the General Classification?"

Ben looked at a page containing a series of equations in Thierry's neat handwriting. At the bottom was a list of names and times. Ben was still in third, behind Gunter and Kyle. His deficit was a whopping one-minute-and-twenty-nine seconds. Despite his great performance, he stood six seconds deeper in the hole than when the day started. It was small consolation that Kyle led him by just twenty-four seconds.

"The finishing bonus killed you. Gunter stole eight seconds right there. Add that to the two-second gap he opened in the closing meters and you have a ten-second swing," Thierry said. "I warned you. You needed to beat him."

Ben ached with anger. Focusing on Kyle wouldn't be enough. He'd allowed himself to be used as another man's stepping stone. Watching Gunter interact with the media, for the first time he zeroed in on the threat the German presented. This anger would do him good. They'd finished together twice, and Gunter had won both times. Ben shouldn't have let that happen. If he meant to earn the maillot jaune, he needed to wrestle it from Gunter's grasp as well as Kyle's.

Chapter Twenty-Six

Two and a half hours after his valet had accidentally discovered Bridgette's location, Robidoux eased his way down the narrow staircase leading into the Top Ski Pizzaria. Rock music assaulted his ears. The dark siding made the place seem cramped. Vintage alpine gear hung on the walls. Though Robidoux disliked dingy places, particularly ones that housed video games, this dark room served him well. He soon spotted Bridgette and a blonde sitting at a corner table. He caught a glimpse of her left hand. No ring.

She glanced his way, then did a double take. "Monsieur Robidoux? What are you ... What a surprise."

"I'm sure it is." He walked over and looked at the blonde. "Will you excuse us?"

Bridgette nodded to her friend, cautiously.

The blonde stood, dragging her hand along Bridgette's arm as she walked away.

"Shouldn't you be somewhere else right now, my little flower?"

Bridgette shook her head. "I can't give Ben the good stuff if I don't have it."

"You've given up?"

"*Non*. But I might have to if you make a habit of chasing my suppliers away."

Robidoux turned to look for the blonde. He couldn't see her.

"You may as well sit. You've chased her away for now," Bridgette said.

Puffing on his cigar, he dropped into the vacant chair. "So, are you telling me that Ben has finally decided to take his game to the next level?"

"I wouldn't put it that way."

He felt his brow crease.

Bridgette leaned close. "I've decided to take it there for him."

Could this be? He tapped his ash into a tray, buying time. On reflection, her strategy made sense. It wasn't the route he'd prefer, though. Without proof Ben meant to dope, Robidoux wouldn't gain the leverage he sought. He could end up with an uncontrollable superstar on his hands. "You ought to tell him what you're doing."

"Are you kidding? I tried that, and he almost kicked me out."

"Did he take your ring back?"

She nodded.

He didn't like the way this was unfolding. Too much felt out of his control. It couldn't hurt to remind her that his blackmail card was still in play. "Have you read your paperwork, beautiful Bridgette?"

She hesitated. "*Non.* I wasn't going to ask you to pay me. I didn't even keep my copy of the contract. I'm doing this purely for Ben."

She'd thrown her copy of the document away? It boggled the mind how freely people signed agreements. Their carelessness was often his gain. "That wasn't just a contract you threw away, my little flower. You should have read the signature page."

She shrugged. "What was it?"

"An admission of guilt for the DuPonte affair, of course. Having such papers at my fingertips simplifies things if I'm forced to increase the pressure."

"You wouldn't!"

Robidoux spread his palms. "I'm a reasonable man. I won't share your secret unless you force me to. Tell Ben what you're up to, and give me proof."

"If I put him in that corner, he'll pull out and we'll all lose. I won't risk it. He's worked too hard for this victory."

"Not hard enough. Remember, he hasn't won yet," Robidoux said. "He's not even in the lead."

Bridgette looked thoughtful as she considered his words. "I think the time has come for me to leave Ben's side. I ought to admit publicly to what I've done and accept the consequences."

He puffed on his cigar. "I'd advise you not to make that decision as hastily as you signed our contract. Think about it. What's going to happen to Benjamin if your secrets are exposed now? I can guarantee such a story would run directly beneath that famous photo of you two kissing at the Alpe d'Huez finish line."

She narrowed her gaze.

"That's right. You see, I'm very pleased that Benjamin has been strong for a few stages, but I want assurances that he'll stay that way. And frankly, I also need proof that he's willing to do as I ask. I've invested a lot in him. I can't keep opening my wallet if I don't know where his heart lies. I'm sure you can explain that to him."

Bridgette shivered. "Give me until the end of the race. You've ridden it yourself. You've got to recognize that messing with his head before it's over could backfire, big time."

How had this gotten so complicated? He longed for the good old days. He clenched his teeth. "All right, Bridgette. I'll give you some more time, but not until the end of the race. Don't test my patience. If Ben doesn't produce results, both of you are going to be very sorry."

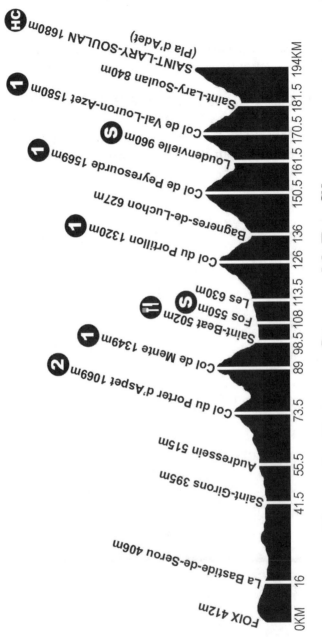

Tour de France Stage 16 Profile

FOIX 412m

La Bastide-de-Serou 406m

Saint-Girons 395m

Audressein 515m

Col du Portet d'Aspet 1069m (2)

Col de Menté 1349m (1)

Saint-Béat 502m

Fos 550m (S)

Les 630m

Col du Portillon 1320m (1)

Bagnères-de-Luchon 627m

Col de Peyresourde 1569m (1)

Loudenvielle 960m (S)

Col de Val-Louron-Azet 1580m (1)

Saint-Lary-Soulan 840m

SAINT-LARY-SOULAN 1680m (HC) (Pla d'Adet)

0KM   16   41.5   55.5   73.5   89   98.5 108 113.5   126   136   150.5   161.5 170.5 181.5   194KM

Chapter Twenty-Seven

Ben tried to relax at a café near the starting line in Foix. Looking down the street, he spotted Frodie headed in his direction. He lifted the menu in front of his face, but the Austrian came to his table anyway.

"You don't need to hide from me. I know what you're up to."

Ben looked at him. "You do?"

Frodie nodded. "I bumped into Bridgette rushing out of the hotel this morning. Nice rock on her finger, by the way."

"What are you talking about? I haven't seen Bridgette in days."

"Oh really? She was carrying a cooler and when I asked what was in it she said, 'It's between Ben and me.'"

"You've spent too much time over a hot stove."

The Austrian chuckled. "If that's how you want to spin things I'm okay with it. You don't need to hide anything from me. I support how your strategy."

"Whatever," Ben said. "I've got to go." He handed the waitress a couple of euro, and headed to the start line.

A three-turreted medieval castle dominated the view from the staging area. The cold, grey edifice sat atop a high knoll in the center of the village. Stage sixteen began in this town's main square beside an enormous red, wrought-iron pavilion. The cyclists would soon spill onto the high-speed roads of the countryside. It would be a monumentally difficult route, the toughest of the three Pyrenean days.

The weather was ideal. A cold front had swept through overnight. Today's high would be fifteen degrees Fahrenheit below seasonal averages. The starter's pistol went off, and the peloton began to roll.

The route began with sixty kilometers of undulating terrain. Land like this didn't look so tough on the profile, but the endless rolling hills were murder. To make things worse, the attacks came relentlessly. Ben wished Rikard and Philippe were available to help control the pack. Instead, he was at the mercy of the battle raging around him. Ultimately one of Kyle's key assistants broke free with a group of four others. As soon as they were out of sight the fire left the peloton's belly.

Ben didn't like seeing these guys build an advantage, but without its strongest flatlanders, Banque Fédérale didn't have the manpower to manage the peloton over this sort of terrain. No point worrying about it. Instead, he'd keep his eye on Kyle. It looked like Megatronics planned to shake things up today. That man up the road gave them some dangerous options.

The cyclists screamed down one of the wickedest descents in all of cycling, the winding seventeen percent plummet off the Col du Portet d' Aspet. Ben heaved a sigh of relief when he reached the bottom.

Approaching the Col de Mente summit the motorcyclist carrying the time-gap chalkboard informed them the breakaway had built a five-minute gap, but since all the elite climbers remained in the main pack, nobody panicked. Thousands of fans screamed from above where the views of the sinuous climb and the rugged peaks beyond must be spectacular. In a steep field beside the road a herd of agitated cows searched for peace, their big neck bells clanging like aluminum garbage can lids.

Ben crested the hill, realizing how cold it was only when he noticed people huddled around a bonfire. A fan handed him a newspaper and he tucked it beneath his shirt for insulation on another rapid descent. Four big ascents remained, culminating on the out-of-category Pla d'Adet, the second consecutive uphill finish.

The peloton thinned as the road crossed into Spain, lining up for the Col du Portillon. Orange-clad Basques made up a huge portion of the crowd. These people, who considered their homeland independent from Spain, supported cycling in droves. They qualified as the most bicycle-crazed culture on earth, at least where climbing was concerned.

Eventually the riders entered the clouds, just like the previous day. Toma was near the summit. He ran with the cyclists the same as before. "Go Ben, go!"

Emotion, which is suffering, Ben thought to himself, *ceases to be suffering as soon as we form a clear and precise picture of it*. All too soon, he left Toma behind.

The gap to the lead group had fallen by a minute as they crested the hill and returned to France. Still no move by Kyle. Deutscher Aufbau controlled the pace and seemed content for the breakaway to remain out front. Were they forgetting about Kyle's teammate who'd gone with it?

This had the markings of trouble as clearly as if it was painted on the road beside the athlete's names.

The group surrounding the yellow jersey became more elite as they shed pretenders off the back on the slopes of the Col de Peyresourde. Ben looked behind himself to assess the damage before he re-entered the fog. Cyclists were scattered all the way down the slope. Waves of moisture enveloped him. On the grassy incline above, thousands of gauzy cobwebs sagged under heavy loads of dew. By the time the cyclists reached the pass fewer than two dozen men remained, and every one of them knew the big horsepower was yet to be unleashed.

They raced down the backside of the hill, blitzing through a speck of a town called Germ, too fast to focus. Frightening corners came one after another. A slight error might send a cyclist airborne off the unprotected shoulder of the road. Ben's grip relaxed as he neared Loudenveille in the valley bottom. On the opposite shore of a shimmering reservoir he caught sight of the leaders. Ben's group shredded a path around the water's perimeter, then charged toward the foothills of the Col de Val-Louron-Azet. As they neared, something changed. Like impala approaching a watering hole, the atmosphere became hesitant. Instinct screamed that attack was unavoidable. Who would the victims be this time?

Thierry came over the radio. "Kyle's man just dropped from the lead pack. Watch out."

No sooner had the words been spoken than Kyle sprang from the front, rapidly distancing himself from the pack. Ben looked to Gunter. The German didn't respond, apparently content to be surrounded by his team and confident they could bring things back together when necessary.

Ben's gut said they couldn't. Kyle had picked the right moment, and now Ben must counter. He stomped on his pedals, pushing big chunks of the mountain behind him with each revolution. For the moment he had more spring, and in a short time he'd gained his rival's wheel. It felt empowering to match Kyle's strength while playing within the rules. Drugs might be capable of increasing performance, but they couldn't substitute for heart.

Somehow, despite the massive stress, Ben felt at peace. He thought through strategy as they climbed. It would be foolish to leave Kyle behind at this point because, within a few kilometers, they'd come upon his teammate. Kyle obviously planned to let his domestique work while he caught his breath. If Ben stayed with Kyle, Megatronics would be forced either to abandon the attack, or to let Ben take advantage of the second Megatronics man as well. Gunter probably didn't think that the former teammates could get along well enough to cooperate against him, but if Ben did his fair share of the work it was unlikely that Kyle would abandon his advantage over Gunter. Today, Ben's perfect ally was the man he liked least.

The unlikely cohorts exchanged a conspiratorial grin as Ben pulled into the lead. While they worked their way up the slope, he recalled training rides with Kyle back when they were teammates. For the first few months, he'd liked the guy. As long as Kyle was working too hard to speak, Ben could pretend they were friends testing one another's resolve on a training ride.

Kyle did his share of the pace setting and appeared comfortable with the relationship as well. Three kilometers from the summit, they reached Kyle's domestique. The man set a brisk tempo, staying in the lead position for over two kilometers. Once he was spent, Kyle and Ben rotated with him so that all three men could remain together on the descent. They blasted over the top of the mountain, sending the crowd into a frenzy.

The trio had once been teammates, and they cruised down the slopes in practiced perfection, careening around corners and sprinting on even the shortest of straightaways.

The route dipped into Saint Lary-Soulan. Then it rebounded up the final climb of the day—the monstrous Pla d'Adet. Kyle's domestique again took the lead. Before the first switchback, they could see the straggler from the now fractured breakaway. The pace increased with this man in their sights. They closed the gap more quickly than Ben would have liked. He enjoyed having someone ahead to chase down. The trio sprinted past the beaten cyclist, and then slowed a little. Three more breakaway riders were still somewhere up the road.

The Megatronics domestique dropped into second position instead of falling behind Ben in normal rotation. The move set Ben's nerves on edge. Had their directeur instructed him to interfere while Kyle made a break up the road?

Ben drifted wide. Kyle took off. Ben knew he could catch up. Instinct told him to follow the domestique's wheel a moment longer. If he bridged the gap immediately, Kyle would shut down the attack to let the domestique catch back on. It would still be two men against one. Besides, if he let Kyle think his plan had worked, it might be more demoralizing when Ben caught up.

A motorcycle chalkboard informed them of the gaps. Gunter rode fifty-two seconds behind Ben. The last fragments of the breakaway were forty-five seconds ahead. Kyle was five seconds up the road. The domestique had set up camp on Ben's wheel, preparing to counter whatever move might come next.

Let's see if he was prepared for this, Ben thought. He shifted to a higher gear, stood for extra leverage, and drove through each full pedal revolution. He flexed his ankle at the bottom of his stroke, as if running on tiptoes, contracting his muscles on every uptake. His cleats allowed him to drive power into the pedals for the entire 360 degrees. Charging, straining, gasping, reaching, capturing. In thirty seconds of all-out aerobic effort Ben dropped into his saddle and quit pedaling. His momentum brought him abreast of his nemesis.

Kyle looked confused. Ben had glided right past him, uphill. But then Kyle collected himself and attacked with renewed vigor. Ben settled in and glanced over his shoulder. The domestique was no longer in sight. Good.

Kyle pushed very hard, and Ben wondered if he'd closed the gap too fast. His lungs, heart, and legs were molten. But he had to hang on to his foe's wheel until Kyle realized escape was impossible. Win the mind game, and you win the race.

He kept pace, despite the pain. Finally, Kyle's chain climbed three rings higher on the rear cassette. Relieved, Ben switched to a matching cog. The resistance decreased by a third.

Kyle looked back. Ben returned a poker face, hiding his discomfort, attempting to look as if the change in effort made no difference to him.

Two more breakaway cyclists came into view on the road ahead.

"Besides that pair, there's one more thirty-five seconds beyond," Thierry said over the radio. "Three and a half kilometers to go. He may be uncatchable."

Ben couldn't worry about that for now. It was more important to beat Kyle than to stand on the winner's podium today. He enjoyed seeing his rival so concerned about their relative strength.

With athletes uphill serving as carrots, Kyle's pace ratcheted higher again. He couldn't seem to control his need to dominate other men, even when it wasn't in his best interests. Seeing cyclists up the road somehow triggered a Pavlovian response.

Ben didn't mind. He let Kyle to do the hard work of pacing the climb while conserving his own energy for a more critical moment.

A kilometer and a half later they captured the two trailing men. Kyle and Ben continued up the road. Still thirty seconds to the leader, and only two kilometers left.

Ben thought about the importance of beating Kyle in the overall. Time to stuff the doper.

"Think you can win?" Ben asked.

Kyle nodded.

"Then catch me." With that he repeated his efforts from the lower slopes, only this time conserving more oxygen.

"*Allez! Allez! Allez!*" Thierry yelled from the car behind.

"Go Ben, go!" Coach pleaded over the headset.

Thirty seconds up the slope he settled onto his saddle, but he didn't look back to gauge Kyle's reaction. He kept his cadence as high as he could, waiting for time gap info to come over his headset.

"Five seconds back to Kyle. Twenty-one forward to the leader. Dig deeper."

"Put a Tiger in your tank!" Fritz said.

Hardly a kilometer left. The remaining road represented not pain, but opportunity. He should cross the line without regret.

He stood on his pedals, defeating the slope. With each revolution more young athletes rode on his back. With each new passenger the burden became more bearable, more important, and more urgent.

"Eight seconds to Kyle. Fourteen seconds to the lead. Half a kilometer to go," Thierry reported.

Hold nothing back. The finish line meant recovery. He drove with all his might.

Ahead he saw the leader. Visual contact energized him. He rose again and pushed even harder. His quarry passed the two-hundred kilometer marker.

"Twenty second bonus for the winner," Thierry said.

Ben gave everything he had. At the hundred-meter line his hamstring seized. He grimaced, losing momentum. He forced the leg forward but the tendon contracted even tighter. He couldn't stop pedaling, though, even though his normal position would no longer work. He rowed with his head low, rocking the bike from side to side, leveraging his upper body over the stem, knees wide like a frog. He hauled himself toward the line, but the gap to the leader grew.

"Kyle can still catch you!"

Coach's words hit like a two by four. Ben hung his head even farther, looking beneath his body. Here came his rival, charging like a Pamplona bull.

Ben rose from his seat again. With each painful revolution, the finish banner neared, but three meters before he reached the line, Kyle blew past on the left-hand side.

Chapter Twenty-Eight

Ben fell forward onto his handlebars as he gained the finish line, third place on the day. His front wheel broke the plane before Kyle's rear wheel cleared the line, so he'd be awarded the same time. Still, he'd failed to damage his rival's confidence. In fact, the opposite had happened. He'd given everything he had, but his body had betrayed him at the end. Kyle must have seen it in Ben's body language. The result was more than the minor loss. It was even more than the handful of bonus seconds at the line. The real damage was Kyle's mental boost.

Unlike yesterday, Ben didn't go near his competitor as he waited for others to finish. Gunter's placement was all that interested him. How much time had he gained on the German?

Forty-one seconds after Ben's finish he had his answer. Moments later, Thierry handed Ben his handwritten calculation. When bonuses were computed Gunter still held the overall lead, but by only twelve seconds over Kyle. Ben had made up lots of ground too, now forty seconds back of the leader, but the effort had the feel of failure. He should have been within a half minute at this point.

He glanced to his right and noticed Bridgette standing near the media tent. Where had she come from? Her auburn hair blew in the breeze. He took an almost involuntary step toward her before remembering that she couldn't be trusted. Was Frodie's claim that she'd been hanging around the team true, after all? What was she up to now?

She was speaking with reporters, including the man from *au Fond* and the ever-present Simone Sardou. He stopped and watched. Why were the microphones in Bridgette's face?

A strong hand gripped Ben's left shoulder and pulled him back. Keeping his balance on his weakened leg forced him to turn away from Bridgette. "You made me very proud today," Thierry said.

Ben looked at his mentor. "I didn't have any more to give."

Thierry shook his head. "Don't dwell on it. I learned as much in my most recent race as in my first. Cycling has lots of moving parts. Every action changes the dynamics. Just make sure your experiences benefit you the next time. If you keep riding like this we'll be fine."

When Thierry walked away, Ben looked back toward the media. Bridgette was gone. Reporters headed toward him. Pushing Bridgette from his mind, he prepared to describe the day's racing to the journalists.

"Do you plan to withdraw from the race now that your fiancée has been exposed?"

Ben stared at the reporter. "What?"

"Now that Bridgette LeBlanc has admitted to administering dope."

"Bridgette never doped anybody."

A reporter gazed at him piteously. "That's not what she says."

Ben looked left and then right. Everybody was riveted by this bizarre line of questioning. In Simone Sardou's eyes he saw a shred of compassion, so he spoke to her. "Where is this story coming from?"

"It broke in the last hour. A signed admission showed up. Many of us assumed it was a forgery, but when we confronted her she came clean."

Ben's mind raced. What type of twisted game was he being reeled into now? "What did she admit to?"

Simone Sardou glanced at her notes. "She procured illegal performance-enhancing drugs and administered them to Christoff DuPonte in preparation for his Liege-Baston-Liege victory four years ago."

Could this be true? Until recently he would have thought it was impossible. Ben hadn't known Bridgette at that time, but they had met shortly afterwards. "Have you spoken to Christoff?"

"We asked him about it before we talked to her. He denied everything. Maybe his story will change now that she's confirmed things, but probably not."

Ben nodded, realizing his word wouldn't be given any more credence than Christoff's. If anything, there was greater reason not to believe him.

"So, has Bridgette administered drugs to you as well?"

He started to speak, but stopped himself. Of course she had administered drugs. The question's implication was *did she give him illegal drugs*, but saying 'no' would allow unscrupulous reporters to twist his answer into a lie. Would clarifying the question raise more suspicions? He didn't know what to say. Finally he whispered, "*Oui*. Bridgette gave me legal drugs. That was her job. Now, I won't discuss this further until I've had a chance to look at the facts."

"When will that be?" someone yelled.

Ben didn't answer. Why was Bridgette suddenly trying to destroy all they'd worked for? He walked away feeling heat on his back from the glaring eyes and flashing cameras. He reached the bus in a state of shock. If the claims were true, then Bridgette had been a doping specialist for years. He couldn't imagine how he'd misjudged her so drastically. Given this information, her act had been Oscar caliber. Even then, he'd been a buffoon to be duped so completely.

His extremities were numb as he climbed the stairs into the vehicle. Bridgette, her mascara streaked and her shoulders quivering, stepped toward him. He backed up.

"It's not how it sounds, Ben."

"Is that right?" His anger sharpened his words. "You just threw me under a train, Bridgette. I don't know if I could deal with this garbage under ordinary circumstances, let alone now. It's the worst possible time."

"I made it clear you haven't done anything."

Ben pulled off his jersey and tossed it onto the couch. "They didn't mention that, and I doubt they care. Let's see how innocent I look in tomorrow's headlines."

"Ben, please listen."

"Why? So you can mess things up even more?" He took her by the shoulders and moved her toward the door. "You know how hard I've worked to reach this point. You, of all people, should understand the consequences of what you've done. What would happen if I spent my energy defending myself while the race is still on?"

"You might lose."

"I probably would. So do I turn my attention to answering these accusations—losing the race in the process, or do I devote my strength to winning while getting fried in the court of public opinion? I can't believe you've forced me into this corner."

Tears rolled down her face. "You don't understand my side."

"I can't afford to try."

She shook her head. "Ben, listen! I lied to Robidoux to protect you, but it backfired when he investigated my old roommate and discovered she's not who I claimed."

"Bridgette, enough! I don't know what you're talking about, and I don't care. My teammates have given me everything they have. They deserve my full effort in return. The only way to deliver that is to get on with my preparation and forget about this nightmare."

Bridgette's face glistened behind a sheen of tears. "Please *Minet*, hear me out."

She seemed so genuine, so vulnerable, but trusting her is what had drawn him into this mess in the first place. He spoke softly. "No."

With a shattered expression, she removed the ring from her finger and handed it to him. "I guess you should have this."

He took it, and then watched her move down the stairs. "*Au revoir*, Bridgette." He closed the door, making sure it shut completely.

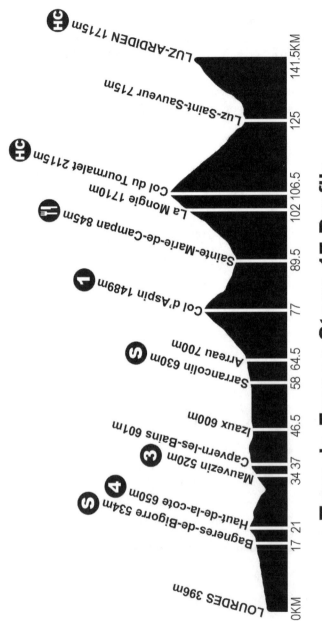

Tour de France Stage 17 Profile

Chapter Twenty-Nine

Stage seventeen began in the pilgrimage city of Lourdes. Its cathedral was the most impressive Ben had ever seen, an ornate masterpiece set in a wide-open space. The previous night he'd watched pilgrims circle the grounds singing "Ave Maria." Today the soaring spire pointed to the blackened belly of a boiling cloud. Ben couldn't believe he'd been forced to break out arm warmers for a July race in Southern France. The sleeves could be removed once the weather heated up.

He noticed an equally gloomy headline on a fan's newspaper: "Ben Barnes' Fiancée Admits to Doping Crimes." Talking to journalists was his job. Listening to them wasn't. He recalled advice often given by Coach: "Control your thoughts and you control your destiny." His mind ought to be on winning this race. That was the destiny he sought.

Luigi had done Ben one better, wearing leg warmers as well. "Are you preparing for a blizzard, *il mio amico?*"

"*Sì,*" said Luigi. "It's a possibility."

At the sound of a pistol, the race began. The cyclists headed off through the historic district, and then climbed a curving hill. It led to a bridge that crossed through the center of the same town, only this time four stories above the ground. It was startling proof of this village's unique location, deep in the bottom of a ravine.

The course continued with seventy kilometers of moderate road, but the route profile forewarned that seventy kilometers of Hell followed. The first of three monstrous climbs would be the category one Col d' Aspin.

On the approach, Gunter, Kyle, and Ben eyed each other like rival gang leaders staking out territory. Each group of teammates took on their respective leader's personality as they rallied around their squad's cause. Members of the other teams seemed anxious to do their own sorts of damage. Cool weather had invigorated everybody.

The cyclists charged up the mountainside as if starved for discomfort. Everyone wanted to be there when the first of the big guns went off. One by one, though, the pretenders were scattered about the hillside behind the main fight.

Thunder cracked just as the peloton crested the Col d'Aspin. The route led straight into the heart of the lightning strikes. Ahead, charcoal clouds darkened the countryside. Soon, the rain began to fall. Normally Ben would dread descending this ruthless road in the rain, but today his mind turned to strategy. Where did the advantages lie?

Rain soaked the cyclists. By now they all wore leg warmers, long-fingered gloves, shoe covers, rain jackets, and helmet covers. Even with the extra clothing, Ben shivered. He rode practically blind due to the spray coming off the wheels in front of him. The upcoming climbs would be welcome relief because the slower speeds would diminish the spray and reduce the wind, but the downhill slope would be hideous. Under such conditions virtually every other sporting event would have been canceled, but not so with cycling. The organizers of the Tour de France had no mercy.

Neither did the weather. As he watched the others struggle, Ben imagined Mother Nature had stepped in to break down his rivals. He smiled at the thought. Any help was appreciated.

They reached the bottom of the descent. Looking like sopping wet sponges, life-sized stuffed dolls were positioned to watch the race in Sainte-Marie-de-Campan. The town was famous for them. Meanwhile, the human spectators peered from beneath umbrellas and out of apartment windows. Once the peloton passed, they would watch the remainder of the race on televisions in homes and bars, excited to have experienced the conditions for themselves. If they only knew.

Ahead, the Tormalet rose far into the clouds. The group climbed, more slowly than usual. Thunder became more frequent. Then the droplets turned solid. Hail! Bouncing white ice balls as far as the eye could see resembled popping corn. The icy projectiles stung. Kyle had a broader back. He would be stinging more. Mother Nature was a devious ally.

As the men gained elevation the violence of the storm increased. A spectator carrying a shredded umbrella ran across the street in front of the peloton, searching for shelter. Other fans huddled inside and beneath vehicles. A few of them hurried to the roadside as the cyclists passed, laughing at the onslaught.

From time to time the road ducked beneath avalanche sheds, giving the men a moment to recover. The respites made it tough to head out and face the elements again.

Ben's earpiece hissed. Thierry spoke: "Five abandons so far today, none from any key teams. I guess they didn't have enough at stake to make it worth enduring the abuse. Just remember, one day you'll laugh."

Ben chuckled now. Kyle's dour expression made him happy.

"Only 140 men left in the race, and a lot fewer than that will make it to the end of this stage," Thierry said.

Ben trudged on, tilting his head forward so that the brow of his helmet protected his eyes from the diagonal assault. Keeping track of competitors was a chore. Their jersey numbers were invisible beneath rain gear, and he could only see the tags on their bikes when he was alongside them. He would identify a man as Gunter, and then pedal alongside only to find he'd lost track in one reshuffling or another. No one looked familiar in the soggy conditions.

The route passed through the ski station of La Mongie. Beyond the high-rise hotels the road entered the clouds. Visibility dropped to less than ten meters. Ben couldn't even see the entire group he rode within.

Now above tree line, safety seemed an even bigger concern. The only things on this hillside more prominent than the cyclists' heads would be the ski lift towers. Did that make the men targets for a lightning strike? Should they go on?

It wasn't Ben's call. The alternatives to continuing weren't good, anyway. If they canceled the stage thousands of spectators would be stuck on the hillside for no reason at all.

The hairs on Ben's arm stood on end. He looked at them.

Suddenly, a pillar of light the diameter of a tree-trunk jackhammered the mountainside, not more than twenty meters ahead. He blinked, but his eyelids didn't stop the brilliant yellow from overwhelming his brain. Before his eyes opened a bone-bone jarring crack of thunder all but threw him from his bicycle. His heart palpitated. Had it been knocked off rhythm by massive electrical interference?

"Holy…"

Gunter put a foot down, scared and confused.

"Keep riding!" Ben yelled. "Don't ground yourself!"

Were they safer on the bikes? Would an inch of inflated rubber and a carbon frame protect them? Ben wasn't certain. He did know, though, that getting away from this place was better than staying.

As they continued to climb there were many more strikes, but they seemed tame in comparison to the near miss. Nothing but a direct hit could out-do what they'd just experienced.

The road wound higher and higher and the visibility became lower and lower. Time and again Ben's sense of place told him he'd reached the top, but his cyclometer reading proved he had farther to go.

He tracked down Gunter again. Based on recent performances both in the rain and on steep roads, Ben was the most likely to benefit from the upcoming descent. That meant he was in the best position to suggest sanity.

"We shouldn't race down the slope. Someone could get killed," Ben said. He was giving up an advantage, but it wasn't worth ending a career over.

The German nodded. "*Ja, wier stimmen zu.*"

Ben had been blindsided when truces were shattered before, so this time he'd remain wary. "Kyle is more likely to listen to you than me," he said.

Gunter rode over to the Megatronics cyclist and got an agreement. Word spread throughout the group. It surprised Ben to find that fewer than two-dozen cyclists remained in the lead peloton. The pace hadn't seemed tough, but many men had slackened under the punishment. All the usual mountain men, though, were among the remaining players.

In the last kilometer spectators were absent. Cars were parked bumper to bumper, but there weren't any people. Ben crossed the mountain's spine and realized why. It was a different world: partly cloudy skies and patchy rain showers, wet roads and water running off the hillside, but nothing near the severity of the other side. A firm breeze blew from below. The mountain directed it skyward where dozens of large birds surfed the current. Did the wind and rock form a wall the hailstorm couldn't cross?

The warm light ahead looked inviting. Ben had never seen so many spectators on a downhill stretch of road. The humming of wet brakes—strangely reminiscent of an orchestra tuning instruments to begin a concerto—accompanied the peloton as it skated down the mountain. The volume rose at each bend. It felt strange to hold back so near the finish, but the soaked pavement remained treacherous, especially with reactions deadened by cold. The drop-offs were enormous. Ben shivered, wishing a truce hadn't been necessary but knowing it was the sporting move.

A group of cyclists shot past them on the left-hand side of the road, throwing a cold mist into the air. Ben looked at Kyle and Gunter. They glanced back nervously. Trailing athletes, unaware of the truce, had overtaken the lead peloton.

After a moment's hesitation, Kyle flew off the front in hot pursuit. Gunter and Ben looked at one another. With Kyle building a lead they came to immediate agreement.

"Close the gap," Ben yelled.

The teams joined forces and the chase was on.

The fast wheels threw water into the air. The peloton carried its mist cloud wherever it went. Conditions at the rear of the pack were far worse than the front, a shower coming from every direction. For Ben, conserving energy was more important than drying out, though. He remained behind his teammates and got soaked.

His cold hands ached from squeezing the handlebars so tightly, and the patchy condition of the pavement made it even tougher. He leaned into a corner, willing his machine to hold the road. The front tire hit a puddle and hydroplaned, but recaptured its grip with a shudder. Ben squeezed the brakes, but with little effect. Water lubricated the aluminum rims, so the rubber pads couldn't slow him much. He pumped the levers; finally checking the bicycle just enough to bring it around the corner and point it down the next straightaway.

Ben trampled the pedals, anxious to rejoin the group. His frigid body wouldn't react quickly, but he couldn't sit back and let victory escape. He watched the forward portion of the pack for signs of splintering as the riders prepared for the next corner. If the group split, he'd better bridge to Gunter immediately.

They rounded a sharp left-hander. Two bloodied cyclists stood near the edge of the road, urgently untangling their bikes. They were casualties of the group that had started this madness. They'd been fortunate to slide off on a turn with a wide shoulder. It could have been much worse.

Over the radio Thierry said, "Kyle caught the men from the lead group. It includes one of his teammates. He's got a twenty-second gap. Don't let it go over thirty."

Ben judged the remaining vertical to the town. If his group was going to stay within a half-minute they'd better speed up. He headed toward the front.

His two remaining teammates joined him as they threaded their way forward. They reached the base, streamed through Luz St. Sauveur, and then navigated a scenic detour to cross the soaring stone Pont Napoléon bridge. Tour organizers always sent the peloton across the river on this historic landmark, no matter from which of three possible directions the race entered the town.

Riders bolted toward the last major mountain of this year's tour like stallions charging for an open gate. They hit the foothills full bore. A chalkboard told them Kyle had passed twenty-five seconds earlier. Ben caught a glimpse of Gunter's face. The German's determination encouraged him. Both teams would work together to neutralize their enemy. Ever-changing race conditions had aligned their needs once again.

The group settled into an organized pattern. One of Gunter's Duetscher Aufbau teammates led. A Banque Fédérale cyclist sat on his wheel. Albert and another Deutscher Aufbau man rode side-by-side behind them. Gunter and Ben rode shoulder-to-shoulder one place back. Luigi tagged along in the next position. Two of Kyle's Megatronics men were at the rear.

Normally on the final climb, the cyclists would have passed their helmets into their support vehicles, but today, with rain beginning again and the hailstones beating fresh in their minds they kept them on.

Each day on the final mountain Ben found himself surrounded by the same, familiar faces, as if grouped by a mathematical algorithm. Long ago he'd owned a coin-sorting piggy bank. Dimes fell into the smallest slot. Pennies, nickels, and quarters rolled farther. Half-dollars made it nearly to the end. But only those rare dollar coins got all the way to the final slot. Ben looked onto switchbacks below where the half-dollars climbed together. Somewhere far behind he was sure the dimes did to. It might be nice to join them. It took a lot more effort to travel with the big coins.

A kilometer into the climb, Gunter's lead man cracked. The gap to Kyle stood at twenty seconds. Ben's domestique took over. Men from Kyle's lead group failed one by one. The chasers drew energy from picking them off. After another kilometer Ben's man moved aside, spent, and Gunter's first lieutenant took over. Kyle came into view on the long straightaways. With the aid of a visible target, the chasers gained even more rapidly. Both groups were being shredded. Besides the remaining Fédérale and Aufbau riders, only Luigi and one Megatronics man still remained in Ben's pack. In another kilometer they were on the verge of capturing Kyle and the two final members of his group.

"Bury them," Ben said.

Gunter nodded. His lieutenant had no more to give and swung wide to let the others pass.

Dense crowds squeezed in from both sides of the road. Basque flags were everywhere. Half the people who didn't carry a banner declared

Basque allegiance by wearing orange shirts. They'd converged on this hill in hopes that a countryman would win the day, but their devotion to cycling was so great that they'd cheer anybody who challenged the mountain by bike.

Ben pumped his machine through the human corridor, comforting himself with the now familiar site of Albert sacrificing himself in the attack. At full redline they sailed past Kyle. Despite the chilling wetness, Ben warmed inside when Gunter threw a scowl Kyle's way. The menacing look would have melted a less self-assured competitor.

The Megatronics man who'd been hitching a ride behind Ben yelled, "Stick with me, Kyle!"

Ben didn't look back. In this vortex moment every athlete was on the verge of fracture. This level of effort wasn't sustainable for long. Who would crack first?

Toma sprinted beside them, dripping wet. "You can do it, Ben! This is your stage!"

Ben couldn't spare the strength to respond. He concentrated on the road.

Ahead, Albert pumped furiously. Ben and Gunter climbed side by side. They chose the same moment to turn for a look through the gap between them. There, only a couple of meters behind Luigi, was the Megatronics domestique, and right behind him rode Kyle. Damn.

With a final surge Albert moved out of the path of the contenders. Ben took the lead, his heart thundering, as if the storm had moved within his body. Torrents of blood rushed through his arteries, pulsating in his fingertips and toes. His chest heaved, drawing and discarding liter after liter of humid air.

Despite being soaked, he needed more to drink. He grabbed his water bottle. He could take in only a small amount at a time because his craving for oxygen was too great to close his mouth. Most of the liquid ran down his chin.

Only five kilometers to go. Kyle's teammate fell back as the rain storm strengthened. Four men remained. Ben looked up, but the visibility was so low that he couldn't even see to the next turn, let alone the distinctive scraggly peaks that dominated this famous finishing stretch.

Luigi swept wide and attacked. Ben swung across the road and followed, ignoring the rain. He could feel the other men on his tail. Luigi's charge lasted a couple of hundred meters.

When the pace fell, Gunter gave it a try. This time Kyle was quickest to respond and Ben had to chase, but it wasn't long before that attack was abandoned as well.

The four men alternated their assaults, but at the three-kilometer mark there had only been one casualty—Luigi.

The top three men remained locked in combat. Ben could now see the time bonuses at the line were going to be more significant than the gaps any of them could open over the other two. Further attacks were a waste of energy. He'd mark his rivals; then he'd beat them across the line. Of course, they probably had the same plan. It would all be in the execution.

They entered the barricaded section of the course. With the fans behind fences and their important rivals within arms reach, strategy changed. The ideal position would be following the other two men. The last guy in line could judge the effort of his rivals, utilize their draft, and choose the perfect moment to slingshot himself past for the win.

The group slowed to a crawl as Kyle tried to force the other men into the lead. Ben gathered energy for the burst. His thigh muscles had been branded by the searing effort, but even in this tiny lull he could feel the beginning of recuperation.

They approached the half-kilometer mark, moving slower and slower, like track cyclists setting up a sprint. Ben looked back. No sign of Luigi. At four-hundred meters it became a matter of balance. Ben doubted that either of his competitors could steady themselves on a motionless bicycle as well as he could. He refused to lose this contest.

Finally Gunter relented and led the group toward the line. Ben held off long enough to force Kyle into second position. As he brought up the rear, he looked back. There came Luigi, closing fast.

Gunter and Kyle glanced back at Ben, and at Luigi's rapid approach. At three hundred meters Gunter opened his sprint. Kyle charged to match him. Ben glided along behind. Two hundred meters out Kyle blew past the German, Ben moved by as well.

Seventy-five meters from the line Ben ducked his head and wrestled speed from his machine. Stroke by stroke he moved alongside Kyle. With fifteen meters to go he edged into the lead. Kyle made another surge, but Ben held him off and crossed the line first. He threw both palms to the sky.

Ahh, victory. He savored the taste. He'd only eked out a couple of bonus seconds, but it felt like the most satisfying of accomplishments. He'd finally won a close contest against his top rivals.

Ben looked back. Kyle had obviously taken second. Gunter still struggled toward the line. Luigi passed him, grabbing the eight-second third place bonus. The German had no more to give and finished fourth. It was the sort of failure Ben could sympathize with. With hundreds of riders per race, even the best cyclists lost far more often than they won.

Ben was still gasping for breath when Thierry arrived. "Congratulations, Ben!"

"What are the standings now?"

"With the time bonus, Kyle retook the yellow jersey. Gunter is behind by five seconds and you're just fifteen seconds farther back."

Twenty seconds from the lead. No more mountains left.

The press corps moved in. The Tour had reached a crescendo. Some were calling it the greatest race ever.

A reporter from one of the biggest European cycling publications spoke first. "Is it true that you and Bridgette LeBlanc broke up six days ago?"

"What? How did you hear that?"

"So it's true? She claims she couldn't have been administering drugs to you because she hasn't been in contact with you. When did you last see her?"

Ben wished the truth wasn't so suggestive, but he wasn't going to lie. "Yesterday evening, briefly."

The reporter's face lit up. "What did you talk about?"

"It was a private conversation. Does anybody have questions about today's race?"

The *au Fond* man's voice rose above the others. "Do you honestly expect us to believe that after years of dating, you separated two days after getting engaged on world-wide television? How come neither of you said anything until now?"

"Nobody asked. Unfortunately, we're through," Ben said, irritated. "Now, since nobody wants to talk about cycling, please excuse me."

He walked toward the doping control trailer, ignoring the questions being shouted after him. As stage winner, he was required to provide a urine sample. He'd never looked forward to medical controls before, but today they meant an opportunity to provide evidence of his innocence, and also a reason to get away from certain journalists intent on manufacturing a scoop.

"You can't hide from the questions," someone yelled.

What difference did it make if the reporters had already made up their minds about the answers?

Chapter Thirty

Thierry scanned the maps and documents spread before him on his hotel bed. Ben's energy must be preserved for getting his bike across that final line in first place. Somewhere in these papers might be the key to that victory.

Nicolas DePerdiux, Thierry's younger brother, had died racing bicycles. Over the past nine days Ben had begun to fill that vacant spot. He had the same courageous demeanor and single-minded determination as Nicolas. Watching Ben discover his capabilities day-by-day had been a rare pleasure.

Tomorrow's pancake-flat eighteenth stage might feature a long breakaway, but it would ultimately be a day for the sprinters. Still, opportunities to gain time might spring up, and there would be risks of losing time, too. Could the Banque Fédérale boys protect Ben within the peloton all day, or were alliances needed to assure his safety? Damn Robidoux for stealing Rikard and Philippe! Without those two workhorses it was probably necessary to find help of some kind. What could Banque Fédérale give in return?

The next day, Saturday, was a time trial. The final "race of truth" ought to decide the yellow jersey. Thierry studied the route in minute detail, looking for potential pitfalls and advantages. He would put each man under strict instructions, testing different theories about the best way to attack the course. Was it better to start out fast or slow? How would the prevailing winds affect the athletes on that particular day? Which corners hid deceptive dangers and how much strength must be preserved to get home? Unlike regular stages, time trial rules prohibited passing food or drink to the rider, so the balance between carrying too little fuel versus the extra weight of too much was another critical factor.

Then, on Sunday, the entourage rolled into Paris for a final battle on the Champs-Elysées. Typically it was merely a celebratory parade with an extremely prestigious sprint tacked onto the end, but if things were still close there would be fireworks all day long. Parade or not, it always got intense on the final rushing laps.

Thierry's hotel phone rang. "*Bonjour.*"

"I wish it was a good day," Robidoux said. "This race has consumed me. I'm not sleeping well."

"Neither am I. It was easier as an athlete. As directeur, nothing is truly in your control." Thierry moved some maps aside and sat down on the bed.

"Watch what you say. I ought to be annoyed at you for such a comment. If you think your job is so hard, you should try to be the *patron* sometime."

Thierry had often wondered what life must be like sailing on a yacht full of beautiful women and jetting from one exotic location to another. It seemed like a great gig, but he knew better than to suggest that to the team owner. Robidoux had the world at his fingertips, but for some reason he despised the suggestion that his life was good. "No thanks, I'll leave that to you. I prefer to prepare for my return to the bike. I'll race again as soon as I've recovered."

"I'm pleased to hear that. I'll be as relieved as anybody once you are leading our team again. Ben's unpredictability exhausts me."

"Despite your lack of sleep, have you enjoyed the race?"

"I'd prefer to see it sewn up much earlier, the way you always have."

Thierry laughed. "You overestimate me. I'm not sure how I'd be holding up if I were still in this race."

"Really?" Robidoux elongated the word. "Are these men better than you?"

Thierry stood and walked to the window, stretching the phone cord to its full length. He looked out on the black night. "You know I'd never admit that. They've gone through hell out there, though. Ben has shown me something, but so have the other two."

"And which one is going to win?"

Thierry thought for a moment. "The time-trial should decide things. If Ben performs like he did in Cannes he can take it."

"Is that in our best interests?"

Thierry didn't know how to answer the surprising question. Finally he said, "Why wouldn't it be?"

"Some commentators say it would be best for the sport if Benjamin withdrew. Is he bringing us more bad publicity than good? Maybe the team should distance itself from him, tainted as he is by the drug controversy."

Was Robidoux uncomfortable working with Ben? Didn't he trust him? Avoiding the growing speculation had become impossible. Thierry understood why Robidoux didn't like the headlines, but it wasn't Ben's fault. "He's a good kid. He'll clear his name once the race is over. Ben has remained focused on the goal, despite the distractions, and I think we should too. After the spokes stop spinning I'll arrange an interview for him with Simone Sardou. She'll treat us fairly."

Robidoux harrumphed. "Benjamin Barnes is a loose cannon. I cringe every time he talks to the media. I worry he'll start thinking he's bigger than our team, or even the race. Tell the press he has a stomach virus and pull him out. There's not much anybody could say to that."

Where was this coming from? Why had Robidoux's opinion of Ben soured so completely? A little over a week ago, after Ben pulled off the inspirational victory on 'l Alpe d'Huez, the team owner had aligned the squad behind the American. Several days later Robidoux stole the two best flatlanders from the effort for no apparent reason, though Thierry had guessed the meaning of the veiled threats that laced that conversation. The team owner despised defiance, and Ben must have crossed the line.

Thierry had never stood up to Robidoux before, but he couldn't allow Ben's quest to end like this. He stared at the maps outlining the last three stages. "Who's going to believe that indigestion could stop this kid from finishing? You're right that some journalists aren't crazy about him, but most of the fans are. They would be stunned if he abandoned the race, and that would turn to fury against Banque Fédérale once he told the world it wasn't his decision. Ben is a warrior, and the viewers know it."

"Then they know something I don't. True warriors follow the chief's orders, just like you've always done," Robidoux said.

"I'm only telling you the way I see it."

Robidoux was silent for a long time. Then he said, "You're right about the dangers of pulling Benjamin from the race. It would be better to expose him as a loser and allow him to fade into oblivion."

"He's no loser," Thierry said, emboldened. "I've seen great performances before, but nothing like this. I've watched Ben give me all he can, and then I've heard Bill ask him for more. Do you know what's happened?"

"*Non.*"

"Neither do I. It's as if Ben's soul has taken over. He's ridden the past two weeks on more determination than any man I've ever seen. He isn't the most gifted athlete, but he makes up for it in grit. He's exposed himself so completely that the fans can see what holds him together, and they love him —"

"Enough of this hogwash. You'll do as I say. I want Ben stopped, and I want it done in a way that reveals his weakness to the public."

Thierry held the phone tight to his ear. "It almost seems like you're looking forward to sabotaging your own athlete. I don't understand why you seem so happy."

"*Content? Non.* Yet there's always a measure of satisfaction in reaching resolution, even if it isn't ideal."

"A resolution of what?"

"You're the sort of cornerstone employee a successful company can be built upon. Customers will continue to love and identify with you long after your retirement. More important, management can rely on your professionalism, your commitment to the whole. You've made yourself into one of my most valuable assets."

"Thank you, but what does that have to do with Ben?"

"Benjamin is different. He's uncontrollable ... unpredictable. He doesn't understand his role in the big picture. I've caught him deceiving me to pursue his own agenda. His friend Bridgette has done the same. If I continued to invest in people like that I'd create a monster. Eventually Benjamin would take the good will he built using our generosity and head to the competition. That's why I've decided our team shouldn't support his efforts any longer. Sure, the short-term loss hurts, but weighed against where I see this going in the long-term, it's a price I'm willing to pay. Now, show the world his weakness."

Thierry rolled the request over in his mind. "I'm not sure I can do that."

"Need I remind you, Thierry, of the compromises you made to win last year's tour?"

Robidoux had ordered him to accept illegal treatment, and he'd relented. "*Non.* I'll never forget them."

"*Bon.* You made necessary and professional decisions, but we both know that you'd be road kill if the story ever got out. Now the time has come for you to do as I ask or it will."

Thierry shut his eyes. His worst nightmare was coming true.

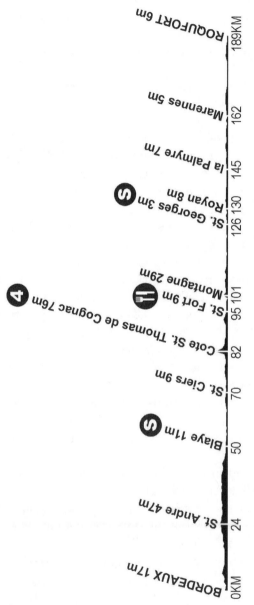

Tour de France Stage 18 Profile

Chapter Thirty-One

Ben positioned himself behind the Bordeaux starting line. The eighteenth stage was being hyped as a beautiful journey through some of the most famous vineyards in the world, but scenery wasn't on the athletes' minds. Their attention was on the wind. On the bus ride there they had watched every tree strain eastward. Now and then an entire branch went flying in that direction. Offshore Atlantic winds were typical for this region. Today's were extreme. This had the makings of another brutal stage.

As the yellow jersey wearer, Kyle had the honor of starting the stage up front along with the other ceremonial jersey wearers like Luigi in red "King of the Mountains" polka dots, and the man who led the sprint competition wearing solid green. Ben and Gunter also started nearby. They would hold those positions until the official start took place. Kyle's team had positioned themselves near the front of the pack as well.

The gun went off, and the bikes rolled through narrow, cobbled streets, past churches and historic sights, then exited the historic city beneath Porte Bourgogne, a soaring city gate that marked the medieval entrance to old Bordeaux. Next they crossed the swirling brown Garonne river on the Pont de Pierre Bridge. There, the wind hit them full force. Conditions became chaotic. They'd soon reenter the suburbs on the opposite bank, but every man knew that echelons would form the moment the race left town. Without buildings to protect them from crosswinds, the cyclists would be forced into these unique formations. Spectators sometimes commented on the beauty of echelons, comparing them to billowing banners built of men. Pro bicycle riders weren't so enamored. To them, echelons meant pain. They only existed while going all out in epic conditions.

An echelon is a peloton built sideways in response to wind direction, but that one change introduces a host of complications. Unlike a peloton, where a column of unlimited length can find a protected position behind the men battling the wind at the front, echelons use rows.

Instead of gaining an advantage by riding behind someone, today a rider could only hide from the wind by having another cyclist to his left; the space for men riding shoulder-to-shoulder, however, is limited by the width of the road.

On an average country route about ten cyclists can fit curb to curb. An echelon consists of two rows of athletes, roughly twenty participants per group. Even though the attrition rate had been exceptionally high this year, there were still 131 men in the race. That meant seven echelons at least. The men who got stuck in the last few groups were almost certain to lose big time.

Ben had to make sure he was near the two other General Classification contenders before the echelons formed. Otherwise, massive gaps could open, and the winner of the yellow jersey would be decided before tomorrow's time trial got underway.

He jockeyed for position at the front of the pack. He'd asked his teammates to join him, but in the frantic conditions it was impossible to look back and see how things were working out.

The Megatronics boys knifed into the top spots with surgical precision. Luigi found a place among their ranks, as did a hodge-podge of men from other teams, but Ben picked the wrong spot. When he tried to squeeze in, he found no room at the inn.

He looked behind. No teammates. Gunter and Duetscher Aufbau had built a second echelon. Positions were filling fast. Ben stood in no man's land. He reduced his effort, and the Aufbau line caught up on his downwind side. He increased his cadence to keep abreast. Thankfully, Albert and another Banque Fédérale teammate joined from behind, taking spots near Ben.

In another moment the remaining places filled. Behind, further ranks would be forming. Hopefully the rest of Ben's teammates would grab a ride in the next echelon; otherwise, there was a good chance he wouldn't see them for the rest of the day. Ben concentrated on his role in the group. The battle was a complex ballet requiring full attention.

An echelon operates like a chain-saw blade, with each man equivalent to an independent link. With the wind blowing from the west and the cyclists moving north, like today, the rotation was counter-clockwise. The cutting position was at the western edge of the formation. The man in that spot battled the gale for as long as he could before dropping into the rear echelon to drift eastward. He moved, link by link, into increasingly protected positions. Meanwhile, rested men moved west in the front row. When they reached the forward corner of the echelon they took their turns confronting the wind. Thus, the chain moved round and round, biting its way through the tempest.

Two positions to Ben's left, the man at the western edge of the road dropped back a bike length, leaving Albert in the wind. The Frenchman swayed as the storm crashed into him. He corrected his course and eased west. Ben moved with him, staying as close as possible to his lieutenant's lee side for maximum shelter.

Fifteen meters ahead, the Megatronics team set a blistering pace. The possibility of opening gaps over Kyle's main rivals to win the yellow jersey competition here and now was all the motivation they needed to justify flat-out effort. The drag race was on. Advantage Kyle.

If the Megatronics group made any errors they might slow momentarily, but because they formed a virtual rolling roadblock, the second-place group containing Ben and Gunter would be unable to overtake them. On the other hand, if Ben's group slipped up, the gap between echelon one and two would widen.

A fist of wind slammed into Ben. Albert had dropped back. Ben corrected course, narrowly avoiding contact with the man to his right. He took a long, steady pull. Consistent pace was the key. If a strong man pushed too fast the echelon would collapse as weaker riders fell out of position. The disruption would slow the chase, and the loss of men would mean less rest between pulls for every remaining cyclist. It required a delicate balance.

The pedaling was difficult, and fighting to control his machine under the relentless cross-block of air made it even harder. The larger surface area exposed to the elements resulted in resistance greatly exceeding that faced when leading a peloton. A moment's inattention could topple the riders like dominos. Exhausted, Ben fell back. The chain rotated another click counter-clockwise.

The Deutscher Aufbau men weren't about to let Kyle out of their sight, and neither were Ben and his two teammates. As insecure as Ben felt about the early developments in this stage, at least he was the beneficiary of the work the Germans were doing for Gunter.

Two riders from the lead echelon drifted back. The road had narrowed, forcing them out of their places.

"Follow me," Ben yelled to his two teammates.

They burst through the front row of their echelon and sprinted beside the two men shut out of echelon one. A new group started to form.

Gunter and two of his teammates recognized the danger and quickly moved into the new formation as well. A ripple effect of repositioning would continue on down the road. Meanwhile, Kyle remained in the best position of the race.

"Sprint bonus coming up in two kilometers," said Thierry over the radio. "You've got to get into that lead group. Otherwise Kyle will cherry-pick the bonus seconds."

There were two sprint bonuses on today's stage. These incentives were sprinkled throughout all the stages to keep competition hot. Normally, they were primarily of interest to the men pursuing the green jersey sprinter's competition, but today the yellow jersey guys had to pay close attention as well. With six bonus seconds awarded for first place at each sprint, they could have a major impact on the final standings.

As Ben and his teammates worked their way toward the windward point of their group, the Megatronics echelon sped. "Go for it!" Ben yelled.

His two men knew what he meant. They bolted ahead of him. They needed to break through the lead echelon before the sprint bonus was decided. The teammates charged toward the tiny bit of unused pavement to the west of the Megatronics group. Ben glued himself in Albert's draft. He sensed another man taking position downwind of him, probably Gunter.

An alert spectator saw the cyclists coming. Recognizing that their destination was the tiny piece of real estate he occupied, he jumped back.

The first of Ben's attackers gave out, having covered the ground between the two groups. He dropped back. Albert jammed through the small slot at the western edge of the Megatronics echelon. He surprised Kyle's teammate as he squeezed by. The Megatronics man, realizing what was happening, drifted west to slam the door shut.

Ben charged like an enraged bull, but the piece of pavement he'd aimed at disappeared beneath the wheels of the Megatronics pacemaker. He swerved onto the dirt shoulder, hoping his ultra-pressurized wheels could survive a jolt or two.

More fans scurried out of the way. Ben gritted his teeth and drove his pedals. A moment later he veered back onto the blacktop ahead of the Megatronics team. He slid downwind of Albert again and slingshotted past. Twisting his machine for everything he was worth, he burst over the intermediate sprint line in first place.

He looked back. Gunter had broken through behind him and captured second. Albert had fended off Kyle for third. That meant six seconds bonus for Ben, four for Gunter, and none for Kyle. Albert had stolen the last two. The differential put Gunter a scant second out of the lead and Ben only fourteen seconds behind Kyle.

Now the echelons reshuffled again. This time there was no way Ben was getting left out of the first group. Despite the jostling, he held solid, as did Gunter and Albert. Ben wondered how he could foil Kyle's efforts at the next sprint bonus, fifty kilometers up the road. A similar surprise attack wouldn't work again.

Now that both of Kyle's key rivals held positions in their echelon, the Megatronics men lost their incentive to go all out. Maximum effort was pointless when the men they were trying to hurt were hitching a ride. Pretty soon the distressed cyclists in the trailing echelons were stacking themselves back into the main pack and a peloton formed.

The category-four Côte St. Thomas de Cognac removed a bit more pressure. As the road rounded the leeward side, seven men from lesser teams charged up the right-hand edge of the road. If these athletes stayed out front, they would sweep up the remaining sprint bonus along the way. Ben wouldn't gain any more time, but neither would Kyle or Gunter. He didn't feel the strength to contest another sprint, so he'd prefer to give the breakaway a long leash. Gunter and Kyle apparently saw things the same way because soon the escapists were out of sight.

With the slower pace came a greater sense of his environment. On a swale ahead Ben saw storybook France. A graceful château overlooked acres of perfect vineyards. Three men wearing tam hats and two women with rosy cheeks raised wine glasses in salute. Similar groups dotted the road.

The route moved to parallel the northeast bank of the Gironde. The shipyards near Royan were visible on the horizon. In some places, cliffs lined the riverbank. Crosswinds off the water were harsh, but none of the teams seemed to have the strength to take advantage. Ben dreamed of Paris. He felt exhaustion clear to his core, a sensation unlike any he'd ever experienced. The kilometers still separating him from the Parisian avenues filled him with anxiety and dread.

For long stretches, the highway traveled among thick stands of trees. The relief from the wind put a smile on every man's face, but the friendly air didn't last long. When the river opened to the Atlantic at the beaches of St. Georges the zephyr hit harder than ever. Stunt kites swirled in the rushing air, windsurfers skipped across the tops of waves, balloons fought to escape the grips of toddlers.

The crowded beaches went on and on. Laughter from happy vacationers filled the air. Thirty kilometers from the finish, the sprinters' teams cranked things up again. They rode hard, fracturing the field into echelons for a second time. Once again, Ben found membership in the second group on the road. This time Kyle rode with him. Gunter managed a position in the first group. He and his men opened a gap the second echelon couldn't close.

"Five kilometers to go," Thierry reported over the headset. "Gunter has you by twenty-two seconds. He's about to overtake the breakaway. You can't let him get the finishing bonus."

That was unlikely, given the powerhouse sprinters he rode with, but catching up was urgent. Even the slightest gap would change the standings. The road swung east, putting the wind at their back and negating the need for echelons.

Ben nodded to Kyle, shifting alliances again. Without words they dropped beside the second place competitor in the sprinter's competition.

"Our teams will help if your men chase," Kyle said.

The peloton transformed. Ben took his share of pulls. Kyle did too. In just over two kilometers they overtook the leaders.

The sprinters began jostling for victory. Just like in Marseille, conditions up front were about to become insane. Rikard would have loved this moment, but Ben got out of the way. He kept his eyes on Gunter and Kyle, relieved that they didn't appear to want any part of it, either.

The peloton zoomed onto the streets of Rochefort, frenzied fans cheering their every move. Somewhere in front, complex reshufflings would be taking place. The sound of grating aluminum broadcast a crash. Ben swerved, threading through downed bodies and machines. Safely past, he sprinted hard to maintain contact with the lead pack. Gunter and Kyle remained nearby. They passed under the flamme rouge within arm's length of one another and approached the finish line sitting up.

After Ben crossed the line he watched the big screen replay. The man wearing the green jersey had won again. The points he received would be enough to clinch the overall sprinter's competition. His team would celebrate tonight.

The cyclists faced an airplane transfer to Paris ahead of them. Ideally, Ben would sleep the whole way. He handed his bike to Fritz, went straight to the vehicle, and collapsed. The tour would probably be decided by this time tomorrow.

Chapter Thirty-Two

As Ben rode his bike through the arched carriageway that passed beneath the Château de Versaille, he wondered if the butterflies in his stomach were visible to everyone. The team had spent the night in the Trianon Palace hotel. Its grounds abutted those of Versailles, but the portion he could see from his window didn't hold a candle to these perfectly manicured gardens. Breakfast had been in a hotel salon where, the better part of a century before, Georges Clemenceau had dictated conditions for the Treaty of Versailles. Several days later the document had been signed in the building behind him now. Today would be his opportunity to enter the history books in a different sort of way.

He unclipped his foot and stopped the bike, taking in the beauty of the palace grounds. What a setting for a race start. There was a time when only the most powerful people on earth experienced this sight. Now, the world was seeing it as never before.

Ben gazed over the geometric gardens and rectangular pools and wondered whether his name belonged alongside the greatest champions of this sport. He believed it did.

He returned to the front of the Palace where the festivities were well under way. Some of the early starters had already completed the course. The weather was clear and the humidity extremely low. The gentle breeze felt scratchy in its pristine clarity. Temperatures were still cooler than average for this time of year at a pleasant twenty degrees Celsius, or about seventy degrees Fahrenheit. In short, it was a perfect day for a bike race.

Ben climbed the steps of the podium to sign in for the stage. This daily ceremony was particularly significant on time trials. Because of the staggered start, every minute or two another athlete would be introduced and interviewed. It made for great pre-race hype.

As Ben reached the highest step the race announcer bellowed to the crowd: "*Mesdames et messieurs!* Now begins the moment you've all been waiting for. One of the remaining three competitors will become your Tour de France champion! Who will rise to the occasion? Starting first of the trio, just fourteen seconds off of the lead, please welcome Banque Fédérale's Ben Barnes!"

The crowd cheered. Ben soaked in the encouragement as he scrawled his name on the sign-in sheet.

"What sort of strategy will we see from you today, Ben?" the announcer asked.

"I'll take it one revolution at a time. I have to turn in my best performance ever. Nothing else will do."

"Do you believe you can go even faster than your previous time-trial?"

"I hope to. Last week's race is fresh in my mind. I know where I was slow. I plan to correct my mistakes and go even faster."

The fans roared in anticipation.

Ben descended the steps and returned to the staging area. He climbed onto his stationary trainer and continued his warm-up, pedaling with light resistance just to stay loose. While he spun he meditated, but his reverie was broken by the announcement over the PA system: "Next, a mere thirteen seconds ahead of Ben Barnes and only a single second out of the lead, please put your hands together for Deutscher Aufbau's Gunter von Reinholdt!"

The crowed erupted in applause.

"Do you have anything special up your sleeve today, Gunter?"

Gunter took a look at his sleeve and the crowd laughed. "Only to follow Ben as closely as we can. We get to see his split times, and we will take full advantage of that information."

"What about Kyle?"

"We can't worry about what happens behind us. Hopefully it will take care of itself."

As amusing as it was to hear Gunter call himself "we," it was even funnier to hear him refer to Kyle as "it." Ben didn't even allow himself a smile, though. He reached for his headphones. He'd better take advantage of this last moment of peace. For some reason, Coach had been adamant that today he use the Walkman Thelma had brought along. He pressed play.

"The Theme from *Rocky*" thundered over the headset. He hadn't listened to this tape in years. Thelma had given him a copy years ago, and he'd devoted a specific ride to listening to it. Memories flooded back.

Southeast of his boyhood home in Hanksville, Ben had claimed the area around the goosenecks of the Dirty Devil River as his own personal playground. He'd spent hundreds of hours cycling the network of abandoned uranium prospecting roads that criss-crossed the Burr Desert, and he'd come to know the region more intimately than any other human on the planet. Rarely did he see anybody in that forgotten corner of the world. It had to be one of the least traveled areas in the lower forty-eight states. The vistas over the gorge were of national park caliber, but with so many scenic wonders in the vicinity, the place went unnoticed.

He named the area Ben Canyon National Recreation Area because there was another place just down the road called Glen Canyon National Recreation Area. Ben figured if Glen, whoever that was, got such treatment, why shouldn't he?

Out in Ben Canyon, his favorite test was to race the sun to the horizon at the end of the day. He'd wait, perched atop an enormous white rock creased with labyrinths of folds. He called the formation "The Brain." He sat on the frontal lobe, soaking in the aura until his target time before sunset arrived. When the golden orb reached the designated spot he'd hit the play button on his Walkman. The supercharged refrain from "The Theme from *Rocky*" filled his head, and his self-imposed time-trial began. Gunna' fly now.

The rules were that if the last visible fragment of the sun disappeared before he pulled onto the paved highway leading to Hanksville, then Mother Nature got a point. If the reverse happened, then Ben got a point, but he had to begin the race ten seconds closer to sunset the next time. For the better part of a year he'd completed the race three to five times a week. He'd marked the score with notches in the fenceposts on either side of their front gate.

Even though each time he won the next attempt automatically became tougher, he kept on winning. He didn't accomplish it by starting faster. The secret was driving to the finish harder. Bit by bit, his take-off time moved toward sunset. The damage to the left fencepost proved he'd whipped Mother Nature by a wide margin.

As he pedaled the trainer, the music brought desert images to mind. He visualized the places he used to pass during specific moments on the soundtrack almost as clearly as if he were cycling in his old backyard at this very moment.

A soigneur interrupted his boyhood trek, handing him an envelope. On the front his name was written in a graceful hand, below that, "Urgent." He recognized the penmanship. It was a letter from Bridgette.

His heart beating faster, he inspected the envelope. There was no postage or other marks of any kind. She must have delivered it herself. Should he open it? Was there any sort of resolution inside, or was this Pandora's envelope?

Ben was supposed to let Coach handle this sort of thing. The last thing he should allow himself was a distraction just as the race started, but how could he pass this on to anyone else? It might be private and harmless, or it might be neither.

He found it impossible to ignore. He might as well get it over with. Still pedaling, he took both hands off the handlebars. He removed his headphones, tore the envelope open at one end, and drew out a single blue sheet of lined paper. Holding the handlebars with his right hand only, he began reading:

Dearest Ben,

My heart breaks with sorrow over what I've put you through in the last week. I understand how my poor choices complicated an already challenging time. I'm sure that right now you can't see a reason to, but please have faith in me. You don't have the full story. I pray you'll eventually let me explain my actions. I know this isn't the time for that.

So why am I writing you? The reason is urgent. Monsieur Robidoux forced me into some difficult choices. He blackmailed me with my past. I convinced myself that following his orders would be the best move for all of us, but when I didn't get the results he demanded he exposed my errors anyway in order to damage your reputation.

Robidoux is a man to be feared. Now that you've refused to play by his rules, he's determined to destroy your career. Robidoux knows many secrets. He's using them to force Thierry to betray you. I have an inside source on this. Be careful!

I hope you'll receive this message in the spirit it's meant. Just because Thierry can't be trusted for the moment, you shouldn't think any less of him. Robidoux is very persuasive and ruthless. Believe me. Thierry is a good man in a difficult situation. This I know all too well.

Watch out for yourself. My prayers and dreams are with you.

Salut Minet,

Bridgette

Chapter Thirty-Three

Ben put his left hand back on the handlebar of the trainer, squeezing the letter beneath it. Tears welled in his eyes. Bridgette's plea to respect Thierry despite his actions under pressure gained a double meaning. He'd never given her a chance to defend herself, afraid the distraction would make him lose sight of his goal to win this race. He'd wanted to remain true to his teammates and those who helped him get here. And he had. But along the way he'd abandoned Bridgette, his fiancée, the woman he loved. He couldn't believe he'd been so shallow.

She hadn't been blameless, but neither had he. He'd become so caught up in his quest that he'd tossed love aside. That was self-centered and wrong. Meanwhile, she'd never quit believing in him ... never stopped working to help him win. Victory would mean so much less if he couldn't share it with her.

He heard a sound like sandpaper and looked in its direction. Coach approached, rubbing his palms together in heated anticipation. "You ready, son?"

Ben wiped a sleeve across his eyes, mixing sweat and tears. "Yeah. Almost."

"How did you like the music?"

"Perfect choice. It brought back a lot of memories." Ben slapped a palm on Coach's shoulder. "Can you do me a favor?"

"Anything."

Ben watched Luigi, who would leave the start house three positions ahead of him, head for the line. "I have a feeling that Bridgette will be somewhere along the course. Watch out for her. If you see her, have Thierry drop you off. Tell her I can't live without her. Convince her to meet me at the hotel tonight."

Coach nodded slowly. "That's not the sort of favor I expected. I'm anxious for the two of you to clear things up, but she seems a little ... misdirected at the moment. Maybe it's best to wait until after the race is over to talk with her."

Ben handed Coach Bill the letter.

Coach read it, his sliver hair lifting slightly in the breeze. When he reached the end, he looked at Ben. "Oh my, there's so much here. Do you believe Robidoux has dirt on Thierry?"

"I'm not sure." Ben took the letter back. "Thierry might have resorted to drugs one time. Hell, he might use them regularly for all I know. Or Robidoux might be manipulating him with something else, entirely. It doesn't really matter."

"Thierry seems like a straight-up guy to me." Coach watched the team directeur, ten meters away, discussing something with Fritz.

Ben, still pedaling, looked in the same direction. "I can't be sure what's at stake for him. If Robidoux convinced Thierry he can tarnish his legacy he might do something."

"What are you suggesting?"

Ben shrugged. "I haven't had time to think about it, but here he comes. I might as well ask him."

Thierry started speaking before he reached them. "You two are wearing very conspiratorial expressions. What are you plotting?"

"Damn, we've been busted." Ben smiled. "How are we ever going to overthrow the French government with these constant security breaches?"

"Is that what you're up to? Don't waste your time," Thierry said. Then he turned to Coach Bill. "What blockbuster motivational book do you have up your sleeve today?"

Ben interrupted. "Thierry, read this."

Thierry took the letter. His complexion turned grey as his eyes moved down the page. Finally, he looked up, but he didn't say anything.

Ben's heart crumbled. He stared at his idol. Thierry had planned to double-cross him. Then, strangely, relief swept over him. Now he knew without a doubt that Bridgette was telling the truth.

"Is it true?" Coach asked.

Thierry turned in his direction. "I've already put him off for a day. I convinced him there were better ways to handle things, but Robidoux has me by the short hairs. When he pushed harder, I had no choice. It's been eating me inside."

Ben stopped pedaling. He couldn't speak. Thierry must have some serious skeletons in his closet. He'd been planning to cause Ben to lose. It was too much to believe. They were brothers of a sort. The betrayal wounded him.

"What does Robidoux want you to do?" Coach asked.

Thierry's voice quavered. "During the early portion of the time trial, when Ben relies on the information I relay over the radio, I was supposed to give him bad data."

"Like what?" Coach asked.

Thierry seemed to age right before their eyes. Crow's-feet etched his face. "I promised to send Ben out way too fast. I was going to convince him he's slower than he should be, no matter how quickly he goes."

Coach nodded. "Use his early adrenaline surge to exhaust him. He'd have a hard time reaching the finish line at all, especially if he ran out of food and water along the way."

"That was the plan." Thierry looked defeated. "If Robidoux doesn't believe I've done everything possible to prevent Ben from winning, he'll ruin me."

Ben ran a hand through his stubbly hair. If he gave his all to win this stage, he would be killing the man he ought to be carrying on his shoulders. "Are you suggesting I should give up?"

Hope returned to Thierry's expression. "You've already exceeded your highest expectations for this year's event. Next year I'll do everything in my power to help you win."

There wouldn't be a next year. They all knew it. Robidoux probably wanted to avoid pulling Ben, kicking and screaming, from this year's event, but in future seasons he wouldn't allow Ben back on the course. Bridgette's letter had said, "*He's determined to destroy your career.*" The things she'd said about Thierry were true. Her warnings about Robidoux must be, too. The man had enough influence to keep the organizing committee from inviting any squad that meant to bring Ben along. There were always worthy athletes who didn't make the start.

Ben squeezed his handlebars, practically indenting the aluminum. He'd come within reach of his lifelong goal. Was he going to have to give it up over this? If he didn't make the most of his opportunity, it would be forever beyond his reach. "I'm sorry Thierry. I can't quit."

"It wouldn't be right for Ben to forfeit an honest victory so you can hold onto a dishonest one," Coach said.

Thierry chewed on his lip, nodding. "Yeah, I understand."

Fritz walked toward them tapping his watch. "You need to fly, and it shows."

Coach looked at his wrist. "Just over two minutes until you start, Ben!"

Ben's heart jumped. He'd lost track of time. Thierry and Coach hurried toward the team car. Ben climbed off the bike while Fritz removed it from the rollers. He grabbed his aerodynamic helmet, put it on, and then fastened the chinstrap. He ran the earpiece wire through a loop in his helmet and fitted the end into his ear. As he pulled on his gloves, Fritz rolled the time trial bicycle into place. Ben swung a leg over the crossbar.

"Tear it up, *mon ami*."

Ben nodded. He locked his left foot into its pedal, stepped on it, and then clicked in his right. Fritz jogged beside him, clearing space through the crowd as they headed toward the raised start house in the center of the marble court. When he reached the ramp, Ben pedaled up. A race official caught hold of his seat post, steadying the bike. Ben kept both feet clipped in place while he waited for the countdown.

"Good luck," Fritz said, and ran off towards the support vehicle.

The announcer's voice rose above the other sounds: "Now signing in, your current maillot jaune wearer, with a one second lead over Gunter von Reinholdt and a fourteen second margin over Ben Barnes, please welcome Megatronics' Kyle Smith!"

The cheers hit a crescendo. Ben looked around. Palace walls surrounded him on three sides. Ahead spectators lined the fenced-off lane he was about to ride.

"What's your prediction for today, Kyle?" the announcer asked.

"I'll win."

The mere sound of the deep voice raised Ben's hackles. If anybody could set him off it was Kyle. He fought for calm, noticing a television cameraman standing at the base of the start house. The broadcast light shone red, and the lens was trained on Ben's face.

He felt off kilter, not the way he wanted to at the starting line for a race of this magnitude. He began his prerace routine, hoping familiarity would calm him. He inspected his sunglasses and put them on. Closing his eyes, he inhaled. Then he opened his eyes as he expelled air through his nose.

Thierry's voice came sharply over the radio. "I want you to give me the most explosive first five kilometers of your life, Ben. Are you ready?"

The comment broke Ben's concentration. Why was Thierry talking like that after the conversation they'd just had? It sounded almost like he was speaking for Robidoux's benefit.

Ben froze. Could that be it? Was the team owner listening in the background? Of course! Suddenly, he knew the solution. He put his hand to his earpiece. "What?"

"If you want the maillot jaune you need to take this race by the throat and impose your will," Thierry said.

"I'm hearing mostly static." Ben took out the earpiece, looked at it, and reinserted it. He was acutely aware of the cameraman, crouching lower for a better angle, but he didn't look directly at him.

"Everything all right?" asked the starter. "Ten seconds to go."

"What do you mean you can't hear me?" Thierry asked.

Ben gnashed his teeth. He reached into his back pocket and grabbed the radio. The earpiece wire prevented him from clearly seeing what he was doing. It ran through a hole in his shirt and up his back. Ben twisted dials and flipped switches. "Dammit! This thing's gone dead!"

The starter extended five fingers on his right hand as he began the count down. "*Cinq ...*"

"We can hear you," Thierry yelled. "Check your volume."

"*... quatre ...*"

Ben unplugged the earpiece wire and fumbled the radio away. The receiver fell to the ground.

"*... trois ...*"

Plastic pieces skittered across the floor.

"*... deux ...*"

The cameraman's eyes opened wide. He obviously bought the act.

"*... un ...*"

The starter pointed to the road ahead.

"*... partez!*"

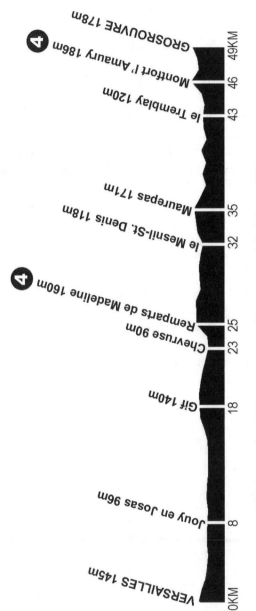

Tour de France Stage 19 Profile

VERSAILLES 145m
Jouy en Josas 96m
Gif 140m
Chevruse 90m
Remparts de Madeline 160m
le Mesnil-St. Denis 118m
Maurepas 171m
le Tremblay 120m
Montfort l' Amaury 186m
GROSROUVRE 178m

0KM   8   18   23 25   32 35   43   46   49KM

Chapter Thirty-Four

Ben's rear wheel bounced over the broken radio as he left the start house. He exploded onto the course. His cyclometer readout climbed like the "Total Sale" readout on a gas pump during an energy crisis. The crowd cheered. He descended a second ramp built over the five stairs to the cobbled royal courtyard, careful to line up with the four-inch central vein of stones that ran the half-kilometer length of the plaza. Even balanced on this prime pathway it was a teeth-chattering ride. Out of the corner of his eye, he saw the Banque Fédérale car pull out from an adjacent pathway and take its position behind him.

So much for communicating over the radio. The men in the support vehicle, Thierry, Coach, and Fritz, had just been relegated to fans with great seats. Ben removed the earpiece. Television spectators probably knew the wire led nowhere, but Ben didn't want to leave any question for Monsieur Laurent Robidoux. He wasn't going to be obeying Thierry's instructions today, and it wasn't Thierry's fault. Robidoux might still bring down his wrath, just like he'd done with Bridgette, but maybe the last-second twist would force the team owner to reconsider trashing a reputation irrevocably tied to his bank.

Ben veered around the equestrian statue of Louis XIV, then back onto the central vein. At the moment, Robidoux was probably pretty happy about things. To him, this setback might look every bit as good as the one he'd planned. It was Ben's job to make sure Robidoux's day didn't end in a satisfying way.

He passed through the golden entrance gate, across the worst 175 meters of cobbles, and onto the Avenue de Paris. Smooth pavement at last. Everything in sync, *en fuego*. Now he would lay it all on the line.

The earpiece tapped him on the cheek from time to time, still swinging from where he'd threaded it through his helmet. He was the only cyclist in this race who would have no idea how he compared to his competition. Time checks were considered critical. Could he overcome this new disadvantage?

Where the avenue bent right, the course turned hard left onto a narrower road. It gradually came around on itself until Ben was heading west. He noticed a faint "C" in the azure sky, a waning crescent moon only fifteen degrees above the horizon. He'd always found daytime moons to be so incongruous, so beautiful.

Maybe Ben could make use of this one. After turning south for a couple more kilometers, today's route would head due west for the remainder of the day. *Rocky's* theme song played in his mind. The moon would set in about an hour, approximately the same amount of time it should take him to finish this course. Could he beat it? In place of Thierry's voice, he'd use memory as his coach.

He felt powerful, driving the bicycle forward with smooth efficiency. The crowds were massive, a half dozen people or more deep on both sides of the road. Every window of every building, plus every patio and rooftop held fans. He settled in, tearing up asphalt at just under fifty kilometers per hour.

As he flew down corridors that separated buildings hundreds of years old, he imagined himself cruising alongside the vast abyss of the monument-filled Dirty Devil Valley where shadowy million-year-old sandstone edifices rose in front of ageless red rock walls. The environment energized him, just as it had when he was a boy. He'd drive hard here, but temper the effort to renew his strength. The road cleared the city and Ben imagined easing away from the Dirty Devil at the same moment.

He charged past the man who'd left the start house two minutes in front of him, and then caught a glimpse of the moon, a fraction lower in the sky.

The next important landmark on his boyhood journey was an old plane wreck. He'd often wondered what sort of trouble had caused this crash in the middle of nowhere. In tribute, he'd gathered fragments of the disaster into a makeshift monument. It marked the point he always forced himself to increase to ninety-five percent effort.

The crumbling church in Jouy-en-Josas represented the corresponding spot on this day. In front of it, children sang. Memory forced Ben to ratchet his effort to the next level. He increased his cadence. The bike moved faster. Pushing harder was a requirement of the game; pain was a byproduct he must ignore.

He shot down an ancient corridor packed with cheering fans, but he imagined himself on a vacant dirt road in the desert southwest. In those days he'd pushed his limits to discover himself, oblivious to anyone else's opinion of his strength. In the desert, if he pedaled efficiently enough he might come upon spectators of a sort. His reward might be to surprise a wandering cougar, a pack of coyote pups, or an enormous buck. More often, he'd startle jackrabbits and kangaroo mice. Sometimes the only animal life he saw all day was a handful of bewildered cows munching sage grass.

The route bent hard right. From here on it would head west for the remainder of its course. He saw the moon again, slightly lower than before. Driving the pedals, he neared Cheveruse.

Before he hit the town's center, a right turn pointed him toward the Remparts de la Madeleine, the edifice that had dominated this valley since the eleventh century. A brutal kilometer of road at sixteen percent gradient separated him from where the gray turret sat atop the ridgeline. He stood on the pedals to conquer the slope.

This hill corresponded in his mind to the ragged ascent to the high desert, a road so obscured by erosion that it had taken him an hour of careful plotting to follow its course the first time through. The trail's atrocious condition assured that no four-wheeled vehicle would ever find its way into Ben Canyon. Getting up the hill quickly required intense concentration. Selecting the wrong way around any given boulder might mean confronting an unscalable wall.

Ben crested the summit and skirted the castle. In his mind's eye, the bleak vastness of the sagebrush-filled Burr Desert was all that remained. This was far and away the least scenic and most important part of the journey. As a youth, the high desert was where he'd bury himself, charging for the highway with everything he had.

He eyed the moon. The crescent's angle to the horizon had decreased by more than a third since he'd first seen it.

The road entered a forest so thick that the trees met overhead to form a nearly opaque roof. With his shoulders tucked in and his head low, Ben sliced into the wind. His legs churned, forcing road behind him at a faster and faster rate. Kilometer after kilometer he kept up his private battle with time. He passed a second competitor on the road, but he didn't even acknowledge the accomplishment. His race was with the heavens.

Exiting the forest, he got another clear view of the moon. He darted through picturesque villages and continued picking up speed. The roads in Montfort l'Amaury were smooth, worn cobbles. The type cyclists didn't mind, at least when dry. The one-lane road climbed past a small chapel, and then threaded through a graceful stone archway that seemed to serve no function other than its beauty. Flowering vines accentuated the ancient rocks.

Ben caught sight of the moon again, low on the horizon, as he passed the ten-kilometer marker. The angle panicked him. He had to go faster or it would drop from view before he crossed the line. He clicked the chain onto a smaller rear cog. Through raw necessity, he found the strength to keep his legs churning at the same cadence. The bike's speed increased in mathematical precision, the gear ratio multiplied by his effort. He devoured pavement faster than ever.

Ben's muscles pleaded with his brain. Exhausted fibers screamed for relief. He ignored the signals and concentrated on keeping his profile as slight as possible. The less wind he pushed, the less work was required to maintain the same speed. Efficiency was everything. He kept his head in perfect alignment with his body, glancing side to side by moving only his eyes. He assessed terrain and conditions, giving extended attention only to those elements that might impact his performance. Was the pavement smoother and faster on the opposite side of the road? Could he gain wind protection by traveling closer to the crowd on the upcoming stretch?

Cresting a knoll, he hugged the flower-speckled wall below a church and cemetery. Though his arms and back ached, he kept them in the same position. They should stay loose and relaxed. Any tension would draw blood flow from muscles required to attack this course. Only his legs moved, flexing at hip, knee, and ankle in a pattern of practiced ergonomics. He extracted every available ounce of power from each stroke. He minimized even the slightest distraction from the effort. Every fiber was committed to the only thing that mattered: beating the moon.

Amid fields of rolled hay sat an ancient stone barn. Beyond it, the white sickle blade hovered just above the edge of the earth. Six kilometers to go.

He passed through another dense forest, anxious for a sight of his target. When he finally got it, with three kilometers remaining, the moon was balanced on the horizon. He pedaled faster, clenching his teeth to extract strength from punished muscles. He passed Luigi, obliterating the six-minute gap, but the moon didn't care. Only a sliver remained.

Ben scorched beneath the flamme rouge. A speck of moon was still visible, but with seven hundred meters to go, the last fragment disappeared.

He hammered for the line. The final 200-meter stretch sat atop a knoll overlooking rolling farmland. The view to the west was perfect.

Could he move fast enough to force the satellite back into the sky? No.

He shattered the plane of the finish line. The crowd erupted. If they'd been making noise before, he'd been deaf to it. Caving onto his handlebars, he saw his name and time take over top position on the board, a full three minutes faster than the previous best.

Gulping oxygen, he turned to see Luigi's finish. Only a minute later another cyclist appeared in the final straight. Not Gunter. Ben breathed a sigh of relief. This was the man Ben had overtaken on the high desert.

Next came the German, driving for the line with single-minded determination. He roared into the finish area, posting a time eighteen seconds slower than Ben's.

Another competitor finished, the first of the three men Ben had passed. The time since Ben had crossed the line approached four minutes.

Coach grabbed Ben and squeezed. "Marvelous performance, son. Simply marvelous!"

"Did you see Bridgette?"

Coach shook his head. "In that sea of people? Impossible."

Ben looked at the ground feeling desperate. He had to speak to her soon.

"Look at the clock," Coach said. "Kyle doesn't have much longer."

As if hearing his name, the leader of the Megatronics team burst onto the straightaway. He powered toward the finish line like a freight train. When he crossed it the clock froze in place. The number was ten seconds greater than Ben's time. Pleasure and pain swirled together in a bizarre combination. He had won the stage, yet he remained four seconds behind Kyle in the chase for the yellow jersey. Gunter was in third place, nine seconds off the lead.

Commotion surrounded Ben as cameramen and journalists converged.

"Are you disappointed that you didn't take yellow?" asked a reporter.

"Are we standing in the shadow of the Arc de Triomphe?" Ben asked.

"No."

"Good. That means the finish line is still over a hundred miles off." He looked west and whispered, "Still time for me to catch the moon."

Chapter Thirty-Five

Ben walked past the hotel bar and noticed footage of himself on the television screen, charging for the line during today's stage. He stopped to watch.

Kyle's image appeared on the screen, speaking in a taped interview. "A back-of-the-pack athlete suddenly starts matching multiple winners in the mountains plus mastering time-trials. Draw your own conclusions."

What hypocrisy! It infuriated him that Kyle would attempt to spin the rumors to his advantage. He turned away and headed for his room. The swirling stories weren't worthy of response, but avoiding them had been nearly impossible.

Ben couldn't wait to reach his bed, the same one he'd spent last night in. For a cyclist in competition, consecutive nights in the same hotel room were a rare pleasure. Because neither the time-trial nor the ride to Paris moved the race too far along the map, it made sense to choose a hotel and stay there. The Banque Fédérale team would remain in the Trianon Palace Hotel for three glorious nights. They'd return here again tomorrow to sleep off the hangover awaiting them at the finish line.

For now, Ben had only three recurring thoughts. When could he lie down? When would he see Bridgette? Would Robidoux punish Ben or Thierry for today's performance? He opened the hotel room door, took two steps past the bathroom, and stopped in his tracks.

Someone had dumped the contents of his suitcase onto the floor. The bedding lay in a corner. The dresser and nightstand drawers were also overturned on the floor. Had an overly aggressive reporter broken into his room? Was this Robidoux's work? Somebody must be looking for the ring!

His momentary panic subsided when he remembered that he'd locked it in the hotel safe. What else of value was he carrying? His heart pounded as he ran to the clothes. He dug through them in search of the tattered yellow jersey he'd worn for one day in the Alps. He found his maillot jaune, bloodied and road weary as ever. Grabbing his prize, he kissed it.

He spotted his Walkman and picked it up as well. He selected another of the tapes that he hadn't listened to in years. Rising to his feet, a wave of exhaustion robbed him of the energy to remain offended at the crime. He grabbed a pillow from the corner, dropped onto the bed, and stared at the ceiling. After awhile, he inserted his cassette and pulled on the headphones. As he hit the play button, a light tap at the open door caught his attention. Could it be Bridgette?

He rose on an elbow, hopefully. "Come in." Removing the headphones, he pushed his Walkman beneath the pillow.

The light coming from the hallway changed, eclipsed by a large body. "*Bonsoir,* Benjamin."

Ben tensed at the formal tone. The voice was Robidoux's. He tried to hide his fear by turning his back. "Oh. I mistook you for somebody else."

"*Désolé,* is that who you spruced this place up for?"

Ben suppressed a nervous laugh. "Do I have you to thank for this mess?"

"Of course not. I am your biggest admirer, but I don't need to break in to souvenir hunt." Ben felt Robidoux sit down on the corner of the bed.

He had to brace himself from rolling in that direction. "So, why are you here?"

Robidoux put a hand on Ben's bicep. "You dropped your radio. I thought you might want it back."

Ben's heart froze. What sort of a game was Robidoux playing? He sat up and looked for the first time at the mystery man who ran the team. He'd seen only pictures until now. The real Robidoux was noticeably older and larger than any of the photographs.

Robidoux extended the radio. "Despite being run over, it works perfectly."

Ben took it. The battery cover and volume knob were missing, and the digital display was cracked, but he wasn't about to argue over the radio's condition. "I guess it needed a jolt." He swung his feet to the floor on the opposite side of the bed, surprised at the control he felt.

"Why did Thierry tell you to sabotage it?" the team owner asked.

So, this was a fishing expedition. "He didn't. Why would he?"

"You can't save your friend by playing dumb, so you may as well tell me what happened."

Ben stood up and walked around the bed to face Robidoux. "What do you think I know?"

Robidoux shrugged.

"You're behind the story that came out about Bridgette, aren't you?"

The corners of Robidoux's lips rose.

"What irony. I owe you so much for allowing me to reach this position in the first place and now…" He closed his mouth. The team owner had no idea what Ben knew about the pressures he'd been exerting, and it ought to stay that way.

"What were you going to say?"

Ben shook his head.

"You're correct about one thing. You do owe me," Robidoux said. "As for accusing me of exposing Bridgette, whom have you been talking to?"

"Nobody."

"If people are assassinating my character, I deserve to know about it. If they are employees, maybe they should lose their jobs."

Ben looked out the window. Horse-drawn carriages carried tourists around Louis XIV's royal domain. The Sun King might have beheaded a subject who spoke behind his back. Would Robidoux? "Do you plan to fire me?"

"At the least, I ought to scratch you from tomorrow's start as punishment for the things you've already insinuated."

"Is that why you're here? I won't go quietly."

Robidoux jowls wobbled as he shook his head. "I'm here because I'm inspired by you, Benjamin. I'm glad we've finally met face to face."

"You're angry with me for avoiding your veterinarian, aren't you." Ben picked up a drawer and fit it back into the dresser.

Robidoux chuckled. "You and I are very much alike. Did you know that? We are both tenacious to the extreme. I really do find your persistence inspiring. It amazes me that you've done so well, given your … methods."

Ben replaced another drawer. "You talk as if playing by the rules is unheard of. I signed the same code of ethics you did."

"*Oui.* Everybody signs the code: athletes, support staff, owners. It's a formality." Robidoux waved a dismissive hand.

"One that some of us take seriously," Ben said.

"Would you be surprised to learn that, in my career as a cyclist, I also avoided chemical performance enhancement? That's the main reason for my mediocre results."

Ben looked directly into Robidoux's eyes and, to his astonishment, saw sincerity.

"Regardless," Robidoux continued, "I am a businessman now, and our conversation has only given me further reason to make a tough business decision. Banque Fédérale can no longer afford the impression that you speak for us. You are unpredictable with the media, and I fear that will only get worse once the race ends. On top of that, you seem to be a magnet for the sorts of drug accusations that embarrass the sport."

"I'm not using anything illegal."

"In this world, perception is what matters. One day you'll understand that."

Ben's gut clenched. "What excuse will you give the race officials for my absence?"

"Stomach problems. I can see that you're experiencing them right now." Robidoux pushed himself to his feet. "Thierry has the same thing. He just doesn't know it yet."

Interesting that Robidoux didn't want Thierry around tomorrow. Ben no longer doubted that the owner would follow through with his threats to expose the directeur. Ben stepped in front of the big man. "No need to tell Thierry your decision."

Robidoux's brow creased.

Ben stepped to the bed and pulled his Walkman from beneath the pillow. The wheels turned behind the Plexiglas window. "I have it all on tape. I'd be happy to play it back for him or anybody else who needs to hear it, or would you prefer for me to mail the cassette to you after I cross the finish line tomorrow?"

Robidoux turned red as a pomegranate. "Give that to me, right now."

"No."

The owner's eyes narrowed, as if considering an attack. It wouldn't have worked. Even in his exhausted state, Ben was a thousand times more agile.

"Do you have a death wish?" Robidoux asked.

"*Non.* I have a victory wish. If you don't interfere with that plan, the tape will remain unplayed."

Robidoux pulled back his lips, revealing small, yellow teeth. "I'm going to let you finish the race, but you're playing with explosives. I could destroy you right this moment if I wanted to."

"I don't doubt it." Ben stepped aside.

As soon as Robidoux left the room, Ben shut the door and locked the deadbolt. Then he knocked on the door to Thierry's adjoining room. After a moment the team directeur opened it from his side. Behind him, Ben could see into the open bathroom, but the living quarters were out of view. Thierry's view of Ben's room would be the same.

"Have you seen Robidoux yet," Ben asked.

Thierry swallowed hard. "He's around?"

"Just left my room. He claimed both you and I were going to have the stomach flu tonight. He said he was going to have my name scratched from tomorrow's start. I assume you would have to do the paperwork."

"I won't do it." Thierry looked at his front door. "It serves me right that drugs have come back to bite me. I wish I could erase the whole episode. I'll do my best to clear things up for you when I talk to him."

"Robidoux might have reconsidered." Ben held up the Walkman. "For some reason, he thinks I taped our conversation on this old thing."

Thierry laughed. "Ben, you amaze me."

"Hey, I'm just trying to find a way to finish this race."

"Come on in and sit down. We need to talk," Thierry limped across the room with his plaster encased foot.

Ben followed. Thierry sat on one bed and Ben took the other.

The directeur looked at his hands, first the palms and then the backs. "I owe you an explanation. The reason I almost betrayed you…"

"You don't owe me anything, Thierry."

Thierry nodded. "You should know what happened. You're aware of the pressures I faced as well as anybody. Win or lose, I'm proud of you for resisting."

Ben jostled ideas in his mind for a moment. He hadn't planned to let Thierry in on his ultimate goal, but now the time felt right. "I'd like to speak out about what I've gone through, Thierry. It bothers me that kids might see drugs, or cheating in general, as the route to success. Every pro knows the hard work they put in is a much bigger factor than anything else."

"I hate to burst your bubble, but unless you win, that sort of talk will reek of being a sore loser, and if you do —"

"That's why I have to win." Ben stared into Thierry's eyes.

"You cut me off. If you do win, riding clean is a nonstory. Trust me. I've done it … twice in fact." He stood and walked to the window where he looked out at the royal horses grazing in their pastures. "That's why it wasn't too hard for me to accept performance enhancing treatment as an insurance policy when my next victory fell into doubt."

Ben rose and went to Thierry's side. Five stories below, a small boy and girl fed crumbs to pigeons. "It's not a nonstory. I realize that people normally tune into sports for an escape from the daily grind, not more of the same, but they'll listen to the winner at the finish line. They always do. Some people won't like hearing what I have to say, but it needs to be said."

Thierry laid a hand on Ben's shoulder. "At least you've thought this through."

"If I win this race, I'll emphasize the challenges presented by the course and the opposition, but I'll also let people in on the pressures that occur off the bike. I'm not going to throw blame around. I just want fans to understand why some athletes take shortcuts, and maybe get some of them to think about ways to prevent it."

Thierry put his hands on the windowsill and leaned forward. "It's a worthy goal, Ben. I have my doubts that it will work, but I support the effort. Let's figure out how to make up the last four seconds of your gap to Kyle; then I'll look forward to seeing what you can accomplish."

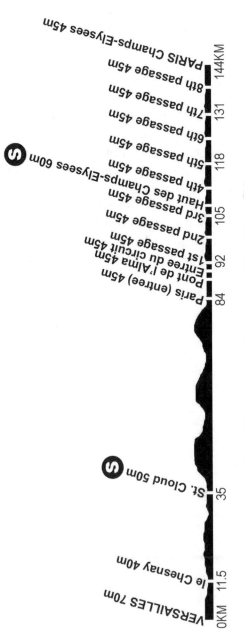

Tour de France Stage 20 Profile

PARIS Champs-Elysees 45m
8th passage 45m
7th passage 45m
6th passage 45m
5th passage 45m
4th passage 45m
Haut des Champs-Elysees 60m
3rd passage 45m
2nd passage 45m
1st passage 45m
Entrée du circuit 45m
Pont de l'Alma 45m
Paris (entrée) 45m

St. Cloud 50m

le Chesnay 40m

VERSAILLES 70m

0KM 11.5 35 84 92 105 118 131 144KM

Chapter Thirty-Six

Sign-in the next morning was uneventful; there was no word from Robidoux, and no indication he'd talked with anybody about removing Ben from the race. For the moment, Ben breathed easier. It was unlikely Robidoux could stop him from crossing the finish line now, but could he cross it in first place?

He checked his jersey pocket and touched Bridgette's ring. He'd run the earpiece wire through it so the transmitter held it in place as a good luck charm.

When Robidoux received the Walkman in the mail and discovered it had no record function he'd be furious, but at least he'd be certain that Ben didn't hold evidence against him. No telling how he'd react to protect his name. He clearly considered himself above the law.

As the race got underway, Ben realized it might be his last day as a pro cyclist. He'd make the most of it. Today was the rarest of Tour de France stages. Seldom were two men still in contention for the overall victory on the last stage. Never before had three men been fighting out the decisive assault on Paris. This year the traditional champagne celebration would have to wait until things sorted themselves out for good on the other side of the finish line. Ben tucked in among the peloton, saving energy for the critical moments to come.

Megatronics refused to take control of the race. Usually the team defending the yellow jersey wanted ownership of the pack, but Kyle's team apparently preferred a breakaway to go up the road. If that happened, the escapists would steal all the sprint bonus time before the General Classification contenders got there. The fewer seconds available to his rivals, the less likely Kyle would lose his yellow jersey.

Deutscher Aufbau took over the pace-making.

"Get up front. Everybody but Ben needs to help set tempo," Thierry called over the radio.

The men moved forward to assist the Germans. Ben wished they could save their energy for later, but there was no alternative. If Banque

Fédérale didn't insure that the pack stayed together, even at the expense of burning their men out before the Champs-Elysées, Ben's slim hope for victory would be gone.

His depleted squad appeared scrawny beside Aufbau. With the three members the team had lost so far, including their two best flatlanders, Banque Fédérale had minimal firepower. Should the peloton split and leave any of the contenders behind, Ben was most likely to be on the wrong end of the deal. He'd have to remain vigilant, watching for key breaks, and then win by grabbing bonus seconds at the sprint.

Those six-, four-, and two-second rewards were likely to be available to the General Classification contenders today. The sprinters would no longer be interested in them because the green jersey competition had been sewn up yesterday.

Larger bonuses were awarded at the finish line, but since a stage win in Paris was enough to transform a man's career, an exhausted General Classification contender had little chance of being in the top three. They simply weren't built to beat the top sprinters on the flats. That probably put the big bonuses of twenty, twelve, and eight seconds at the final finish line out of their reach

Two kilometers before the first sprint, the nine Megatronics men burst ahead on the right-hand side of the road and attempted to hijack the pace-making. Kyle sat in the caboose position of his team train. Deutscher Aufbau responded decisively, organizing their own lead-out on the left. The Banque Fédérale riders found themselves in no man's land between the two groups.

"Organize a charge," Thierry urged over the radio.

The men tried hard, but sandwiched between the other two teams it proved difficult. Streaming past the one-kilometer-to-go mark, Ben's rivals were shedding men, but his small squad was giving out quicker. The disparity increased.

When two spent Banque Fédérale men peeled off together, Ben dove in behind Kyle's wheel. The big American should be able to out sprint Gunter, and if Ben could charge past him at the last moment, he'd move closer to the lead.

The two remaining lead-out trains slapped against one another as they charged forward. The line neared and the pedaling became ferocious. Two hundred meters out, Ben was in third position. Kyle rode immediately in front of him following the wheel of his last remaining Megatronics teammate. Gunter was to Ben's left, in the draft of a teammate of his own.

The Deutscher Aufbau lead-out man pulled off, clearing the way for Gunter. Then the final Megatronics man fell into the jet wash as well. Kyle charged. Ben put his head down and drove. Kyle's rear wheel pulled farther ahead of him, and out of the corner of his eye, he sensed others leaving him behind on the left. He dropped his head and pushed with all he had.

Finally, the white stripe passed beneath his wheel. His legs ached. He looked up. Kyle was way out in front, having grabbed the six bonus seconds for first place. Gunter was next, four seconds to him. Right on his wheel was a Deutscher Aufbau teammate. He'd swept the final two bonus seconds out of Ben's grasp.

Overcoming the strength advantages of the rival teams was going to be a big challenge. Even without the teams, Ben wasn't likely to match Kyle's flatland speed in a head-to-head drag race.

The peloton continued to reel in pavement while Ben worked on replenishing his strength. He squeezed a gooey energy gel into his mouth and followed it with lots of water. He mentally calculated the current General Classification standings. Kyle now had ten seconds on him. Ben could no longer make up the margin using the remaining sprint bonus alone. Gunter stood only a second behind Ben. To win, Ben would need another tactic.

"Listen to me, Ben. You're going to have to risk your second place finish to go for first. Are you sure you're all right with that?"

"Yes."

"Very well. It will take a miracle to save this race for you, and you're going to have to make it for yourself," Thierry said over the radio. "Bill and I have worked through every scenario. Your only shot is a solo breakaway to win the stage. You'll have to go earlier than they expect."

"How early?"

"Somewhere before the last lap of the Champs-Elysées. I'll tell you to attack once I see the right opportunity."

"Okay," Ben answered. It was so much easier to obey somebody else's orders than to impose them on himself. At breakfast that morning in Salon Clemenceau, the team had concluded such a breakaway was impossible. Now it sounded like a simple matter of following directions. Fit "tab A" into "slot B."

Thierry spoke deliberately. "It doesn't matter where you place in the remaining intermediate sprint because you can't gain enough time there to make up the gap to Kyle, nor can you lose enough to eliminate your chance of capturing yellow if you win the twenty-second bonus at the end of the stage. Does that make sense?"

Ben's mind was in no condition to follow complex logic. "Not really."

"Assume that Kyle wins the next sprint and you get no bonus time. You'll be back by sixteen seconds. If you go on to win the stage, you'll take a twenty second bonus, plus any time gap you hold over the field," Thierry said. "That will make you the Tour de France Champion."

"That's assuming neither Kyle nor Gunter gain bonus time at the finish line," Coach added.

"It's a risk we have to take," Thierry said.

"Okay," Ben answered.

The peloton swung onto the Champs-Elysées for the first of its nine six-kilometer laps from the Arc de Triomphe to the Place de la Concorde. Only thirty-four miles remained in this year's Tour de France. Enormous crowds lined the route. It seemed that all of Paris had come to watch. The peloton's energy level skyrocketed in response. The last sprint bonus would be in front of the grandstands the third time around.

"Move up front and force your rivals to work, Ben," Thierry said as the wind up to the sprint began on the second lap. "Make sure they assume you want this bonus."

Ben moved toward the front. As the cyclists rounded the 180-degree turn in front of the Arc de Triomphe, he found himself momentarily at the head of the pack, cruising downhill through the famed shopping district. Kyle and Gunter charged past, organizing their teams on the fly. Ben slid deeper into the group to save energy.

The peloton stretched thin as it headed for the last shot at mid-stage bonus time. They crossed the line in front of the grandstands. Word filtered back that Kyle had taken first yet again and that Gunter was the second man on the road.

Now Ben was sixteen seconds off Kyle's lead and three seconds behind Gunter. All the chips rode on the final lap.

As the peloton headed up the Champs-Elysées for a fourth time, four cyclists sprinted off the front. Ben rode in the eight-inch concrete gutter. This far right edge of the road was the only smooth line. Beside him cyclists shuddered across cobbles as the peloton chased.

The escapists established a twenty-second gap, but that was as far as the peloton let them go. Ben drifted left in preparation for the turn. He eyed the leaders as they flew down the Champs-Elysées on the opposite side of temporary barriers. They bounced around ahead of the main body of cyclists like leashed puppies anxious to reach the park.

He made another U-turn just short of the Arc de Triomphe and charged down the avenue in direct pursuit of the leading cyclists.

For three laps the four men held their gap, but each time they passed close, Ben gauged their faces. They were tiring, while his strength was building.

With a little less than two laps to go, the peloton had had enough. They reeled the miscreants in, and the pace increased even further. Now the sprinter's teams controlled the race, trying to set up their men for the most prestigious sprint victory in the world.

Gunter and Kyle jockeyed. What plans did the German have to overcome his deficit?

Ben inched forward through the pack, bit-by-bit, certain that the command to attack would come at any moment, yet thankful it hadn't. There was a long way to go. Down the Quai des Tuileries, beside the calm waters of the Siene, the cyclists streamed in an ever lengthening line. Men clinging at the back would be under serious stress now.

Ben felt good. He continued to edge forward, waiting, watching. The route dove into a shadowy tunnel beneath the Place de la Concorde. It hit bottom and leveled momentarily.

"Now!" Thierry commanded. "Go! Go! Go! Go! Go!"

Ben threw himself into the pedals as if the finish line were only meters ahead, not seven kilometers distant. He flew up the tunnel ramp, past the leaders, down the Rue de Rivoli, beneath the shadow of the ancient Obélisque de Luxor, and past dozens of pieces of stunning public art.

"Aufbau men are with you, Gunter and two others! Make them take their turn!"

Ben moved to the side and waved them through as he reduced his effort slightly, but no one came. This wasn't the time for games. It was an all or nothing gambit. He returned to full effort.

"Damn them!" Thierry screamed.

Ben had committed himself. He drove with every remaining ounce of power. Nothing could be gained by holding back. If the German had positioned himself to take advantage, so be it. Ben meant to win, but if that didn't happen he'd rather drag Gunter to victory than see the trophy go to Kyle.

They charged between the grandstands for the penultimate time. Confronting the gradual slope of the Champs-Elysées, Ben soared beneath the drooling gargoyles atop buildings erected centuries before his hometown of Hanksville even existed. As before, he tucked into the gutter of the famous avenue where the rough cobbles couldn't cause him damage.

"Ten-second gap. Drive Ben, drive!"

His thighs bellowed in pain, his calves screamed for relief, fire filled his lungs, and his heart pounded on the verge of explosion. He kept his head down and fought for more.

"Eleven seconds Ben! Harder! You've got to give it more!"

He torqued the bike with each revolution. Suddenly his left foot slammed into the ground and he straddled his crossbar. Dizzying pain stunned him, but only for a millisecond. He realized his pedal clip had failed as the handlebars twisted from his grip. His front wheel hit the curb and ricocheted left. He skated across the cobbles on his free foot, somehow recapturing the handlebars. The three Deutscher Aufbau men zinged past him on the right as he regained control of the bike.

In a smooth motion he clipped his left foot back in place and drove the pedals again, but his momentum was lost, and he had nothing in reserve. In the next moment the leading edge of the peloton screamed by on his right. He sensed the pressure of more men from behind, overcoming him like a crashing wave. He glanced over his shoulder and saw an opening to the left. The moment he took it, more men swarmed by.

Now faster cyclists flooded past on both sides. They poured by in a disorienting array of color. Ben couldn't push hard enough to stem the flow. Something glanced off his right shoulder. He steered left, just retaining his balance, as the man in the yellow jersey passed. Had Kyle purposely bumped into him?

He finally found clear passage to the unused left-hand side of the road as the stream of cyclists changed to cars and motorcycles. Still, Ben had no strength to match their pace. He wasn't merely burnt toast; he was a smoldering cinder. Turning the pedals even a single revolution was a gargantuan task.

The next thing he knew, the cyclists were coming toward him again, on the opposite side of the temporary barriers that divided the Champs-Elysées. Two Aufbau men and Gunter came first, about ten seconds ahead of the enraged peloton. Led by the sprinter's teams, the beast gnashed its from head side to side as it made its serpentine charge down the opposite side of the road. It stretched its neck and worked its jowls.

Then came the passengers in this thrill ride to glory, the men who meant to finish with the pack but stay clear of the sprint. Ben's eyes locked onto Kyle's as the two headed toward one another. The other man's expression of dominance shattered him. This was Ben's moment of supreme failure. He'd ridden to win, but instead he would drop a step lower on the final podium. He was destined to finish the Tour de France in third place. There was no longer any way to catch the two men ahead of him in the overall standings, and no way he'd be caught by any of the one hundred plus men who were behind him.

Not only had he failed to do as Thierry had asked, but he was going to cross the line dead last for the stage. He had no more race left in him. Moving his bike at about half the speed of the peloton was the best he could do. He struggled on.

"Damn, damn, damn, damn, damn! They beat us," Thierry said.

Ben had taken last place in a race only one other time in his life, and the memory of that moment flooded over him now. Just like today, he'd been in the lead in his very first race in the Wasatch Cyclists Criterium Series in Salt Lake City, and just like today he'd been passed by every single competitor before he reached the finish line. At that time he hadn't had a clue about the dynamics of drafting or any of the other subtleties of cycling. What had he been clueless about today? He didn't have the energy to search for an answer.

The last of the hangers-on and the vehicle caravan poured past on the other side of the barriers, and then Ben was alone. He drifted to the right and pedaled up the empty gutter, all but overlooked by the massive crowds on either side of the road.

He reached the U-turn and headed back toward the Place de la Concord. One last length of this street plus a loop toward the Louvre and back, and his quest would come to a close, unfulfilled. Still, he kept pushing the pedals as hard as he could.

Winning would have given him a voice to shine light on the problem he'd seen. Seventeen seconds worth of unexploited opportunities had ended it all. He thought back across the journey, wondering how much time he'd allowed to escape. Had he let victory slip from his grasp, or had he done everything in his power and simply fallen short?

He rode alongside the river and into the tunnel where his ill-fated attack had begun. Now the grandstands were just a kilometer away. By the time he arrived the crowd would have fallen from its crescendo. Maybe he could sneak through unseen.

But as he neared the cheers were at an incomprehensible volume. What was going on? He ducked his head as he sprinted for the finish. Rolling across the line he realized he wore the only sour expression in a field of joy. Even the man with the slowest overall time, the lanterne rouge, was thrilled with his accomplishment. Ben wanted that feeling as well. Instead he'd been buried under an avalanche of remorse. He'd never allowed himself to believe it could end this way. Now that it had, it was too much to bear.

He spotted Bridgette standing in the finish area. What was she doing here? Her skin seemed to glow. He rode straight toward her. He had to squeeze his brakes when he nearly ran over a pair of cameramen taking his picture.

He climbed off his machine, and Bridgette ran toward him. Fritz rescued $7500 worth of high-tech bicycle an instant before Ben would be forced to either hang onto his machine or catch a flying woman. She leaped into his arms, kissing him. He closed his eyes and ignored the photographers as they hungrily recorded this moment of reconciliation that he'd told them wouldn't happen. They were together again, and that's all that mattered.

He soaked in her feel, her smell, her aura. This was the person he was meant to be with. "Will you forgive me, Bridgette? I should have had more faith in you."

She laughed. "I'm here to apologize to you. Do you have time to hear it now?"

He squeezed her tighter. "Apology accepted. We'll talk things through later. It's so good to have you back." He reached into his back pocket and pulled his earpiece wire from the transmitter, freeing the ring. He handed it to her.

Bridgette put it on her finger with a smile. "Ben, do you hear them cheering for you? Isn't it wonderful?"

The cheering was for him? "What about the winner? Who finished first?"

"Gunter, in a photo. The sprinters missed it by a millisecond."

Gunter won the stage? He was down nine seconds to start the day. He'd lost two more in each of two sprints, putting him down thirteen. Then he gained twenty at the line. "He took yellow! Why didn't you say so? That's terrific!"

Bridgette laughed. "Tell him yourself."

When she released him he opened his eyes to a sea of microphones. He'd stumbled into Gunter's victory press conference without even realizing it.

The German extended his hand through a wall of reporters. "No hard feelings?"

"You beat me, fair and square. Perfect tactics at the finish," Ben said.

"We couldn't possibly have won if we hadn't taken advantage of your launch. Simply *fantastisch!*" Gunter plowed through the crowd.

Ben hugged him. "Nice work, man!"

"You look happy, Ben," said Simone Sardou.

"Yeah? I guess I am." Bridgette had transformed his mood in the revolution of a pedal. He'd dreaded facing the media while feeling spiteful; thanks to her he didn't have to.

"You put in an incredible attack, even though it failed. Do you wish you'd done anything differently?" Simone Sardou asked.

"I wish I'd won, but now it's over." Ben pointed to the digital readout. "I'm satisfied with third overall."

"Will you be back?"

"If I get another opportunity. I'm not smart enough to know any better."

A reporter yelled over the group. "We've just seen you passionately kissing an admitted drug cheat. Why?"

Even grizzled journalists booed the question.

The *au Fond* man pressed. "Isn't it true that —"

"I'm clean. I know I'm clean, and so does everybody close to me," Ben said. "That's going to have to be enough. Now it's time for me to get out of Gunter's way. This is his moment."

Chapter Thirty-Seven

Ben lay exhausted on the hotel bed. He was vaguely aware of Bridgette walking around the room. The thought of moving a finger, let alone getting out of bed, was more than he could bear. Yesterday's closing ceremonies had sapped his last bit of strength. Surprisingly, he'd never felt so at peace as he did right now.

He felt Bridgette sit beside him with her back against the headboard, and then five delicate fingers caressed his face. A moan escaped his lips.

"I thought you were awake," Bridgette said. "It's noon already. You've got an hour until the post-race press conference you promised to attend."

"I made a promise for today? What was I thinking?"

Bridgette must have activated the remote control because the television popped on. After several commercials, Ben recognized Simone Sardou's voice. He pried open an eye and peeked at the screen. She stood on yesterday's finish line. In the background, an army of men and machines disassembled the tinker toy remnants of the closing ceremony festivities.

"The cycling world is reeling this morning," said the woman in a grave tone, "and the circle of impact grows larger and larger. So far, at least twenty elite athletes have corroborated and even expanded on the statements first made by three-time Tour de France champion Thierry DePerdiux, and while others have refuted his claims, there can be no doubt that something big is afoot. It's like a dam has given way and floodwaters are reshaping the canyons below. We're going to take you back a couple of hours and show you how it all started. Monsiuer DePerdiux called early this morning and invited me to his hotel room for an exclusive interview."

Ben opened the other eye. "What is this?"

Bridgette leaned forward beside him. "I have no idea."

The shot switched to an image of Thierry sitting in front of Louis

XIV's Royal Domain, the same panorama that would have been visible out of Ben's window had he opened the curtains. Thierry had done this interview no more than six feet from where Ben lay at this very moment. What in the world had he said to cause such an uproar?

"It's hard for fans to appreciate the pressure athletes are under in an event like the Tour de France," Thierry said. "Having won twice, I knew what it was going to take to do it again. Since I'd put enormous pressures on myself and felt I'd be letting down my sponsors, supporters, teammates, friends, family, countrymen, and God knows who else, I accepted a hemoglobin transfusion when Laurent Robidoux demanded it of me, hours prior to the final time-trial of last year's Tour de France."

"What is he doing?" Ben imagined Robidoux's reaction. His blackmail had suddenly backfired in the worst conceivable way. Thierry had just jammed a bicycle pump into the cogs of Banque Fédérale's massive marketing machine. Would it seize? "Robidoux's probably having a stroke right now!"

"Shhh," Bridgette whispered.

"You'll face an automatic suspension for admitting to this, won't you?" Simone Sardou asked.

"Yes, a long one, but I deserve it. I cheated. Recent events have convinced me that I need to pay the price, even though I didn't get caught."

"Do you believe your were a victim?"

"I take full responsibility for my decisions, but your implication is fair. Certain advisors took advantage of my trust. I definitely don't want to see them do the same to others. They ought to be punished just like me. A year ago, when I broke these rules, I believed I had nothing to lose. I'd put in the suffering, knowing that some competitors were benefiting from techniques I hadn't allowed myself to use in the previous years, and I could see clearly enough that they weren't getting caught."

"If you had known specifics for years, why didn't you ever say anything?"

"Cyclists are bound by an *omertà*, a code of silence. It's fine to compete clean but not to destroy the livelihood or reputation of friends who've been forced into other decisions. The public isn't likely to understand the reasons for their choices because the pressures are more complex than they appear.

"We endure a lot. Our mutual respect is one of the things that gets us through, so, over time, my thinking changed. My job was to do the impossible, to push the boundaries of human performance. Using cutting edge medication seemed the professional thing to do."

The camera slowly zoomed out and Ben recognized the back of Simone Sardou's head. "What motivated you to speak out now?"

Thierry rubbed his cheek with an open palm as if loosening his jaw to release difficult words. "In this year's contest, after being knocked out of the race, I've been treated to a performance I'll never forget. I watched Ben Barnes endure unimaginable pressures. The course was tough, conditions were miserable, and the competition was fierce. The three men battling for the lead put on a display unlike anything I've ever witnessed.

"I sat silent when I knew that banned drugs, drugs that might have reduced Ben's suffering, were not merely being offered, but practically forced on him. I scratched my head at his naïveté when he refused the help, time and again, even though everybody in the peloton knew that some competitors were taking advantage of these same techniques."

Simone looked up from her notepad. "Ben was accused of using drugs. What did you think of that?"

"It's disgraceful that certain journalists were reporting speculation as fact. I guess we shouldn't be surprised that some people will stoop to any level to get the story they want, even if they have to manufacture it. There are reporters who believe it's their job to shape public opinion, so they pick and choose between the facts. Have you ever heard of *Schadenfreude?*"

"No."

"In German *Schaden* is damage and *Freude* is joy, so this is the pleasure derived by watching other's troubles. Sadly, it's one of modern society's greatest pastimes. Knocking heroes off pedestals is a sure way to sell papers."

Simone nodded sympathetically. "But it wasn't just papers. As the race progressed, an increasing number of people were calling for Ben to withdraw."

"Suggestions like that come easily to people with nothing at stake. It's simple for strangers to tell a man to toss his ambitions in the trashcan, but do they really believe he should give up on his dreams just because someone planted suspicions? I'm proud of Ben for finishing, and he should be proud of third place. He was beaten by worthy men."

"But you just suggested that some of his competitors used drugs."

"Nobody failed any tests. I won't call results into question without evidence."

Simone shifted in her seat. "So why speak out? If you feel that the right man won, that the competitors are all playing by the same set of rules, then why admit to drug use you've never even been accused of?"

A warm smile spread across Thierry's face. "Thirty-six hours ago Ben taught me a lesson. He reminded me of arguments I'd set aside to support my world view. His heart burned with the fiercest fire I've ever seen. He wanted to win this race so badly, but the reason he wanted to win was a new one in my experience."

"What was it?"

"He believed he could deliver a message that would instigate change. He thought the world would listen to the man standing on the podium's top step."

"Would they?" Her tone communicated doubt.

"I don't know. They might shoot the messenger. But last week I read a quote from an Auschwitz survivor. He said that those who survived did so partly because of their willingness to do anything necessary to stay alive, sometimes even at the expense of fellow prisoners with greater scruples. Can you imagine the honesty it took to admit to that? I may be risking a lot by telling the truth, but it pales compared to what he did."

Simone nodded thoughtfully. "I think you're doing the right thing."

"Not everyone will see it that way, and some might have a point." He sipped his water. "I know a young man from Eastern Czechoslovakia who's battling to enter cycling's pro ranks. If he makes it, he'll become rich by his family's standards. He'll also be a hero in his country. If he misses, he'll spend his life underground as a coal miner, breathing toxic dust seven days a week. He'll die at a young age from either accident or disease. What lengths should he go to in order to break through?"

Simone paused. A flock of pigeons banked just outside the window. "He'll probably do whatever it takes."

"So am I at fault for going to similar lengths to protect my job?"

"I've never thought of it that way. I'm not sure." Simone rocked back.

"Neither was I, but the evening before last Ben reminded me who the victims are. He couldn't stand the thought that he might inspire a child to take a path that led, inevitably, to drug use, and now I can't either. So, in this blink of an eye when the world is paying attention, while the ratings are sky high from Beijing to Botswana, I owe it to myself to tell the truth. It's my job to say, 'Here's why the Tour de France is the greatest human contest ever devised, cheating and all, and here is what it can teach us.' It goes beyond the confines of sport. If I can accomplish that I'll have made the most of my successes and my failures."

The shot switched back to Simone Sardou standing at the finish line, "So there you have it. Tough talk from a popular champion. What effect will it have? I believe Thierry DePierdeu has just handed us a tremendous opportunity."

Bridgette turned to Ben. "Thierry is my hero. That was incredible!"

"I agree," Ben said. "There's not another man alive with the credentials to deliver that message so effectively. His confession is more powerful than any claim of innocence I could have made. I can't believe he's risking so much."

The phone rang. Bridgette answered it, and then handed the receiver to Ben. "It's Toma."

Ben put the phone to his ear.

"Hello Ben. Are you feeling okay yet?"

"Yeah pal. I feel great."

"You sure made me proud."

Ben smiled to himself, thinking about the huge role the boy had played in his most important decisions. "Thanks for saying that, Toma."

"You would have really liked my dad."

Ben looked at Bridgette. "How come?"

"You remind me of him."

"What do you know about your father?" It excited Ben to hear Toma talk about this hidden part of his past.

"He used to take me for rides on his bike. I'd sit on the handlebars and dream about riding a bike like him. Thanks to you, now I can."

Ben heard love in Toma's voice, and recognized why bicycles were so important to the boy. "What happened to your dad?"

"He was my hero. One day he got on a train and went away to the war."

"You never heard from him after that?"

"No. Well, not exactly." Toma paused. "I mean, I wasn't sure ... until he sent you."

The End

Acknowledgment

No one deserves more credit for this book's existence than my wife, Elle. She's been both a motivator and a sounding board since my novel writing quest began. What an amazing journey it has been!

I owe debts of gratitude to many other people, as well. The members of NovelPro.com who critiqued various drafts of the manuscript, especially founder J.R. Lankford, Kate Johnston, Susan Asher, Alan Jackson, Alistair Potter, Paula Jolin, Lynn Hoffman, and Christopher Hoare, are responsible for taking this novel to a higher level than I ever could have on my own. Keith Pyatt deserves special recognition. Time and again he has pointed out potential in my stories beyond their initial scope. I also want to thank Joylene Butler for the incredible work she's done for me. Each one of these people have pushed me to stretch my limits. Thanks for the shove.

I'm grateful for all of the help I've received with research, but one name stands above all others. Marty Jemison has given me more of his time and thoughtful feedback than I could ever have asked for. A two-time Tour de France finisher, and winner of the 1999 U.S. Pro Cycling Championship, he's one of the premier cyclists America has ever produced. Working with him has been a great honor.

Every member of my family has helped me in one way or another, and every member of the Morris family has as well. I'll never be able to properly communicate all the ways these people have motivated me, nor will I be able to repay them for all the times they have assisted me. I can't possibly thank them enough.

Finally, I want to thank the thousands of readers who have helped spread the word about my books, and who have also encouraged me to keep writing novels. I've enjoyed being a guest at your book clubs, attending your bicycle events, and meeting you at signings. Your e-mails and letters are always gratefully received.

The more stories I write, the more stories that I dream of writing. Thank you all for helping to make my adventure possible.

Tailwinds,
Dave Shields

p.s. Please don't hesitate to get in touch with me by visiting DaveShields.com and clicking the contact link.